CRIMES OF HONOR

THE BUREAU BOOK SEVEN

MICHAEL NEWTON

WOLFPACK
PUBLISHING
— EST 2013 —

Crimes Of Honor is a work of fiction. Any references to historical events, real people or real places are used fictitiously. Other names, characters, places and events are products of the author's imagination, and any resemblance to actual events, places or persons, living or dead, is entirely coincidental.

Published in the United States by Wolfpack Publishing

Wolfpack Publishing
6032 Wheat Penny Avenue
Las Vegas, NV 89122

wolfpackpublishing.com

Paperback ISBN: 978-1-64119-471-6
Ebook ISBN: 978-1-64119-470-9

Library of Congress Number: 2018964376

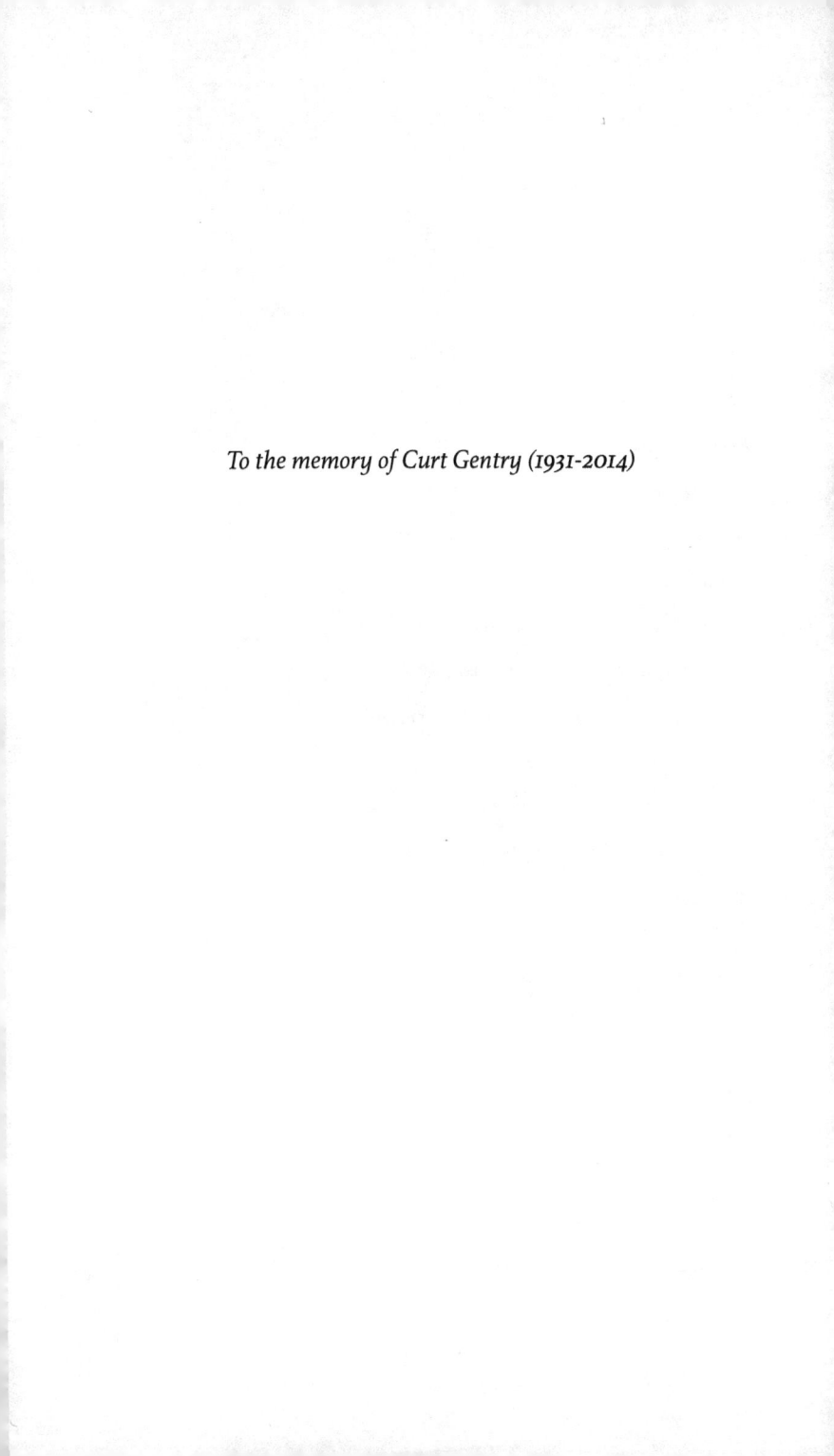

To the memory of Curt Gentry (1931-2014)

DRAMATIS PERSONÆ

Aloysius Gantt: agent of the Federal Bureau of Investigation.

Colby Gantt: his son, agent of the CIA.

Devon Gantt: his son, agent of the FBI.

Declan O'Hara: retired FBI agent.

Nolan O'Hara: his son, an FBI agent.

Fiona O'Hara: Declan's daughter, an attorney.

David Jordan: an attorney.

Carlo Giordano: Jordan's uncle, a *mafioso*.

Dominic Giordano: Carlo's son, also a *mafioso*.

Angelo Giordano: his second son, also a *mafioso*.

Payton Sawyer: an NYPD officer.

Frederick Douglass Sawyer: Payton's brother, an FBI agent.

Stephen Barnes: a KGB sleeper agent living in America.

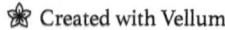 Created with Vellum

To the memory of Curt Gentry (1931-2014)

DRAMATIS PERSONÆ

Aloysius Gantt: agent of the Federal Bureau of Investigation.

Colby Gantt: his son, agent of the CIA.

Devon Gantt: his son, agent of the FBI.

Declan O'Hara: retired FBI agent.

Nolan O'Hara: his son, an FBI agent.

Fiona O'Hara: Declan's daughter, an attorney.

David Jordan: an attorney.

Carlo Giordano: Jordan's uncle, a *mafioso*.

Dominic Giordano: Carlo's son, also a *mafioso*.

Angelo Giordano: his second son, also a *mafioso*.

Payton Sawyer: an NYPD officer.

Frederick Douglass Sawyer: Payton's brother, an FBI agent.

Stephen Barnes: a KGB sleeper agent living in America.

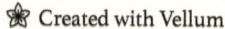 Created with Vellum

AUTHOR'S NOTE

The Bureau is a work of fiction, but real-life public figures, institutions and events often appear within its pages. Where that occurs, personal conversations and actions are the author's invention, except where drawn directly from reliable nonfiction sources. Timelines of historical events, likewise, may be rearranged, compressed or extended as required for dramatic effect. Anachronistic terms now often deemed offensive—"Negro," "colored," "queer" and the like—are used within these pages as they were applied during the years portrayed. Obsolete geographical names are used as they were normally applied during the years of 1965 to 1973 inclusive.

PROLOGUE

Governor's Mansion, Montgomery, Alabama: February 27, 1965

GOVERNOR GEORGE WALLACE WAS IN A RAGE, STRUTTING around his office, walls decorated with a life-sized portrait of General Robert E. Lee and the simplistic state seal designed in 1817 by the first appointed governor of Alabama Territory, two years prior to statehood. Behind his desk, two flags hung limply from their staffs: the state's banner—a red diagonal cross of St. Andrew on a field of white—and the obsolete "Stainless Banner," a Confederate battle flag.

Throughout the room—throughout the capitol, in fact —America's "Old Glory" was missing in action.

Wallace's visitor, Dallas County Sheriff Jim Clark, had given up on tracking the governor's restless movements. He sat in an armchair before the huge desk, 250 pounds of fat and muscle straining the seams of his suit with the proud "NEVER" button pinned to its lapel. Without his trademark helmet or peaked cap, he was a balding fat man who looked years older than forty-two.

"You wanna tell me, Jimbo, what in royal *hell* is goin' on around Selma these days?"

It was rhetorical. The whole world knew what had been happening in Selma, seat of Dallas County, building to a head these past two years.

"Well, Guv'nor, it's them niggers."

"Oh," Wallace stopped short behind his desk, gnawing the stub of a cigar. "I'm fuckin' glad you cleared that up. 'Them niggers,' is it? How'n hell would I have ever guessed that without you? It ain't like they're on television every fuckin' night. You get that from a crystal ball, did you?"

"I meant—"

"Fuck what you *meant*. Tell me about this nigger kilt in Marion."

"First thing," Clark said, "he had it comin', tryin' to attack an officer. Plus, those were state troopers, and Marion ain't even in my county."

Wallace gaped at Clark as if the sheriff had sprouted a second head. "Son of a bitch! You tryin' to *correct* me now, puttin' it back on *me* and sayin' it's *my* fault?"

"Nossir, I only meant—"

"It's first thing on the fuckin' TV news this mornin', *Sheriff*. Now I've got Martin Luther Coon on television, tellin' ever'body and his dog that mob you got down there is gonna march from Selma to Montgomery and camp outside here, on my fuckin' doorstep, prayin' for some kinda voting law from Congress."

"We can put a stop to that," Clark said, feeling his booted feet on firmer ground.

"Oh, *can* you? After all the shit the goddamn media has heaped all over you and me since this mess started up?"

"Yessir. I guarantee it."

Wallace paused, sucked in a breath and clearly tried to calm himself.

"I hope you're right, Jimbo," he said at last. "Cuz if you can't, *I* guarantee you'll be out of a job and unemployable statewide. I don't care what your pinhead voters say. You let this march proceed, and you are done in Alabama. By the time I'm through with you, the fuckin' Birch Society won't let you swab their toilets. Are you hearin' me?"

"Yessir. Stop it. That's what I aim to do."

A few beats passed with Wallace staring at him, then the governor bellowed, "Well, why are you still sittin' there? Get off your ass and do your goddamn job!"

CHAPTER 1

Harlem: March 2, 1965

SOME DAYS, LIKE THIS ONE, PAYTON SAWYER FELT AS IF HE'D dropped the ball and hadn't even seen which way it rolled away from him. He'd been with NYPD's "BOSS" unit for nearly fourteen years, reporting weekly on the machinations of Black Muslims and assorted other Negro radicals, but in the past ten days he'd felt it slipping through his fingers, fading out of reach.

The year had started strong for Malcolm X, Sawyer's primary target, and the Organization of Afro-American Unity he'd founded back in June. He had been busy giving speeches all over the map, from Gotham and New England up to Canada, down south to troubled Selma, then to London for the First Congress of the Council of African Organizations. Before leaving the States, he'd flown out to Los Angeles and met with lawyers representing two women who'd filed paternity suits against Nation of Islam "prophet" Elijah Muhammad.

London had gone well enough, but when Malcolm

moved on to Paris, headed for Geneva, he'd been stopped by the law at Charles de Gaulle Airport, denied entry to France amid rumors his name had been placed on a CIA "hit list," marked to go the same way as Patrice Lumumba in the Congo.

So, he'd come home to New York and barely spent twelve hours there before someone firebombed his home in East Elmhurst. Elijah's people owned the place, and they'd been trying to evict Malcolm for months, so journalists were quick to blame the NOI.

But Malcolm wasn't sure. Not anymore.

BOSS eavesdroppers were listening when he phoned Alex Haley, would-be author of Malcolm's biography in progress. Tape spun, capturing his words as he told Haley, "The more I keep thinking about this thing, the things that have been happening lately, I'm not at all sure it's the Muslims. I know what they can do, and what they can't, and they can't do some of the stuff recently going on. The more I keep thinking about what happened to me in France, I think I'm going to quit saying it's the Muslims."

But if not them, who?

At that point, Payton hadn't known if it could be the Agency, the FBI, someone from BOSS itself—not shy about breaking the law—or other players that he couldn't even name.

Two days after that conversation on the phone, a long-time friend had asked Malcolm and family to stay at his apartment. Malcolm had demurred, as an informer noted, saying, "You have a family. I don't want anyone hurt on my account. I always knew it would end like this."

And one day later, it *had* ended.

At 3:10 p.m. on February 21, Malcolm stepped to the podium at Gotham's Audubon Ballroom. The place was packed to overflowing, and as he began to speak, a man had risen from the audience, shouting, "Nigger, get your hand outa my pocket!" At the same instant, a smoke bomb detonated in the middle of the crowd and people started fleeing toward the exits—just as three men rushed the stage, blazing away at Malcolm with two pistols and a cut-down shotgun, literally blowing him away.

The audience mobbed one of the gunmen, identified as Talmadge X Hayer, né Thomas Hagan, beating him before police arrived, and while his two accomplices escaped. No matter. Members of the audience identified the vanished pair as NOI members Norman 3X Butler and Thomas 15X Johnson. Both were now in custody, Hayer denying either one of them had been involved in the shooting. Ironically, another NOI member, Reuben X Francis, had exchanged fire with the killers, wounding Hayer before he was mobbed. For "balance," NYPD charged him with felonious assault against the killer.

What a shit show that had been, and in its aftermath, "Allah," the Five Percenter's founder previously known as Clarence 13X, was trying to fill Malcolm's empty shoes. Payton didn't like his chances, knowing that BOSS and the FBI both had him pinned in their crosshairs, Director Hoover branding Clarence as a "Harlem rowdy," warning that his faction might hook up with other radicals unless it was destroyed forthwith.

NYPD had plans in mind for him. In fact, he was already facing trial on charges of assault and drug possession. Sixty followers had been ejected from Allah's arraignment when they started shouting, "Peace!" His judge was unimpressed by Allah's threats to rain divine fire on Manhattan, packing him off to the psych ward at Bellevue for observation. Now it looked like Clarence might evade the pending charges on a loony plea, but he was sane enough to have his followers resisting bids by Malcolm's evident successor at the NOI to win back the defectors.

"Christ all Friday," Payton muttered, falling back on one of his old man's bemused expressions. What in hell would he be facing next?

———

Manhattan: March 25, 1965

As SOON AS the phone rang, Dave Jordan guessed it would be Fee O'Hara on the line from Washington. Who else except his friend and sometime lover would be calling on a Thursday afternoon, when Jordan had no court dates scheduled, and for what reason but the Alabama demonstrations that were dominating all three networks from ground zero in Montgomery?

It clearly wouldn't be Dave's father, missing now for five months and presumed dead by police, Dave's grieving mother, and the whole damned Giordano family. Greg Jordan might've changed his name before he went away to college, in the hazy days preceding World War One, but he had never managed to escape what mobsters blandly called "The Life."

Dave grabbed the phone before it rang a third time. Said, "Hello?"

"Dave, are you watching this?" Fiona asked.

"What else? The networks haven't given me much choice."

"It's *history*," she told him. "We can actually *see* it being made."

"It's something," he agreed. On his TV screen, Martin

Luther King was speaking from the state capitol steps, exhorting a multiracial horde of followers that they must keep on fighting, taking any risks required of them, until all citizens were equal under law as they were in the eyes of God. Governor Wallace was in hiding, his state troopers in their helmets, clutching billy clubs, watching the crowd with wary eyes.

The last time Fee had phoned him from D.C. had been on Selma's "Bloody Sunday," not quite three weeks earlier. On that day, Alabama troopers and a sheriff's mounted posse had attacked 600 marchers on the Edmund Pettus Bridge, tear-gassing them and beating them down with nightsticks, some of the county deputies flailing with hoses wrapped in barbed wire, cracking bullwhips like the antebellum slave drivers they sought to emulate.

That clash had landed sixty demonstrators in the hospital and brought an influx of replacements from the North, including nuns and clergymen of all denominations, people of all races, from all walks of life. One of those volunteers, a minister from Boston, had been slain in Selma four days later, walking with two colleagues past a Selma dive, the Silver Moon Café. Four Klansmen were in custody for that killing, but no one in his right mind thought they'd ever be convicted.

"I'm thinking I should go down there," Fee said, sounding breathless.

"What? Fiona, why on Earth—"

"I can't just sit here, watching. You see that, don't you?"

"Have you discussed it with your family?"

Dave hadn't met her parents, even though her dad and his were law school classmates in the old days, before Dave's father went off to fight in France and Fee's had joined the Bureau of Investigation, now known as the FBI.

MICHAEL NEWTON

"My parents think I'm crazy," she replied. "But Nolan's in the thick of it already."

Nolan was her brother, and a G-man like their dad. He was four years older than Fiona, and before joining the Bureau he'd won damned near every medal the Marine Corps had to offer, during the Pacific War. They hadn't talked about him much, but Dave recalled a bit of data now, from months gone by.

"He's there in Alabama, right?"

"Not anymore. They transferred him to Mississippi, which is even worse, if you can picture that. They're bombing, burning, killing people every time you turn around down there."

"Excellent reasons to stay where you are and help the folks you can through Legal Aid."

"I'm being left *behind*. Can't you see that?" She sounded on the verge of anger now.

"I hear you, but—"

"Oh, just forget it! Never mind!"

The line went dead, and David fought the urge to call her back immediately, try to reason with her, maybe give the bees a chance to leave her bonnet and fly off. He stopped himself before he started dialing, knew it would be futile until Fee's temper had cooled a bit.

And if she really did it, really went to Dixie's war zone, what could Jordan do about it? Squat. But was it possible for him to help her in some other way, before she took a dangerous, perhaps irrevocable step?

———

Atlanta, Georgia: August 20, 1965

FRED SAWYER STOOD on Auburn Avenue Northeast, staring across traffic toward Southern Christian Leadership Conference headquarters. It wasn't far to walk, across four lanes of blacktop, but he saw it as crossing the Rubicon, passing a point of no return.

The Bureau didn't know he was in Georgia—not yet, anyway. He'd mailed his resignation back to D.C. from a postbox on the concourse of Atlanta International Airport, after deplaning in mid-morning. It wouldn't reach headquarters until Monday, at the earliest, but Sawyer knew that bridge was well and truly burned.

His taxi driver on the ten-mile ride to Auburn Avenue had run his mouth in competition with the radio, a newscaster announcing two more ministers, both white, had been gunned down in Alabama. One was dead, the other touch-and-go, some kind of "special deputy" already out on bail for blasting them inside a store they'd tried to patronize after they'd been released from jail for demonstrating in some jerk-water town called Hayneville.

That crime would have the SCLC staffers buzzing, planning some reaction. Fred supposed he could've picked a better time to drop in unannounced, but would there ever *really* be a better time in Dixie, while that kind of shit was going on?

Besides, it was another murder—and the grim events that followed after it—which brought him to this place, right now, forsaking a four-year career in law enforcement, all for...what?

Fred had been present at the Audubon Ballroom in February, when assassins gunned down Malcolm X. He'd spotted brother Payton, doubtless covering the scene for NYPD, but he'd slipped away unnoticed in the chaos that ensued. He'd thought about quitting the Bureau then, disgusted with its handling of "racial matters" and his own role in that travesty, but he'd required another shove before he made the final break.

That push had come from California, the Watts ghetto of Los Angeles exploding into flames this very month. LAPD had managed to restore uneasy order just four days before Fred's flight from Washington to Georgia, but the cost was steep: thirty-four people dead over the span of six days, including one white cop shot accidentally by another, headed for the riot zone aboard a bus; more than 1,000 others injured; 4,000 arrested; destruction of 1,000 buildings tabulated at $40 million in damages. Of course, police and National Guardsmen had seized the occasion to shoot up NOI Mosque No. 27, while LAPD Chief Bill Parker went on television, blaming Muslims for the riot, likening Watts inhabitants to "monkeys in a zoo."

That firestorm, finally, had pushed Fred into the irrevocable step he was completing now.

He crossed the street, entered the SCLC's lobby, and was greeted by beefed-up security. The man in charge, confronting him, was six foot five or six, 200 pounds at least, like something carved from ebony.

"Help you?" he asked.

"I need to speak with somebody about protecting Dr. King."

A frosty smile greeted that overture. "I think we've got that covered, Mister—?"

"Frederick Douglass Sawyer. Until half an hour ago, I've been working against your people for the FBI."

FBI Headquarters: August 25, 1965

ALOYSIUS GANTT HAD FINALLY DECIDED: he was definitely bailing out, age sixty-nine and sick of dealing with the bullshit he'd been plowing through for damned near half a century.

Clyde Tolson, for example. Virtually crippled by a stroke last year, he still hung on as Number Two inside the Bureau, Edgar Hoover's faithful pet. On top of that, he'd just received the President's Award for Distinguished Federal Civilian Service, LBJ praising Clyde as "a vital force in raising the proficiency of law enforcement at all levels and in guiding the Federal Bureau of Investigation to new heights of accomplishment through periods of great National challenge."

And what a crock of shit that was.

While Tolson clung to his position, Assistant Director Alan Belmont had retired after nineteen years in harness, replaced by Hoover sycophant Cartha DeLoach. Belmont moved on to serve as assistant director of the Hoover Institution on War, Revolution and Peace, a right-wing think tank in Manhattan founded in 1919 by Herbert Hoover—no relation to Edgar, though the irony still tickled Gantt.

Intent of wrapping up his tenure with a flourish, likely wasted on the Boss, Gantt was reviewing some of the outstanding files heaped on his desk. One bore the name of Negro agitator Hubert "Rap" Brown, lately inducted by the army, who had wreaked such havoc at his physical in Baltimore that he was finally rejected by the military, heading back to D.C. and dual occupations as spokesman for the Student Nonviolent Coordinating Committee, doubling as a neighborhood anti-poverty worker.

Another dossier belonged to Richard Bullock Henry, aka "Imari Obadele," born in Philadelphia, now living in Detroit, leading the Malcolm X Society until he craved more action and began recruiting for another outfit labeled the Republic of New Afrika.

Out west, two other Negro radicals—Ron "Maulana" Karenga and Allen Donaldson, aka "Hakim Abdullah Jamal"—had formed a group called the US Organization in the wake of the Watts rioting. Depending who you asked, "US" either stood for *us* (Negroes), opposing *them* (white people), or perhaps was an abbreviation of "United Slaves." Jamal was on the letterhead as founder, while Karenga ranked as chairman, pushing an "US School of Afroamerican Culture" among other things. The group's alleged ideals were summed up in seven Swahili words, as translated by Karenga: *Imani* (faith), *Kujichagulia* (self-determination), *Kuumba* (creativity), *Nia* (purpose), *Ujamaa* (cooperative economics) *Ujima* (collective work and responsibility), and *Umoja* (unity).

Last but not least on the Bureau's latest hit list was Pedro Albizu Campos, founder of Puerto Rico's Nationalist Party. Edgar Hoover longed to tap his phone, but by the time Bill Sullivan's gremlins realized the target didn't own one, Albizu Campos had died on April 21, at age seventy-three. Loath to give up a wild goose chase, G-men had tapped a neighbor's phone in San Juan, seeking a scoop on "plans to foment assassination attempts and other violence at the time of subject's death."

Sometimes, Gantt marveled at how long he'd spent under the Bureau's sway, remembering the crimes he'd committed on behalf of "national security," but it was finally enough. As soon as he'd disposed of the remaining files in hand, he planned to follow Declan O'Hara's example by pulling the pin.

———

STARTING his sophomore year at age nineteen, Stephen Barnes had no reason to think his classes would be any more daunting than those he'd aced, making the dean's list, as a freshman. Granted, nearly one-fifth of the university's students had placed on that list, but he'd shared the year's Freshman First Honor Prize with a coed from the Science Department, putting him well on track for graduating Summa Cum Laude downrange.

Princeton considered its first year "a time for exploration and discovery," while the sophomore year was tagged "a time for reflection, consolidation, and decision-making." That meant formally choosing a major, which Barnes had selected before he enrolled. He was sticking with history, keeping his eyes on law school and, beyond that, ultimate acceptance to the ranks of Edgar Hoover's FBI. If Hoover did the universe a favor and expired before then, it was all the same to Barnes.

He had a debt to pay in equal measures to the father he could not recall from life, to his adoptive parents—and, of course, to Mother Russia.

Oddly—it had come as a surprise to Barnes—Princeton was one of three Ivy League universities without a law school, the others being Brown and Dartmouth. Princeton had *tried* to start one, back in 1847, consisting of three professors, but it closed five years later, after graduating only seven students. Now, Barnes had his eye on Yale.

In the meantime, nothing said he couldn't kick back and enjoy himself within accepted limits: drink a bit, get laid as much as he could manage—though it held no great appeal for him—and avoid any blowback from dumb mistakes.

His roommate, Jack Edmonds, had mourned the Goldwater defeat last fall but seemed to have learned nothing from it. He was hooked on Ronald Reagan now, a third-rate movie actor—and, Barnes knew, a former undercover stoolie for the FBI in Hollywood—who'd scored big with Republicans for an emotive speech supporting Barry called "A Time for Choosing," Reagan had delivered it via TV's *General Electric Theater* six days before November's balloting. It hadn't helped the senator from Arizona, thankfully, but party leaders were already raising Reagan's name among potential White House candidates for 1968.

Some country, Stephen thought, and snatched a handy quote from Proverbs. *Pride goeth before a fall.*

———

FBI Field Office, New Orleans: October 13, 1965

DEVON GANTT WISHED he could say the Bureau's COIN-TELPRO—WHITE HATE schemes had put a dent in Ku Klux operations, but he didn't see it happening. At least, not yet. They had recruited more informers, granted, and discredited some loyal Klansmen via smear campaigns, but so far there'd been no letup in violence statewide.

Gantt counted three known dead for 1965, so far. The first on file had been Oneal Moore, appointed in June with friend Creed Rogers as the first Negro sheriff's deputies since Reconstruction in Washington Parish. Hired in 1964, they'd lasted one year on the job before a June ambush killed Moore and blinded Rogers in one eye. Rogers survived to radio a good description of the shooters' pickup truck, stopped by police in Mississippi shortly afterward. The driver, Ernest Ray McElveen, was a Bogalusa Klansman and National States Rights Party member, a paper mill worker, and part-time insurance salesman. Police caught him with two pistols, but the deputies were blasted with a rifle and shotgun, both weapons missing along with McElveen's cohorts. Gantt would've bet good money that the murder's wheelman would escape unpunished for his crime.

The other dead so far were both civilians, killed by white police. The first, John Wesley Wilder, had been shot five times by a Ruston patrolman during a vaguely described altercation. One week later to the day, Ferriday police and Concordia Parish deputies blasted William Piercefield, claiming he'd brandished a .22-caliber rifle during a family argument.

Devon knew the DOJ would never try to prosecute those cops, so he was focused chiefly on the Klan. An informer from Concordia Parish identified James Seale, his father Clyde, and brother Jack as members of the Silver Dollar Group, flashing their recognition coins at a Ku Klux picnic while James faced charges of a double murder in Mississippi. Too bad the stupid bastard had confessed in custody, but that apparently meant little to his Franklin County prosecutor.

Their informer placed the Seales at as guests at the home of SDG member James "Red" Glover, prime suspect in an August car bombing that had nearly killed NAACP activist George Metcalfe in Natchez. Metcalfe's mistake—aside from advocating Negro civil rights—was working as an Armstrong Tire employee at the Natchez plant, where a majority of white coworkers were identified as members of one Klan faction or another troubling Adams County with a rash of dynamite explosions, targets ranging from black agitators to the town's white mayor.

Another Bureau stoolie, named in various reports as

"JN-348," described James Seale attending an SDG meeting on a sandbar in the Homochitto River, Franklin County, where he'd demonstrated use of "bologna sized" TNT sticks. More recently, Seale and other terrorists had packed the funeral of SDG member Ernest Finley, Seale and a comrade clipping a silver dollar onto one of Finley's wreaths—their only public demonstration so far that the group existed.

Gantt hoped to dig up more dirt on another murder, this one of a Klansman named Earl Hodges from Eddiceton, Mississippi. Branded as a traitor, thanks in part to FBI "bad-jacketing" harassment, Hodges tried to quit the Klan but took a fatal beating for his trouble, allegedly on orders from Clyde Seal, "exalted cyclops" of White Knights Unit No. 2 in Meadville. Evidence showed Hodges had been clubbed over the head and whipped with a leather strap studded with 1/8-inch rivets, ripping his flesh, before he staggered off and collapsed beside a rural well, trying to wash blood from his face. Despite the clear-cut evidence of murder, Franklin County's coroner and sheriff deemed the homicide "an accident."

Two days ago, Louisiana's premier Klan, the Original Knights, had suffered yet another rift. The "Grand Dragon" had terminated charters for his units based in Ferriday and Vidalia, citing Silver Dollar defections and chastising Red Glover for looting the till. With one foot out the door already, Glover threw himself into the SDG full-time, joined by a Kluxer known as "Scrapman"—birth name Elden Glenn Hester—who served the group as its resident explosive expert. Another member of the clique, E. D. Morace, stockpiled stolen dynamite at various locations where the SDG could call for it at need.

One thing about the Klan, Gantt mused: no matter what changes it made in name or leadership, somebody in the ranks was always ready to sell out his fellow goons for thirty pieces of federal silver.

As if Klan violence wasn't enough to occupy the Bureau in Louisiana, Edgar Hoover had gone apeshit on them back in February, when the *New York Times* published a piece about the Deacons for Defense and Justice, headquartered in Jonesboro. Director Hoover fired a memo off, demanding all available intelligence on the new group, noting, "Because of the potential for violence indicated, you are instructed to immediately initiate an investigation of the DDJ." So far, the file had plumped to 1,500 pages with no evidence of any crimes committed, while enough G-men were sidelined from important cases to ensure no end of eavesdropping and spying.

More business as usual, Gantt thought, and turned his focus back onto the Klan.

———

FBI Field Office, Jackson, Mississippi: October 25, 1965

NOLAN O'HARA HADN'T BEEN SURPRISED in January, when Franklin County District Attorney Lenox Forman filed a motion to dismiss the affidavits from confessed Klan killers Charles Edwards and James Ford Seale. Justice of the Peace Willie Bedford, who'd signed the Klansmen's arrest warrants, happily reneged "in the interest of justice and in order to fully develop the facts in this case," presumably letting it die from neglect. Both ex-defendants now swore they'd been "brutally beaten" by lawmen, despite emerging from jail without so much as hangnail.

That was Mississippi justice for you: one version for Negroes and another for the whites who murdered them.

And the state's death toll kept mounting. In January, a white Winona farmer shot Jessie Brown with no apparent questions asked. Eight days later, Mrs. Selma Triggs died in a suspicious Hattiesburg house fire. One day after that, police shot and killed Ollie Shelby inside the Hinds County jail. In late February, officers found William Lee beaten to death beside a railroad track near Canton. Two days later, a plantation boss in Okolona shot employee Donald Rasberry. In August, an off-duty constable shot Johnny Queen in Fayette, followed by Freddie Thomas, slain as a warning to other black voters in Sidon. Jimmie Lee Griffin was September's victim, killed by a hit-and-run driver near Sturgis, run over at least twice in the coroner's opinion. Another constable killed Robert McNair in November, at Pelahatchie, and police shot Lillie Power four days later, as she sat with friends in a parked car.

Of course, the bombings and arsons continued with no sign of letup: a freedom school and library in Indianola; a newly integrated Vicksburg café; two Negro churches near Natchez. George Metcalfe had survived his car bombing in August, though it fractured one arm and one leg, nearly costing him the sight in one eye. Charles Evers—brother of the martyred Medgar—had stepped up to lead the state's NAACP at great personal risk, pulling no punches in his condemnation of white violence.

By August 30, with the fires of Watts still fresh in mind, FBI headquarters warned Governor Paul Johnson that a cadre of Deacons for Defense were en route from Louisiana to defend embattled brethren in Natchez. Johnson, fearful of martial law being imposed under his reign, dispatched National Guardsmen led by Adjutant General Walter Johnson, armed with heavy weapons.

On arrival in Natchez, General Johnson summoned

ranking Klansmen to an upstairs room in the Adams County courthouse, overlooking its parking lot. Below, his soldiers manned an anti-aircraft battery with four .50-caliber machine guns. At a signal from their general, the troops swiveled their weapon's turret, elevating and depressing its guns, while Johnson told the Klansmen they could hear the guns up close and personal they next time any of their men stepped out of line. For emphasis, all major Natchez intersections sported sandbags and at least one light machine gun with a crew on watch.

And so peace was restored—at least, that is, for the two weeks before the Guard pulled out.

The "Mississippi Burning Case" from Philadelphia was still up in the air. A federal grand jury had indicted eighteen defendants on January 15, but six weeks later those charges were dismissed by U.S. District Judge Harold Cox, appointed to the bench as Senator James Eastland's reward for allowing Thurgood Marshall's confirmation to the Second Circuit Court of Appeals. Cox was no better than a Klansman himself, often berating Negroes in his courtroom as "apes" or "baboons," and Nolan saw no future for the case while he remained in charge.

Meanwhile, in July, Congress had passed the Voting Rights Act of 1965, and three months later, HUAC had broken its long tradition of willful blindness by opening a full-scale investigation of the several active Klans.

Although he had his hands full, working out of Jackson, Nolan still kept a proprietary eye on Alabama from a distance. Things were little better there than where he was, in the Magnolia State, but frequent calls to Keely and their children reassured them they were safe and sound, his private threat against Birmingham's top Klansman still holding firm.

Klan membership had topped out at an estimated 30,000, with Bob Shelton's UKA by far the strongest faction in the state and in the South at large. The year's death toll fell short of Mississippi's, but police and their collaborators from the KKK had done the best they could.

In February one of "Colonel" Lingo's troopers had killed Jimmie Lee Jackson during a protest march in Marion. Next up, in March, four drunken "knights" had beaten Reverend James Reeb to death in Selma, also battering two other northern clergymen. Two weeks later, a volunteer from Detroit named Viola Liuzzo was shot while driving marchers back to Selma from Montgomery. Chief Hoover passed a file loaded with lies about her sex life on to Sheriff Clark down there, before G-men busted Liuzzo's killers. One of those who'd ridden in the murder car was Gary Rowe, an FBI informer Nolan wouldn't trust as far as he could throw the guy, a drunken brawler who had boasted of his role in 1963's fatal church bombing. Now, three of Liuzzo's slayers were awaiting trial, but they had visited North Carolina for a stopover in May, signing autographs for some 6,000 fans at a Klan rally.

Skip from there to July, when three yahoos left an NSRP gathering in Anniston and shot a Negro, Willie Brewster, who was driving home from work. They faced manslaughter charges, bomber-lawyer Jesse Stoner ready to defend them.

August chalked up three more shooting victims, with two dead. At Hayneville, the seat of "Bloody Lowndes" County, Tom Coleman—a Klan member and part-time sheriff's deputy—had shot two white clergymen, killing Jonathan Daniels and leaving Father Richard Morrisroe in critical condition but expected to survive. Al Lingo had supplied a bondsman for the killer, chauffeured from Montgomery by a state trooper who was also Coleman's son. Six days after that incident, persons unknown had slain Thad Christian with a shotgun blast near Anniston, as he walked home from fishing at a nearby pond.

Before that, in Demopolis, four redneck bastards sprayed a pair of teenage Negro girls and a small boy with acid on a streetcorner, then drove off, laughing. Thankfully, while the three victims suffered burns, none proved to be disfiguring. Police, of course, had "no leads" in that case.

In "Bombingham," it seemed the terrorists were getting clumsy. Out of nine devices planted citywide in March and April, only one exploded, shattering a Negro family's home. Six more were found in black or integrated neighborhoods but failed to detonate, two other duds uncovered at the mayor's house and a city councilwoman's place. Agents had questioned UKA "klokan" Floyd Simpson—nearly charged two years ago when "someone" used his gun to murder freedom marcher William Moore—but Simpson answered that he knew nothing about the bombs "and wouldn't tell y'all if I did."

More G-men were assigned to tracking Stokely Carmichael and his Lowndes County Freedom Movement, a spin-off from SNCC that had registered an amazing 2,600 Negro voters—up from seventy in 1960, now 300 more than the county's registered white tally. Edgar Hoover hated Carmichael, his upstart movement, and its letterhead emblazoned with a snarling black panther. That was too much black and too much nascent militancy for the Chief, sparking demands for new and fatter dossiers.

The "BAPBOM" file was thick enough already, in Nolan's opinion, but Hoover was leery of arrests that likely wouldn't pad the FBI's conviction stats. Four suspects had emerged as likely murderers: Klansmen Tom Blanton Jr., Herman Cash, "Dynamite Bob" Chambliss, and Bobby Cherry—or five, if you believed repeated boasts from Gary Rowe that he had been among the Sunday morning bombers. Headquarters had wiretap evidence enough to send the main four up for life, or land them all in "Yellow Mama," Kilby Prison's fifty-eight-year-old electric chair, but it was holding back that proof so far.

O'Hara wondered how much longer Hoover could retain his job, but with the rumored glee President Johnson felt while listening to bedroom tapes of Martin Luther King, the Chief should be secure for three more years, at least.

Too bad, thought Nolan, *when an old man's pride lets murderers walk free.*

———

Little Italy, Manhattan: November 25, 1965

DOMINIC GIORDANO FIGURED this would be his last Thanksgiving with both parents, given how his father had been fading over the past thirteen months. The disappearance of *Don* Carlo's only living brother—Uncle Greg to Dominic and Angelo, who'd changed his name to "Jordan" years before they made their squalling entries to the world—still hadn't surfaced, and it didn't look like he was coming back.

As *consigliere* and accountant for the Giordano family, Greg was a vital cog in its machinery, though by all accounts, he hadn't got his hands dirty since 1931, a job that Papa Carlo still wouldn't discuss with either of his sons. Gotham's five families had been at war back then, some of the top men killed along with their *soldatos* before Charley Luciano finally came out on top and set up *La Commissione* to run the show.

Of course, some hassles still went on. In January,

Vincent Rao agreed to testify against Lucchese family leaders, but he'd lied to the grand jury and was serving five years now, for perjury. In Chicago, Momo Giancana had been jailed for contempt of another grand jury. Gotham's Bonanno family had split into competing factions, one led by the missing Joe Bonanno's son, another by Commission-sanctioned Gaspar DiGregorio, both sides arming for war. Carlo Gambino learned that underboss Joseph Biondo had been hiding income from their family but spared him, busting him down to a common soldier's rank, replacing him with Aniello Dellacroce. Just two days ago, back in Chi-Town, a heart attack killed Murray Humphreys moments after he had pulled a gun on G-men at his own apartment, taking off on foot. A tiny laceration on his neck sparked rumors of a lethal hypodermic, bolstering Mob talk that Humphreys had been "losing it" of late.

Now losing it another way was weighing heavily upon Dominic's mind. He hadn't voiced those fears, but worried that when Papa Carlo kicked the bucket, likely leaving him in charge, the family would go downhill under his leadership and maybe get wiped off the map.

In which case, Dom decided, he might just as well be dead himself.

———

Fairlawn, Southeast Washington, D.C.: December 19, 1965

Declan O'Hara sat watching *Andy of Mayberry* on CBS and half imagined he could feel Abigail's irritation radiating at him from the kitchen where she was preparing lunch, likely more of the same salami sandwiches they eaten yesterday.

I need to get out more, he thought, already planning some

excuse for slipping off to hit Maguire's his favored local bar. Retirement wasn't all he'd hoped for, but at seventy and counting, what in hell could he expect? He and his wife had taken a vacation down to Florida, two months ago, but even traveling for pleasure these days felt like too much work.

And what *was* pleasure for a man his age? Forget about the bedroom frolics, even makeup sex after an argument, although they didn't bicker much. Fighting required more energy than he possessed.

Mostly, when not watching TV or sipping Jameson with one or two fellow retirees at Maguire's, Declan kept up with news about the Bureau he'd abandoned. Congress had approved a whole new Quantico complex, but actual construction wouldn't start till 1969, from the projected estimates. Hoover and Tolson still held power at headquarters, and the Ten Most Wanted list was still ticking along, still mostly tracking robbers and escaped prisoners, but more fugitives were eluding capture for longer periods, and hitman Fred Tenuto had been scratched, still never found, when Joe Valachi testified he had been killed in 1952.

More interesting to O'Hara was the lengthening JFK "death list." Private physicians blamed three of the year's nine fatalities on "natural causes." Maurice Gatlin, a lawyer and sometime Guy Banister pilot, fell six stories from a New Orleans hotel window, his death ascribed to "heart failure." Two others were struck by vehicles, one by a Dallas bus, the other—Rose Cheramie, who'd foretold the Kennedy assassination in advance—killed by a hit-and-run driver. Journalist Dorothy Kilgallen interviewed Jack Ruby at length, vowing to "break the case" before she died from a supposed overdose. Two days later, Mrs. Earl Smith, a friend of Kilgallen and columnist for the *New York Journal-American*, dropped dead from an alleged "cerebral hemorrhage."

Finally, just yesterday, Dallas cabbie William Whaley had died in a crackup that also killed his fare, a U.S. Navy lieutenant commander, and the octogenarian driver who struck Whaley's taxi. On the last day of JFK's life, Whaley had driven Lee Oswald home from work to his rooming house. Now, he was the only cab driver killed on duty in Dallas history.

Mysterious, but not my problem, Declan thought, as Abigail called him for lunch.

———

Glover Park, Northwest Washington, D.C.: December 25, 1965

THE NEIGHBORHOOD WAS D.C.'s closest thing to a suburban district, bordered on the west by Glover-Archbold Park, on the south by Whitehaven Park and to the east by Woodley Park. Its northern border was defined by Fulton Street, close to Washington National Cathedral, in case Colby Gantt should feel a sudden urge to pray—or to confess his sins.

As if. Whatever he had done was classified Top Secret or above.

Christmas with wife Eileen and their son Hardy, presently an eighteen-year-old freshman at George Washington, reminded Gantt of most others he'd spent with family, aside from when he'd served the OSS abroad in World War Two. They traded presents all around, and Eileen worked up a dessert for dinner with his parents, his father recently retired and trying to become a golfer even though he didn't seem to like the sport.

At least it got him out in the fresh air to exercise, no small accomplishment for an ex-bureaucrat who'd seen age sixty-nine receding in his rearview mirror.

That could be me in another twenty-something years, thought Colby, *if I last that long.*

In his inaugural address, President Johnson had advised America, "We can never again stand aside, prideful in isolation. Terrific dangers and troubles that we once called 'foreign' now constantly live among us." That meant more money and expanding power for the CIA, whose new director, named in June, was ex-Vice Admiral William Raborn. *Time* magazine hailed his appointment, saying his administrative skills would be invaluable for the Agency at risk of being "drowned in data," but so far, Raborn struck Colby as a bad fit for the job of DCI, just marking time.

Not that Raborn didn't have his plate full, trouble coming at him from all sides. In Cuba, Castro had officially renamed his 26th of July Movement the Communist Party of Cuba. Thirteen thousand miles to the east, the People's Democratic Party of Afghanistan declared itself for Marxism, then settled down to squabbling between the moderate *Parcham* ("banner") and hard-line *Khalq* ("masses") factions. Gantt thought that ought to keep them busy for a while.

In Laos, while would-be *putschists* fought among themselves for power, the U.S. launched "Operation Steel Tiger" the Laotian panhandle and the Vietnamese DMZ, then followed up with "Operation Tiger Hound" to stem enemy traffic on the Hồ Chí Minh Trail. While that succeeded to a point, now full-scale civil war was raging in the country's northern quadrant.

Action in Vietnam was down and dirty, with the CIA's new "Phoenix Program" seeking to destroy the Việt Cộng or NLF by means of infiltration, capture and interrogation, counter-terrorism, and assassination. Langley called it "fighting fire with fire," meaning that they'd embraced Red tactics to defeat the Reds, while "winning hearts and minds."

Air America kept flying guns and drugs, one shipment interrupted when a Huey helicopter crashed and sank into the Mekong River. Three crewmen escaped that wreck, but two others died when ground fire dropped their C-45 Expeditor near Bao Trai Airfield in Hậu Nghĩa Province.

In overt warfare news, by August the U.S. had more than 125,000 ground troops in South Vietnam, with no end to escalation in sight. "Operation Rolling Thunder" spearheaded the first of countless massive bombing raids, followed by "Operation Flaming Dart." LBJ delivered his "Peace Without Conquest" speech at Johns Hopkins University, offering Hanoi "unconditional discussions" to end combat in exchange for massive economic assistance to modernize Vietnam. Despite telling his aides, "Old Hô can't turn that down," the only answer coming from Hanoi was mocking laughter at the Texan's arrogance.

Pissed off at that, Johnson had vowed "to nail that coonskin to the wall." More palatable for his voters, in July he'd doubled monthly draft call-ups to 35,000, telling Americans, "I have asked the commanding general, General Westmoreland, what more he needs to meet this mounting aggression. He has told me. And we will meet his needs. We cannot be defeated by force of arms. We will stand in Vietnam." He claimed to know how weeping mothers mourned their sons, cut down on Asian battlefields, but showed no inclination to desist.

The upshot: Congress delivered another $1.7 billion for the war—that is, the war they *knew* about—and burning draft cards had become a trend, now punishable by five years in prison and a $1,000 fine. Two days after Thanksgiving, 35,000 anti-war protesters circled the White House, then rallied at the Washington Monument.

At home and still unknown to most Americans, Operation MIDNIGHT CLIMAX was shut down for good, and George White had finally retired from both the CIA and FBN, settling in California's Marin County as chief of the Stinson Beach Fire Department. Colby wondered what in hell he knew about firefighting, likely nothing but the thrill he got from speeding in his bright-red Jeep with its lights flashing. As for his longtime dabbling in dope, one thing he had succeeded at was spreading LSD and weed around the Haight-Ashbury neighborhood of San Francisco.

Meanwhile, Operation MKSEARCH had been split up into parallel programs christened MKOFTEN and CHICK-WIT. Research on drugs and mind control continued as before, the Agency collaborating with the U.S. Army Chemical Corps to "test the behavioral and toxicological effects of certain drugs on animals and humans." Dr. Gottlieb, on a tangent of his own, now sought to "explore the world of black magic" and "harness the forces of darkness and challenge the concept that the inner reaches of the mind are beyond reach." To that end, MKOFTEN roped in fortune-tellers, palm-readers, clairvoyants, astrologists, mediums, psychics, specialists in demonology, witches and warlocks, Satanists, and anybody else Gottlieb could lure with cash or dope.

Colby thought he must be as crazy as a fucking bedbug, but so what? It kept black money flowing into CIA coffers, and there was still an outside chance—way, *way* outside—that they would somehow save the world.

CHAPTER 2

New Orleans FBI Field Office: February 5, 1966

DEVON GANTT WAS MAKING LITTLE PROGRESS WITH HIS efforts to investigate Louisiana's Klan, and he was pissed off by the Bureau's failure. Even with informers on the payroll, telling him who'd burned a church or bombed a home sometime, even suggesting suspects in his open murder cases, evidence that would hold up in court was sparse to nonexistent.

Whatever else he might surmise, Gantt knew for sure that Governor McKeithen's half-assed scheme to bribe the Klan for peace and quiet had been money wasted, nothing much achieved besides the Kluckers laughing at McKeithen when his back was turned.

In brutal Bogalusa, sixty-nine miles north of the Big Easy, friends had posted bond for suspected cop-killer Ernest McElveen, lying character witnesses had white-washed his racist record, and the parish prosecutor had dismissed charges of killing one black deputy last year, blinding another. If that case ever wound up in court, Gantt would've been amazed.

In far-off Washington, what Edgar Hoover liked to call the Seat of Government, HUAC Chairman Edmund Willis finally had Klansmen on the hot seat, grilling them the same way his committee once interrogated Reds. Much violence and some embezzlement was on the public record now, but none of it headed for trial. The homicidal Seales—Clyde, Jack and James, all hid behind the Fifth Amendment, as did others such as Houston Morris, recently inducted by the Silver Dollar Group despite his murky history with the home-grown Original Knights.

And the bloodshed continued. James Seale had logged his fourth suspected murder, running down Negro pedestrian Bailey Odell in Franklin County, Mississippi. Add that onto Seale's involvement in the deaths of Henry Dee, Charles Moore, and Frank Morris, it marked Seale as a homicidal lunatic on par with Bob Chambliss in Birmingham, but no one of the side of law enforcement seemed inclined to stop him.

Meanwhile, the first black student at a previously all-white school in Ferriday, 140 miles northwest of Bogalusa, had been targeted last week, a firebomb hurled into his grandmother's home—once again, said informers, a job carried out by the SDG's crack "wrecking crew." Gantt thought he knew the men responsible for that but couldn't get the DOJ to charge them yet.

As far as an indictment by the state, that was a puerile fantasy.

But he'd keep trying, sure. Why not?

These days, what else was there for him to do?

———

Princeton, New Jersey: March 19, 1966

THE LAKESIDE GRILL was situated on Route 27, overlooking Lake Carnegie, a manmade reservoir on the Millstone River in the far northeastern corner of Princeton. It was popular with students from the university who could afford it—meaning nearly all of them—but would be losing customers over the next eight days as many went away for spring recess.

Before they scattered, Stephen Barnes had faked enthusiasm for a double date with roommate Jack Edmonds and two attractive coeds he'd enticed to have a meal of surf and turf. Barnes sat beside a red-haired sophomore, Yvonne Dickens, while Jack was paired off with a blonde freshman, Louise Springer. Barnes recommended oyster appetizers to the girls, and while Jack sniggered, they had gone for it.

Expecting sex on the first date, perhaps?

Barnes hoped so, although, to be honest, he wasn't excited by the prospect. Young Miss Dickens was attractive, relatively "stacked," but on a normal day, Barnes thought no more of sex than, say, blowing his nose.

He wasn't gay, a reference to homosexuals that had appeared during the latter 1940s; women simply didn't *move* him as they did most Princeton males, particularly jocks. Still, he was conscious of the need to "score," guarding against venereal disease and pregnancy, of course. The FBI, like his male classmates, would expect a duly "macho" attitude from applicants.

Louise was talking now, saying, "I'm telling you, they always die in threes."

"Who's 'they,' again?" Barnes asked, feigning interest.

"Celebrities. Two weeks ago or something, it was Fred from *I Love Lucy,* Gladys from *Bewitched,* and Joseph Fields."

Barnes recognized the playwright and movie producer's name. He guessed the other two were stars of television shows he'd never watched, saying, "Is that unusual?"

"Oh, no!" Louise replied. "It *always* happens."

"What's your theory about airline crashes?" Edmonds asked his date. "You know we had a couple two days running, earlier this month, with something like two hundred people dead, both in the Far East."

"Those crazy Asian pilots," said Yvonne, then caught herself. "I didn't mean that like it sounded," she assured them.

"*I* know what you meant," Jack said. "When Goldwater was running—"

Both girls heaved exaggerated, bust-expanding moans, Louise adding, "Enough with Barry G. already, Jack."

"Okay, okay."

When Barnes had time to watch TV, he concentrated on the news. Eleven days ago, Irish Republican Army bombers had blasted Nelson's Pillar on O'Connell Street in Dublin, forcing Brits to raze the part that hadn't been destroyed before it fell and killed pedestrians. Three days later, ex-Harvard professor Timothy Leary had received a thirty-year sentence, together with a $30,000 fine, for smuggling untaxed marijuana into Texas. One week after that, in Moscow, the Presidium had passed three laws further restricting practice of religion, on grounds that ritual displays "disturbed public order." Congressmen in Washington complained about the new statutes, then fled to their saloons and mistresses in time for happy hour.

Leaning toward him, one firm breast nuzzling his arm, Yvonne whispered to Barnes, "I think the oysters worked, Steve. I'm *so* wet!"

He grinned and whispered back to her, "Good thing I saved room for desert."

———

Harlem: June 15, 1966

THE SHOOTERS who'd eliminated Malcolm X, whoever was behind it, hadn't stopped Black Muslims cold, but killing him had hurt the movement, caused large-scale defections from the NOI, and turned a spotlight of suspicion on the group's commanding "prophet." In the meantime, Payton Sawyer had been handed new orders and other fish to fry for BOSS, now under the command of one Inspector Kevin Shaughnessy.

Another Irishman, he thought. *And that was NYPD for you.*

The new "menace" was an outfit known as the Black Guerilla Family, sometimes shortened to the Black Family or switched up to the Black Vanguard. Payton couldn't decide if that was an attempt to mask the group's activities, or if its poorly educated members simply couldn't keep the name straight in their heads.

The group had started out in prison, founded by three California inmates at San Quentin: George Jackson, George Lewis, and ex-boxer William Nolen. Some pegged Nolen as the brains behind the BGF, but most sources named Jackson as its prime mover and public spokesman—if there could be such a thing, penned up behind state prison walls.

Inspired by Marcus Garvey—shades of Payton's late father! —the BGF was down in FBI and BOSS files as a group of Negro Marxist-Leninist revolutionaries, founded in prison, now expanding to the "free world" as some of its members were paroled to roam abroad. Jackson was a Chicago native, born in 1941, whose family moved to Los Angeles in when he was fifteen. In January 1957 he was busted for stealing a motorcycle, released into his father's custody, then rebounded two weeks later, burglarizing a motorcycle shop and assaulting two cops.

Something about the bikes, thought Payton. *All that power rumbling between his legs.*

That same winter, Jackson had joined a gang called the Capones, and a cop shot him six times during a department store burglary. That didn't kill Jackson, but he was sent to juvey for a year, until he slipped out by impersonating a cell-mate earmarked for release. From there, he tried armed robbery, mostly gas stations, and in February 1961 pled guilty to his latest holdup, drawing an indeterminate sentence of one year to life. Parole denials landed him at Soledad in 1962, where he proved to be an equal opportunity brawler, fighting members of both the Aryan Brotherhood and the Mexican Mafia. By May of that year he was at San Quentin, racking up fifty bad-conduct reports from his jailers. Six months ago he'd been denied parole again, then hooked up with a pair of fellow would-be Che Guevaras to create the BGF, and where he'd go from there, nobody knew.

Events in California didn't fall within Sawyer's purview or NYPD's, but the BGF was spreading like a fungus, now infesting New York's prisons for a start, enlisting members who would likely be paroled someday and take their gospel to the ghetto streets. Payton couldn't penetrate the family, but he could still stand watch in Harlem and report if any BGF recruiters showed themselves.

Pile that on top of his continuing attention to the late Malcolm's Organization of Afro-American Unity, pushing a four-point program of restoration, reorientation, education, and economic security, while mutterings of revolution lingered in the background. And now, as if that load wasn't enough, Sawyer had younger brother Fred to think about.

What had possessed him, turning in his resignation from the FBI after a short four years, enlisting with the SCLC as one of Martin Luther King's security people? Payton knew why King and company would want a former G-man on the payroll, spilling all the Bureau's dirty tricks, but what drew Fred to Dr. King? Was it the minister's vaunted charisma, or perhaps the underhanded things Fred witnessed as an agent, tactics going far beyond simple surveillance and outside the law?

Whatever, Payton still recalled the last time he'd spoken to Fred—a bitter argument when Fred briefed Payton on his new career path—and he worried that the quarrel had opened a rift between them that might never heal completely.

Have we grown that far apart? Sawyer questioned himself. *And if we have, which one of us is in the wrong?*

———

Natchez, Mississippi: June 15, 1966

AGENT RYAN O'HARA was still acclimating to the Mississippi Delta, vastly different than anyplace he'd lived before—at least in climate—though he'd had a taste of die-hard racism in Florida, more so in Birmingham, as Edgar Hoover shifted Ryan's dad around field offices in Dixie.

Similar, he recognized, but when it came to hating Negroes and outsiders, Mississippi took the cake.

Nolan O'Hara had raised no objection when his son announced a plan to join the FBI. Ryan's mother was less accepting of the news, likely because she'd been personally threatened by the KKK in Birmingham, before Nolan took care of it in person, off the books, and the harassment was cut short by an "exalted cyclops" fearing for his life.

For that, Ryan hated the Klan, but he hadn't requested posting to the South after he graduated from the FBI Academy in March. That order came down from the Chief's office, maybe from the Old Man himself. Now, here was Ryan, operating from the Jackson field office and covering a Ku Klux murder plot while his father worked other cases, even more notorious but still related to the Bureau's COIN-TELPRO—WHITE HATE network in Dixie.

It had started with James Meredith, the same guy who'd touched off a firestorm back in 1962, when he became the first black student at Ole Miss. The university expelled him two years later, on a charge of carrying a pistol to protect himself after the U.S. marshals finally left Oxford, and so the trailblazer had gone abroad, earning a B.A. in political science from Nigeria's University of Ibadan, then coming back to enter law school at Columbia in '65.

That hadn't been enough for Meredith, of course. June of this year had found him back in Dixie, airing plans for a one-man "March Against Fear" from Memphis to Jackson, covering 220 miles of America's most dangerous highways for a Negro who wouldn't shut up and retire to "his place."

Meredith had set out on his epic walk ten days ago, wearing a pith helmet, armed only with a walking stick, and trailed by members of the media. Maybe he thought they'd keep him safe along the way, but he'd been wrong. Outside Hernando, Memphis Klansman James Norvell had ambushed Meredith on June 6, dropping him with shotgun blasts but failing to inflict a mortal wound. At once, assorted civil rights leaders including Dr. King announced their plan to carry on the march, stopping at towns along the way for rallies and to register black voters.

That was when a splinter of the White Knights planned to lure King off-track and kill him, thus presumably saving Jim Crow or touching off a race war that the Klansmen reckoned they could win.

The tiny clique of morons called itself the Cottonmouth Moccasin Gang, based in Natchez, consisting of redneck numskulls Ernest Avants, Claude Fuller, and James Lloyd Jones. Their brilliant plan: abduct and kill a random Negro, thereby drawing Dr. King to Adams County and his death by long-range rifle fire. Four days after the Meredith ambush, they almost got the first part right.

Almost.

Their chosen victim was Ben Chester White, a sixty-seven-year-old handyman with no connection whatsoever to the civil rights movement. Like Edward Aaron nine years earlier, he was a sacrificial lamb selected for availability. On June 10, the three Cottonmouths offered White two dollars to help them find a missing dog—the same old ruse employed by pedophiles to snare children for decades, maybe centuries. White had agreed, joining his would-be killers on a drive to Pretty Creek in the Homochitto National Forest. There, Fuller riddled White with sixteen rounds from an M2 automatic carbine, while Avants blew White's head off with a twelve-gauge. Finally, they'd dropped his corpse from Pretty Creek Bridge.

And that was when the nitwits realized their master plan was fucked. While blasting White, they'd also shot hell out of Jones's Chevrolet Bel Air and felt compelled to ditch it on in a county supervisor's driveway, setting it afire. Around the same time waders spotted White's body in Pretty Creek. The car was registered to Jones, of course, and early next morning police were grilling him. He cracked after a couple hours, naming his accomplices, telling Adams County's sheriff, "Fuller shot him with a machine gun, and Avants blowed his head off." In jail, Avants told his interrogators, "Yeah, I shot that nigger. I blew his head off with a shotgun."

Those confessions led to murder charges, but the killers quickly changed their minds and pled not guilty at arraignment. Ryan doubted that the case would end with a conviction, but at least James Norville copped a plea to shooting Meredith. His sentence for attempted murder: five years' prison time, with three of those suspended.

Meanwhile, as O'Hara had discovered, FBI headquarters was more interested in tracking Dr. King and SNCC, the student agitators who'd elected Stokely Carmichael to succeed chairman John Lewis. At the same time, draft-dodger Rap Brown was named to lead the group's ongoing work in Alabama, talking more about rebellion, less about nonviolence.

SNCC and the Klan were bound to clash again, as they'd been doing since the freedom rides of 1961, later in Georgia, then in Mississippi's "freedom summer." How long would it be, O'Hara wondered, until Negroes motivated by "Black Power" speeches started fighting back with guns, instead of angry words?

———

Jackson, Mississippi: June 26, 1966

LUCIA RICCA HADN'T KNOWN that it could feel like this, stepping outside her family in New York City and becoming part of something vastly larger than herself. There was a fright factor, of course, but at the same time, it had been exhilarating, and she wanted more of it—as much as possible, in fact.

Last year, at age eighteen, Lucia had belatedly fulfilled her mother's languished dream of study at Columbia, enrolling with the university's School of Journalism, founded by Joseph Pulitzer in 1912, dispensers of the prizes named for Pulitzer since 1917. Reporting hadn't been her mother's goal, of course, but over time that lofty aim had faded to a vague ideal encapsulated in the name "Columbia." Now, bankrolled by her late father's estate—God rest his soul, wherever it had gone—Lucia Jordan Ricca was a college girl and going places.

Granted, when she's started out, there'd been no thought of traveling to darkest Mississippi with a race war going on. She'd started out dabbling in leftist politics with members of the SDS, attending its convention this year, far from home in Clear Lake, Iowa. The open mingling of blacks and whites surprised her, then—as she imagined it—enlightened her to build a better nation and support equality for all downtrodden people on the planet. The clincher for Lucia came with news that Uncle Dave had quit his job with Legal Aid and gone to Birmingham, joining the cause and, incidentally, chasing a sometime girlfriend whom the other members of his family still hadn't met.

Instead of trailing him to Alabama, though, Lucia set her sights on the Magnolia State, eye of the storm engulfing Dixie. She had made that choice three weeks ago, after a sniper wounded bold James Meredith and titans of the movement vowed to carry on the march that started as a one-man effort. She'd hopped a bus and headed south the same day, feeling like a freedom rider, even though her white skin spared her the indignity of sitting in the Greyhound's rear after they'd reached the Mason-Dixon Line.

Lucia hadn't warned her parents of the plan. They wouldn't understand her need to get involved, and might have tried to stop her, suffering from the delusion that they could restrain a bright young woman of her present age.

She'd reached Hernando, in DeSoto County, one day after Meredith was wounded on U.S. Highway 51, just north of town. She'd mingled freely with members of CORE, SNCC, the SCLC, Mississippi's Freedom Democratic Party, and something called the Medical Committee for Human Rights, protected by armed members of Louisiana's Deacons for Defense and Justice. Governor Paul Johnson promised full protection from the state police, unless marchers "broke the law," but no one Lucia encountered thought his public vow was worth a damn.

The march had picked up at the very spot where Meredith was shot, hundreds, then thousands tramping down the highway where one man had meant to do it on his own. By June 9, they had walked twenty-four miles due south to Como, where some marchers peeled off to recruit new voters. Through the next two days, they'd covered sixteen miles to Batesville, then another forty-one miles to Grenada along Highway 51, receiving a surprise when certain whites turned out to cheer the marchers and applaud.

Next came Greenwood, thirty-three miles southwestward of Grenada, home of still unpunished slayer Byron De La Beckwith, star attraction at an endless series of Klan rallies where he boasted of assassinating Medgar Evers, urging other bigots to step up and do likewise. That morning, June 16, the *Greenwood Commonwealth* newspaper had run a front-page editorial comparing Dr. King to Mao Zedong and Stalin. Tipped over the edge, Governor Johnson had withdrawn their state police escort, telling reporters,

"We aren't going to wet nurse a bunch of showmen all over the country." That evening, the first arrests occurred when marchers tried to pitch tents on the grounds of Stone Street Negro Elementary School. Local police grabbed Stokely Carmichael, aware of his preeminence with SNCC, and locked him up for hours while a protest rally organized.

Upon release, Carmichael, furious, had roused the crowd with his now-famous speech that introduced "Black Power" as campaign slogan and, for some, a battle cry. June 21, the second anniversary of Mississippi's triple murder back in 1964, the marchers entered Philadelphia, seat of notorious Neshoba County. Dr. King had joined the group by then, confronting Cecil Price, the deputy who had arrested murder victims Schwerner, Chaney and Goodman, now facing charges of conspiracy to carry out their executions. From the courthouse steps, King told the crowd, "I believe in my heart that the murderers are somewhere around me at this moment." A redneck on the fringe evoked laughter by shouting back at King, "They're right behind you." Three hundred racists waded in at that, some swinging clubs and hurling stones, a couple of them firing pistols in the air, while local cops mostly did nothing. Dr. King escaped, promising to rejoin the march later, but never did.

After their side trip to Neshoba County, marchers doubled back to Canton on June 23 and tried to set up camp again, this time at McNeal Elementary School. Local police and state troopers moved in, tossing teargas grenades and lashing out with clubs, making no effort to arrest the marchers, simply beating them for sport. One grinning oaf was on the verge of striking down Lucia when a white man in a suit had stepped between them, brandishing a badge and snapping, "Back off! FBI!"

The cop had cursed her savior and went off in search of

other targets, while the agent led Lucia to a safe place well away from drifting gas and lashing clubs. He'd given her his name—Agent Ryan O'Hara—and a business card, in case she chose to file charges against the thug in uniform who'd nearly brained her. When she hugged O'Hara, it had been impulsive, likely stupid, but he hadn't seemed to mind, wearing a sheepish smile as he told her, "Take care, now. If you're staying for a while in Mississippi, maybe I'll run into you again."

The march reached Tougaloo, still nine miles short of Jackson, on June 24. They'd rested that day and the next at Tougaloo College, founded in Reconstruction by New York's American Missionary Association, now the repository for a grim museum of American lynchings. Celebrities showed up to speak, including actor Marlon Brando, singer James Brown, and comedian Dick Gregory. Lucia hoped the cause she'd chosen wasn't being turned into a sideshow, and that almost-prayer was answered when some 16,000 demonstrators thronged the streets of Jackson on June 26.

James Meredith was back for the finale of what started as his solo effort, telling the throng, "Governor Johnson and every other person is going to pay attention to the Negro. The system of white supremacy will reign no longer." Lucia found it moving, though she doubted that parading through the capital would mean a lasting victory. What she remembered most was Stokely Carmichael's "Black Power" speech —and now, ironically, the business card she had received from Ryan O'Hara.

That card called him a "special agent," and she couldn't argue with the designation after he had saved her from a beating, maybe even saved her life. By sundown, she'd decided to remain in Jackson, making herself useful to the movement—and if she met up with Ryan once again...well, that would be all right with her.

As for her parents, Lucia would find time to update them on her travels in a week or two.

———

Jackson, Mississippi, FBI Field Office: August 25, 1966

SOMETIMES, Nolan O'Hara felt as if he had been transported back in time to the war, but nobody was firing at him yet. The targets dropping all around him were Negroes, together with their white supporters in the drive against Jim Crow.

The new year had begun with a White Knights attack on Vernon Dahmer, Forrest County's NAACP chapter president, a successful merchant, and promoter of black voter registration since 1949, when Luther Cox, the local registrar, had rejected Dahmer's application, asking as a "literacy" test, "How many bubbles are there in a bar of soap?" Dahmer's mantra since that time had been "If you don't vote, you don't count." And now, he had repeated those words on his hospital deathbed.

The raiding party had attacked in the wee hours, hitting both the Dahmer home and an adjacent store with gunfire and Molotov cocktails. Dahmer fought a rear-guard action with a shotgun while the other members of his family escaped, but like Frank Morris, he had suffered fatal burns. His killers left behind a wealth of clues: one of their cars, shot up in the excitement, a pistol that might prove traceable, cartridge casings, and a weird Halloween mask.

One day after the Dahmer raid, five Negro voting activists were driving near Sidon, ninety-one miles north of Jackson, when a white motorist hit their car head-on. Two passengers in the victims' Plymouth Fury died on impact, while the other three were injured but survived. The white man walked away without a scratch and faced no charges, a suspicious circumstance in Nolan's mind, since the Klan was known to favor tricked-up "accidents" in lieu of outright shootings when they could devise a means.

HUAC was questioning White Knights in Washington, meanwhile, Sam Bowers, Byron De La Beckwith, and assorted others of their ilk hiding behind the Fifth Amendment to protect themselves, but the committee got their crimes on record in a venue where the Kluxers couldn't sue for libel, so O'Hara guessed that had to count for something.

March, in Washington, had been a rugged month for Dixie bigots. First, the Supreme Court banned poll taxes in the landmark case of *Harper v. Virginia Board of Elections*, finally enforcing the Constitution's Twenty-fourth Amendment, which five southern states had openly defied since January 1964. Three days after that body blow to racism, the Warren Court dealt Ku Klux murderers a one-two knockout punch in *United States v. Guest* and *United States v. Cecil Price, et al.*, approving federal conspiracy prosecutions under the Fourteenth Amendment and the 1870 Ku Klux Klan Act. Cases could thus proceed against Lemuel Penn's assassins in Georgia and White Knights indicted for the "Mississippi Burning" triple murders.

The system still wasn't perfect, since it relied on mostly-white juries, but June saw Penn's triggermen sentenced to ten years apiece, while four conspirators were acquitted. Trial of the Neshoba County killers still might be delayed another year or more, but Nolan took whatever progress he could get.

Meanwhile, dead bodies kept on piling up around the state. In July, a Hinds County sheriff's deputy trailed Eddie

James Stewart home from a Crystal Springs tavern, where he'd supposedly "caused a disturbance" but wasn't arrested. The officer preferred to park at Stewart's home, then follow him inside the house and shoot him—so the cop claimed—when the black man tried to grab his gun. Oddly, the bullet that drilled Stewart's heart was fired into his back, a second slug striking his hand, as if he'd raised it to defend himself. His widow had a case in federal court, claiming she'd seen her husband beaten prior to point-blank execution, but O'Hara had his doubts about a white judge letting that proceed.

And so, he didn't mind at all cracking the Dahmer case with help suggested by a G-man from New York. It seemed the Gotham office had a *mafioso* on the hook for sundry charges, offering reduction of his sentence if he'd take a little trip below the Mason-Dixon Line and help out with a bit of dirty work. Long story short, the second-generation member of Brooklyn's Colombo Family flew south, kidnapped the Klansman who had dropped his piece in Vernon Dahmer's yard, and shoved a pistol in his mouth, demanding names of the conspirators. The "knight" had pissed himself and babbled off a list of those involved, while G-men crouched outside the shack and listened in. The DOJ now had indictments in the works, with fancy verbiage to support probable cause, but Nolan guessed another year or two might pass before the cowards went to trial.

So, let them sweat it out, he thought. *Shoe's on the other foot now, and about to kick them in the ass.*

———

Birmingham, Alabama: September 27, 1966

DAVE JORDAN PULLED his suitcase from the taxi's backseat, paid the driver, and stood looking at the storefront office of the People's Legal Center, on Avenue C in Birmingham's Ensley district. Three pockmarks left by bullets striking brickwork had been painted over but were still distinctly visible.

"Welcome to Dixie," Jordan muttered to himself, then took his bag in through the boarded-over front door that had once been made of glass.

Inside, a young Negro receptionist looked up at him, doing a double take at Jordan's pale skin and Brooks Brothers three-piece suit, down to his polished Florsheim shoes, and his suitcase.

"Can I help you?" she asked, uncertainly.

"I'm looking for a Miss O'Hara."

"Ah, Fiona. And your business is...?"

"We used to work together in New York, at Legal Aid. My name's—"

"David?" The voice, familiar, came from somewhere off to Jordan's right. He turned in that direction and saw Fee approaching, eyes wide in surprise. Was it just his imagination, or was it a challenge for her not to gape at him?

"So, *this* is David," the receptionist said, knowingly.

"Denise, I'll handle this," Fiona told her.

"Sho' nuff," the reply came back, faking a field hand's accent through a killer smile.

"Come on with me," Fiona said, leading the way into a room of tiny cubicles before she turned again and asked, "Is that a suitcase?"

"You don't miss a thing, counselor."

"I mean, why...?"

"I like to travel light, but not *that* light. The army taught me to appreciate small comforts in a new location."

"You're confusing me."

"Don't mean to. I'm relocating."

"To Birmingham?" She sounded as if he'd announced a plan to camp on Mars.

"For now, at least. I'll need to see how it works out."

"How did you get here?"

"Caught an airplane headed south. I hear it's all the rage, these days. And they've got taxis at the airport, if you can believe it."

"No. I mean, why Birmingham? Why *now*?"

"I've been all over: Italy, North Africa, I even made it down to Washington a time or two." He cocked a thumb back toward the street entrance. "Maybe I just missed people shooting at me."

"We've got restless rednecks hereabouts," she said.

"I doubt they'd hold a candle to the *Waffen* SS," he replied. "No tanks, at least."

"Sometimes they use patrol cars, though."

"Even with Bull put out to pasture?"

Connor and Art Hanes had lost their bid to stay in power, Jordan knew, rejected by the courts. Bull Connor hadn't gone far, though, elected as president of the Alabama Public Service Commission in 1964, while Hanes kept busy defending Klansmen charged with murder and assorted other felonies in Alabama and neighboring states.

"Mayor Boutwell's an improvement, and the Klansmen hate him. So does Wallace, in Montgomery, but he's tied up running his wife for governor just now. Al Lingo quit his job as head of the state troopers last October, but he's running hard for sheriff here in Jefferson County."

"Never say die, eh?"

"Not yet, but we have others dying who didn't deserve it. You've heard of Sammy Younge?"

"Even up north," Dave said. "No trial in that case yet?"

Samuel Younge Jr. had been a navy veteran, a college student and SNCC activist, shot dead in January when he tried to use the "white" men's room at a gas station in Tuskegee. His slayer, a sixty-eight-year-old redneck, was facing murder charges, but he'd posted bail and was still walking around.

"December now, they think, around Pearl Harbor Day. And now, there's Nathan Johnson, dead in Alabaster, south of here in Shelby County."

"I missed that one. What's his story?"

"He was shot inside the local police station by—get this —the same state trooper who killed Jimmie Jackson back in March of '65. James Bonard Fowler, that would be. He claims the victim tried to grab a billy club, so naturally, Fowler had to kill him. Stick with what you know, I guess."

"And no charges on that, I guess," Dave said.

"No more than if it happened up in Harlem."

"Well, at least I saw the Klansmen who killed the Liuzzo woman will be doing time."

"Three of them were convicted on a federal conspiracy indictment," Fee replied, "but local juries set them free on murder charges. Overall, what really made me angry is the way the FBI reacted to it. You know that my father was an agent, like forever."

Jordan risked a smile. Said, "I believe you mentioned it."

"Retired now, and I'd call it none too soon. On the Liuzzo case, Chief Hoover—pompous bigot that he is—spread vicious lies about Viola, claiming she had puncture marks from hypodermics on her arms, and—let me quote his crap from memory—'was sitting, very, very close to that Negro in the car, that it appeared to be a petting party.' All bullshit, as you might imagine. The autopsy found no needle marks at all, no evidence of any sexual activity. Meanwhile, they cover up for their stool pigeon in the car, who's bragged of other murders to his Bureau handlers."

"And you know that, how?"

"A mole inside the field office," Fiona said.

"Hey, works for me. I read about another case with a conviction in the *Times,* back in December. I believe the victim's name was Brewster."

"Willie Brewster, right, from Anniston. A lunatic named J. B. Stoner fired the shooters up before they killed him, then took up the triggerman's defense in court. Lucky for justice, he's a crappy lawyer. That was offset by Tom Coleman, though, in Hayneville."

"The cop who shot the ministers?" Dave asked.

"A 'special deputy,' the county sheriff claims. Tom's sister runs the school board, like their mother did before her. He's killed once before, we know about: a black state prison inmate guards couldn't control, they said, so Coleman came and shot him. After August's double shooting, Al Lingo brought down a Klan bondsman to bail him out. The jury didn't even spend a half-hour deliberating at his trial. And get this: one of them *winked* at the bastard as they were retiring to deliberate."

"So basically, the court system is rotten."

"Well, our sainted governor was once a judge, so what does that tell you? The one bright light is U.S. District Judge Frank Johnson in Montgomery. He hates the Klan, and Wallace too. They bombed his mother's home last year, mistaking it for his, the stupid pricks."

"How do you really feel?"

Fee blushed and said, "I'm sorry. It just gets me down sometime. *Most* times, in fact."

"Okay. How can I help?"

She frowned at him. "You're serious?"

"It's why I'm here."

"I have to warn you, then. The pay's lousy and nine-tenths of the white people in town will hate you, sight-unseen. I'd make it ninety-nine percent of all the cops."

"Sounds just like Legal Aid back home. I worked for beans up there, and I keep hearing that it's cheaper living in the South."

"Living's the problem," Fee responded. "Not so much the price of it."

"I'll take a chance. There isn't much to keep me in New York. My sister's married with a kid in college, and my mom's been holding up all right since losing Dad."

"Your father? Dave, I didn't know. I'm so sorry."

"We'll talk about it later," he told Fee, thinking, *but maybe not the whole of it.* "Meanwhile, where do I start?"

———

Little Italy, Manhattan: October 6, 1966

"THAT FUCKIN' Joe Bananas, man," Angelo Giordano said. "He shoulda just stayed dead."

"The whole thing was a set-up," Dominic replied. "Givin' himself some room to breathe."

Bonanno's reappearance from his fake kidnapping hadn't stopped the war in Gotham, though. In early spring, Gaspar DiGregorio, anointed as the family's new boss by *La Commissione*, had called a sit-down with Bonanno loyalists to forge a peace treaty. When Bill Bonanno showed up at the house on Brooklyn's Troutman Street, however, shooters cut loose on his group and sparked a battle through the neighborhood. The missing Joe Bonanno had surfaced in May, claiming that Stefano Magaddino had him snatched and held hostage, but most wise guys thought Joe was ducking out on vengeance from the bosses he'd conspired to kill, plus a subpoena issued U.S. Attorney Robert Morgenthau, which could have jailed him on contempt charges for the duration of a federal grand jury's term. While he was AWOL, son Bill ran the business and the ongoing "Banana War," to the delight of bullshit columnists and TV talking heads.

Later, just two weeks ago, cops had raided the La Stella Restaurant in Queens, arresting thirteen ranking *mafiosi* at what headlines called a "little Apalachin meeting." Those detained included *Don* Carlo Gambino and underboss Aniello Dellacroce; Joseph Gallo, their *consigliere,* no relation to imprisoned rebel "Crazy Joe" from the Profaci clan; Tom Eboli and Mike Miranda, presently co-leaders of the Genovese family; Santo Trafficante Jr., up from Florida; Carlos Marcello from New Orleans, with his brother Joe and Anthony Carolla, son of ex-boss Silver Dollar Sam; plus small-fry and La Stella's two owners. Their cumulative bail was $1.3 million, and the law was calling them "material witnesses" to something or other.

More bullshit harassment, Dom thought. He was relieved and disappointed, all at the same time, that he'd received no invitation to the Queens sit-down: relieved because he'd managed to evade another roundup; disappointed that the big boys obviously didn't think enough of Papa Carlo Giordano or his sons to have them at the table.

Wait and see, Dom told himself, managing not to grind his teeth. *When Papa's gone, there'll be some fuckin' changes made.*

———

SCLC Headquarters, Atlanta: October 16, 1966

FRED SAWYER'S new life as part of Dr. King's security team meant travel aplenty and headaches galore. King was a moving target anywhere he went, not only for white racists but also certain black militants, either pursuing what they called their revolution, or else faking it to earn their FBI paychecks. And speaking of the FBI, Fred had to be on guard around the clock against subversion of King's move-ment by his former fellow agents from the Bureau, tapping phones, bugging hotel rooms, agitating sick *agents provoca-teurs* and spreading lies about the minister to anyone who'd listen and repeat them.

So far, Fred thought he was handling it, and there'd been no complaints from King or his second-in-command, the Reverend Ralph Abernathy.

This year's string of crises had begun in Chicago, in late January, when King and his wife occupied a squalid West Side ghetto apartment to publicize wretched housing condi-tions. While there, King met briefly with Black Muslim Elijah Muhammad, but he couldn't faze the "prophet's" commitment to a separate all-black offshoot from the United States.

March found King delivering a speech in Paris, 4,400 miles from home, with a whole new crop of far-right European lunatics for Fred to worry over, in case one of them decided to make history as an assassin. June was mostly eaten up by Mississippi, King and his competing movement leaders picking up the "March Against Fear" where wounded James Meredith fell, plodding along his scripted route of march through hecklers, rowdy mobs, and Klansmen itching for a shot at King.

And elsewhere, the long hot summer began. Chicago's

Division Street riots raged for three days, reported as the first time Puerto Ricans took the lead in a ghetto rebellion. Omaha exploded on July 5, requiring National Guardsmen to quell three days of vandalism against stores owned by Jews. Chicago blazed again for four days in July, leaving two persons dead, thirty more injured, and 244 in jail. The trigger that time: white cops shutting off a fire hydrant black kids has opened for relief from the oppressive heat.

Four days after Chicago took a breather, riots rocked the Hough ghetto in Cleveland, killing four, wounding fifty, and logging 275 arrests. In the wake of the mayhem, white street gangs went public, vowing to defend their neighborhoods against invasion.

Dr. King missed all that action, but he had another brush with danger on July 31, in Raleigh, North Carolina. Two factions of the Klan turned out to countermarch against him, but King's oratory focused on Stokely Carmichael's "Black Power" rumblings from SNCC, condemning visions of "black supremacy." As King declared, "The Negro needs the white man to save him from his fear, and the white man needs the Negro to save him from his guilt."

The same day that Kind spoke in Raleigh, interracial demonstrators marched into Chicago's Marquette Park. White residents met them with flying bricks and bottles, torching cars, while Mayor Richard Daley's police mostly stood on the sidelines, watching. The mêlée left fifty people injured and eighteen blackened cars for wreckers to remove.

Sawyer was at King's side when King returned to Chicago in August, trying to lead some 700 marchers through Marquette Park and neighboring Gage Park to their target, a real estate office on 63rd Street. Between them and their goal stood howling racists, one of whom dropped King with a stone to the head. While Fred and others hustled him out of harm's way, King was preparing for his next press conference, telling reporters, "I have never seen—even in Mississippi and Alabama—mobs as hostile and as hate-filled as I've seen here in Chicago." Police moved in that time, and bigots stood their ground, leaving another thirty persons hurt and forty-plus locked up. After the rioting, George Lincoln Rockwell brought his Nazi Party to recruit new members, some 150 rallying beneath "White Power" signs in Marquette Park.

Soon after Rockwell's grandstand play in Chi-Town, San Francisco police killed a black teenage car thief in the Hunter's Point ghetto, sparking riots that spanned five days, leaving 160 persons injured, 457 arrested, and with property loss estimated at $136,000.

From the ashes rose new angry militants. In Oakland, thirteen miles from Frisco across San Francisco Bay, college students Huey Newton and Bobby Seale founded the Black Panther Party for Self Defense in October, "patrolling pigs"—their term for cops—with guns purchased from campus sales of Mao Zedong's "Little Red Book." FBI agents were already stalking the Panthers, as were cops from every major department across the country, including NYPD's "BOSS." Fred heard that from his brother, Payton, although Payton wouldn't share details since Fred, in his words, had "gone over to the other side."

Funny. Fred only knew of one side in the game of life: human. Some of them simply didn't recognize the rules of common decency.

Far south of Oakland, in Los Angeles, Ron Karenga's US Organization had founded a newspaper titled *Harambee*—Swahili for "all pull together"—and Karenga had also fabricated his own "pan-African holiday," dubbed *Kwanzaa*, allegedly Swahili for "first fruits of the harvest." What that had to do with living in L.A.'s ghetto was anybody's guess, Karenga claiming it promoted "a communitarian African philosophy."

What troubled Fred the most wasn't Karenga's showmanship, but his established record as an FBI informer and perhaps *agent provocateur* under the Bureau's COINTELPRO—BLACK HATE drive against supposed African American "subversives." There were rumblings already of conflict between US and the Panthers, but Fred didn't want to get involved in that.

His job was keeping Dr. King out of the firing line before the guns went off.

———

800 16th Street NW, Washington, D.C.: December 4, 1966

OFF THE RECORD was the kind of bar Declan O'Hara liked. Although it was within a stone's throw of the White House, it was nice and quiet, operating in the basement of the Hay-Adams Hotel since 1928. Adorned in red velvet, with comfy wooden booths, nobody hassled Declan there. In fact, nobody recognized him but the bartenders, who knew his usual was Jameson and kept it coming until he'd acquired a pleasant glow.

Granted, there wasn't much to glow about in what were euphemistically referred to as the golden years. O'Hara often felt that death surrounded him, beginning with May's news from Pennsylvania that a self-styled "mountain man" and kidnapper had killed the first G-man gunned down on duty in nine years. The agent's name was Terry Anderson and he'd been forty-two years old. The teenage victim of his quarry had been found alive, the nut extinguished in a final blaze of gunfire.

Others were dying, too, weaving a thicker web of myth and mystery around the Kennedy assassination. Alleged heart attacks had claimed two persons linked to Dallas: former Oswald landlord Earlene Roberts and Henry Suydam Jr., who had handled the assassination coverage for *Life* magazine, lately Miami bureau chief.

Two more went in the record books as suicides. Car salesman Albert Bogard said he rode with Oswald for a test drive, but the Warren Commission rejected his statement, insisting that Lee couldn't drive. In February, he'd supposedly gassed himself near a cemetery, running a hose from his auto's tailpipe to the cab. Eight months later, a point-blank gunshot killed Navy Lieutenant William Pitzer, JFK's autopsy photographer, at Bethesda's Naval Medical School. He'd called his presidential photo session a "horrifying experience," and news of his death prompted another military man, retired Lieutenant Colonel Dan Marvin, to recall how a CIA spook had asked him to kill Pitzer in the summer of 1965.

One nearly clear-cut murder was the shooting of Marilyn Walle, a former stripper for Jack Ruby—stage name "Delilah"—at his mobbed-up Carousel Club. She'd married in August and moved to Omaha, where her husband of one month had pumped her full of bullets, drilling heart, lungs, liver, arms and legs. Hubby was sitting in the local nuthouse now, presumably intending to plead temporary lunacy.

Traffic crashes had dispatched two Dealey Plaza witnesses who'd logged suspicious sightings on assassination day in '63. Lee Bowers Jr. had reported seeing men, never identified, milling around a fence atop the so-called "grassy knoll," plus puffs of gunsmoke when the fatal shots were fired. The Warren panel managed to dismiss his testimony, and in August of this year, a black car—also unidentified, apparently untraceable—had forced his vehicle into a Highway 67 bridge abutment between Cleburne and Midlothian. He lived just long enough to tell his ambulance attendants he'd been drugged while stopping off for coffee, moments prior to the crash.

The other Dallas witness, James Worrell Jr., swore that he saw a man flee from the Book Depository's rear exit, ignored by federal investigators because "everybody knew" Lee Oswald had gone out the front door, onto Elm Street. This November 9, Worrell "apparently lost control" of his motorcycle in Dallas, killing himself and a female passenger. The driver who'd hit them, some guy from Mesquite, was unharmed.

Besides those maybe accidents and suicides, Declan was keeping track of "sudden cancers" striking those involved with 1963's events. Dallas police captain Frank Martin witnessed Ruby killing Oswald in the precinct basement on November 24. Later, he told the Warren panel, "There's a lot to be said, but it's probably better if I don't say it." The tumor that got him appeared in late May and killed him in June.

Jack Ruby, likewise, was another "sudden cancer" victim living in his cell on borrowed time. It only came about after the Texas Court of Criminal Appeals reversed his 1964 murder conviction and death sentence, ordering a new trial based on adverse, inescapable publicity. That ruling came down in October, and his cancer popped up in December. Ruby's new trial still hadn't been scheduled, but no one expected live that long.

Now Declan wondered, sipping whiskey, whether anything would come of Jim Garrison's investigation in New Orleans. He was claiming new "important evidence" on the assassination, but Warren Commission critics hadn't made their minds up yet: was Garrison a true crusader, or a shill tossing out suspects—some of them already dead, like ex-G-man Guy Banister—to divert attention from Carlos Marcello and his fellow *goombah,* Santo Trafficante Jr.?

Galloping in hot pursuit of Garrison and calling him a fraud was Amos Guidry, a New Orleans tabloid journalist who sniffed around, interrogating and attempting to discredit Garrison's potential witnesses. Instead, so far, he'd turned up links between the Klan and Minutemen, pilot Dave Ferrie, and the CIA's campaign against Castro, now trying busily to sweep them all under the rug.

O'Hara didn't know if anyone would ever learn the whole truth about Dallas, much less share it with the world, but what else did he have to do in his retirement than sit back and watch the show?

———

East Potomac Park Golf Course, Washington: December 18, 1966

ALOYSIUS GANTT SLICED his third drive into the rough and cursed a blue streak, wishing there was someone near enough for him to bend his club over the bastard's head.

Why had he ever taken up the game of golf at his age? That was darling Gwen's idea of "helping" him, insisting it would aid his heart and keep him limber—maybe even put the lead back in his pencil, as if she had any interest in *that.* Gantt knew that what she really wanted was to get him off the couch, out of the house, out of her hair. Sometimes he thought she might feel sweet relief if he keeled over on the green and she could cash a nice fat life insurance check.

That wasn't fair, of course. He knew she loved him in her

way, but that way hadn't worked too well for either one of them in years.

So, he knocked balls to hell and gone around the course, and in his free time kept in touch with former colleagues from the Bureau. Trying to watch over twin sons Colby and Devon was too nerve-wracking for him, one flying around the world's hotspots in service to the CIA, the other somewhere in Louisiana, tracking homicidal rednecks who could barely spell their names.

From headlines, Aloysius knew that LBJ had signed a new Freedom of Information Act on Independence Day, which would start releasing scads of formerly classified federal files to the public in July 1967—but only after they'd been censored to the point where some of them became illegible entirely and the rest only provided sneaky peeks at what various agencies had been doing in God and Country's name since the foundation of America.

No one would catch even a glimpse of COINTELPRO operations, since the bulk of them were patently illegal and a few simply ridiculous. The dumbest plan he'd heard of through his Bureau contacts had been codenamed "Operation Hoodwink." That brilliant idea sought to provoke a shooting war between the Mafia and CPUSA, mailing fraudulent letters from the Party that attacked Mob infiltration of assorted labor unions (true enough) and urged the few surviving Reds to launch guerrilla war against the underworld. It sounded like something Clyde Tolson might've dreamed up since his stroke, and even the most volatile of *mafiosi* seemed to think it was a farce.

The smartest thing I ever did was quit, Gantt thought, and lined another ball up on his tee.

———

Vientiane: December 28, 1966

ON BALANCE, Colby Gantt decided that he thought no more of Laos than he did of Vietnam. His stint in Burma as a young man with the OSS had been exciting. These days, running secret wars in tropic heat came down to drudgery and sweat that smelled increasingly like alcohol.

There had been changes stateside for the Agency, with June's appointment of Richard Helms to succeed incompetent William Raborn as Director of Central Intelligence. Helms had come up like Colby, through the wartime OSS, and favored personal intelligence over the technical, without slighting the new age of spy satellites that could read license plates and newspaper headlines from outer space. He'd served as Raborn's deputy until the former admiral wore out his welcome and was booted from his Langley office after barely fourteen months.

Imagine how long he'd have lasted if Americans knew what was *really* going on.

In Haiti, Papa Doc Duvalier's death toll amongst opponents had topped 60,000, but who cared? He'd welcomed Ethiopian Emperor Haile Selassie I to Port-au-Prince, Haiti's only visit by a foreign head of state, and grinned like crazy as Selassie named him a knight of the Order of the Queen of Sheba.

Meanwhile, 6,100 miles south of Haiti in Montevideo, Uruguay, Agency front man Philip Agee was busy spreading all the right-wing mischief black money could buy, smearing native leftists as tools of Moscow, creating a phony Congress of the People to attack Red demonstrators, fielding agents to fine-tune torture methods used by members of the Uruguayan National Police.

Bolivia was also heating up, with Che Guevara and his

female sidekick "Tania"—née Haydée Tamara Bunke Bider —working overtime to break the country's military junta. Che had even taken on another *nom de guerre* for the occasion, swapping out his name to become "Adolfo Mena González." Either way, his names and famous face were on a WANTED list, and that meant wanted dead. You could forget about alive.

Guevara was, in fact, a hunted man on both sides of the world, having surfaced in the former state of Tanganyika, now called Tanzania after it had merged with Zanzibar two years ago. He'd shown up in the capital, Dar es Salaam, advising leaders of the Mozambique Liberation Front on ways and means of freeing their homeland from Portuguese control. Wherever he went next, the price on Che's head would be haunting him to hell and back.

But Asia...Jesus, what could anybody say?

In May, China had launched its Great Proletarian Cultural Revolution, Mao's fancy name for replacing his failed "Great Leap Forward" with a restoration of the Stalinism he admired so much. The movement was supposed to purge "revisionists"—that is, Mao's rivals within the Communist Party, most notably Liu Shaoqi and Deng Xiaoping. Tactics included harassment and public humiliation, torture, arbitrary imprisonment at hard labor, and often execution. For good measure, Mao was razing cultural and religious sites, while deporting large numbers of urban youth to rural districts in a parallel "Down to the Countryside Movement."

In Laos, where the U.S. military continued its off-the-books "Steel Tiger" and "Tiger Hound" campaigns north of Luang Prabang, the air force was pursuing "Operation Barrel Roll," a new bombing campaign, accompanied by long-range forays into China using "Team Fox," a reconnaissance unit composed of Mien hill tribesmen. None of the secret war was legal, but who cared, as long as the stateside media—thoroughly infiltrated now by spooks—ignored it? Colby viewed most journalists as mushrooms, kept in darkness while their masters fed them shit. As for the few who dug and probed, like those at *Ramparts* magazine, they could be tied up with disinformation and tax audits till the frigging cows came home.

In Vietnam, where LBJ was cashing his blank check from Congress on a war no one had bothered to declare —*aloha* to the Constitution's so-called checks and balances —an ever-escalating conflict had become a fact of life. Officially, the U.S. death toll in combat had reached 6,250 this year, and a super-secret peace initiative codenamed "Marigold" had flopped with a resounding thud in Washington. In his State of the Union address, Johnson tried not to gloat as he called Vietnam a war unlike any other U.S. conflict, then concluded, "Yet, finally, war is always the same. It is young men dying in the fullness of their promise. It is trying to kill a man that you do not even know well enough to hate. Therefore, to know war is to know that there is still madness in this world."

And without that madness, where would the Agency be? Would it even exist?

Before his sudden death in Dallas, still pissed off about the Bay of Pigs, John Kennedy had spoken of dismantling the CIA, "scattering it to the winds." Now, he would never have that chance, and his replacement from the Lone Star State would never dream of trying. Not while he could play policeman to the world at large and reap a fortune in the process.

There was some opposition, of course. In February, rogue columnist Walter Lippmann condemned Johnson's war plans, declaring, "Gestures, propaganda, public relations and bombing and more bombing will not work." A month later, Wisconsin's Senator Wayne Morse tried to repeal the Gulf of Tonkin Resolution. That same month, Buddhists began a paradoxically violent effort to depose South Vietnamese Premier Nguyễn Cao Kỳ after he dismissed a Buddhist general. Stateside, large anti-war protests had occurred in New York City, Washington, Chicago, Philadelphia, and San Francisco.

Have your fun, thought Colby. *No one in control is listening.*

Two weeks after those marches, B-52 bombers made their first raids against North Vietnam, dropping 100 massive bombs apiece from six miles up, striking at utilities, fuel storage dumps, transportation infrastructure, and any other target viewed even vaguely as military.

Buddhist protesters began setting themselves afire in May—a tactic LBJ deplored as "tragic and unnecessary"—but the human sacrifices stopped in June, after sweeping arrests that jailed movement leader Thích Trí Quang and many of his acolytes. July found captured U.S. pilots on parade in Hanoi, jeered and spat upon by furious inhabitants. In August, American jets accidentally struck two "friendly" villages south of the DMZ, killing more sixty-four peasants and wounding more than 100. By November, "Operation Attleboro" concluded a search-and-destroy mission north of Saigon, deemed "successful" with 155 Americans dead and 494 wounded, against Red losses of 1,106.

After a flying visit under heavy guard to Đà Nẵng, President Johnson graced a meeting in Manila of America's allies in Vietnam: Australia, New Zealand, the Philippines, Thailand, and South Korea. Spokesmen left that gathering to pledge complete withdrawal from the country within six months—if Hô Chí Minh pulled his troops back to the north. Responding to that fatuous charade, Moscow immediately promised military and financial aid to Hô. The year closed badly for freedom's defenders in the jungle, with a *New York Times* report that theft was gobbling up 40 percent U.S. money sent to Nguyễn Cao Kỳ's regime.

If people only knew the half of it, Gantt thought, *they'd shit one huge collective brick.*

At home, some folks at Langley showed persistent inability to learn from past mistakes. In June, they'd unleashed another helping of *Serratia marascens*, this time in New York City, sending more innocent subjects into hospitals. Back in the Senate, William Fulbright of Arkansas had turned a spotlight on shady operations by the Office of Public Safety in South America. Brazilian adversaries of the OPS briefed South Dakota Senator James Abourezk on some of the group's worst abuses, and it didn't help the cause when John Hannah—ex-president of Michigan State University, now head of USAID under the Agency's sway— tried to support the OPS by sending a letter of praise for its great work to Louisiana congressman Otto Passman. The operation wasn't dead yet, but it had been gravely wounded in the public eye and mind.

Forget about it, Colby thought. Before the politicians got around to scuttling the OPS, some other group would spring up to replace it, shaped by Langley's planners to propel their tentacles around the world and clutch it in a snug embrace.

CHAPTER 3

H Street Northwest, Washington, D.C.: January 15, 1967

DECLAN O'HARA SAW THE FORD FAIRLANE PULL UP AND climbed into the shotgun seat as quickly as he could, allowing Aloysius Gantt to join the traffic's flow again after only a slight delay, pulling away from the George Washington University campus.

"Thanks, Ally." Declan used the nickname he and Greg Jordan had tagged Gantt with so long ago, when they were law school classmates at GW. "Glad you could make it on short notice."

"Well, you made it sound important, Deck. I have to ask what's up?"

"Just thought we'd have a talk and catch up, like I told you on the phone."

"Right, but we haven't spoken since you left the Bureau, back in '64. I'm coming up on fourteen months myself, and nothing. So, I'll ask again: what's going on?"

"You want to stop somewhere and have a drink, for old time's sake?"

"It isn't even noon, yet. Do I *need* a drink?"

Declan knew *he* wanted one, but didn't push it. "Just a thought," he said. "Something's been bugging me."

"About...?"

"Cuba."

"Say what?"

"Long time ago, Ally." Once started, Declan plunged ahead with it. "I never told you this, but back in 1933, when I was posted to Chicago—you remember?"

"Sure. With Purvis."

"Right. Well, as it happens, I ran into Greg from college."

"Greg? Greg *Jordan*?"

"In the flesh."

"I thought he lived in New York City."

"Did, maybe still does. I haven't kept up with him. He was in Chicago on some legal business—" no need to invoke the name of Mafia—"and I met him accidentally."

That was a lie, of course. O'Hara had been stalking Jordan's cronies from the Syndicate, saw him, and trailed him back to his hotel.

"Okay. And what's that got to do with Cuba?" Gantt inquired.

"While we were catching up, Greg said he'd seen you in Havana, not too long before I met him."

"What? Havana? That's—"

"He sounded positive, Ally. Said you were talking to some military type. That was eight years before the SIS, and you weren't part of that, regardless. I know, since I *was* and you were pissed about being passed over."

"Deck, I don't know what Greg *thought* he saw, but—"

"He was positive about it," Declan interrupted him. "You and an army type in uniform, talking."

"Bullshit. He got it wrong."

O'Hara let that pass. Said, "Then I started thinking, that was right around the time Senator Walsh got hitched in Cuba, then came back to catch the train for Washington. Remember? He'd been nominated as Attorney General, talking about shaking up the Bureau from the top down."

"Sounds vaguely familiar," Gantt acknowledged, "for something that happened over thirty years ago."

"And then he died in transit. You remember that? The way the Boss was suddenly relieved as all get-out?"

"Can't say I like the sound of where you're taking this," Gantt said, tight-lipped behind the Fairlane's wheel. "Way I remember it, the old boy died from too much honeymoon for him to handle, at his age."

"There were...suspicions."

"Oh, I get it now. You met Greg in Chicago, way back when, and he fed you a line about me being in Havana. You put two and two together, coming up with...what, me *killing* Walsh to save Speed's job? And no one's worked it out over the past thirty-four years? Christ, would you listen to yourself?"

"I saw my doctor yesterday," O'Hara said.

"A shrink, I'm hoping."

"An oncologist. It's prostate cancer, Ally. Too advanced for anything beyond what they call palliative care, to ease the pain."

"Well, shit, Deck. That's a bitch. If you need anything..."

"Only the truth, Ally."

Gantt turned to face him as they came up on a red light. "Fine," he said. "You want to know the fucking truth? You want to hear that I—"

A squeal of brakes behind them cut off Ally's words. He glanced up at his rearview mirror, barely having time to mouth a curse before the semi rig plowed into them, rolling as if its driver hadn't seen the light, the cars in front of him, or maybe he was just drunk on his ass.

Declan pitched forward, cracked the windshield with his skull, and everything blacked out. He never saw or felt the flames as they leapt up from underneath the Ford Fairlane.

———

National City Christian Church, Washington: January 19, 1967

DAVID JORDAN HATED FUNERALS, maybe in part because his father's disappearing act had robbed the family of one, but he'd seen no way of avoiding this memorial service. Fiona's father had been killed in a traffic pile-up, with a friend he'd known forever, first from college, then the FBI. She had to be there, and she needed Dave's support

He hadn't told her that *his* father had been close to hers and his companion in the accident, way back before the First World War. Declan O'Hara and the other fellow, Aloysius Gantt, had joined the Bureau to avoid the draft, while Greg Jordan went off to France, won medals for his bravery, and stopped some lead along the way. All that was ancient history, along with Greg Jordan—born Giordano—coming home to serve as lawyer and *consigliere* for his clan's crime family.

Why would he mention that? Why would she even want to know?

The church they occupied for this solemn occasion had been organized in 1843, its present sanctuary built in 1930, numbering around 800 congregants from then until the present day. Its stained-glass windows featured two dead presidents affiliated with the church: James Garfield, slain by an assassin back in 1881, and Lyndon Johnson, elevated to his present office by another gunman in November 1963. The service, honoring two former public servants—and the first two killed in tandem since a plane crash back in 1943, though Gantt and Fee's father were both retired—had been arranged and funded by an outfit known as the Society of Former Special Agents of the FBI.

It was Dave's first meeting with any of Fiona's relatives, and there were four of them on hand: her mother, now a widow, Abigail; Fee's brother Nolan, also with the Bureau; nephew Ryan, yet another special agent; and her niece Erin, a junior at George Washington, her grandpa's alma mater, looking forward to law school.

The Gantts were represented by the dead man's widow, Gwendolyn; their twin sons Colby and Devon, married to Eileen and Camille, respectively. The twins, Fee said, were agents of the CIA and FBI, in that order. Their offspring— Hardy, son of Colby and Eileen; Wyman, the son of Devon and Camille—each planned on signing up with the divergent family businesses as soon as they were able, Hardy with the Agency, Wyman the FBI.

No wonder Dave felt as if he'd been dropped into the middle of a spook convention, and he didn't plan to say a word about his father or *his* family's trade, unless one of his new acquaintances brought up the subject. If his luck held out, Dave's surname would mean nothing to them, no connection drawn between him and a college friendship severed fifty years ago.

Get in, get out, he thought. *Sit through a standard mourning banquet, spend the night in a hotel while Fee stayed with her mom, then head on back to Alabama, where the tide of history was flowing fast and strong.*

Dave couldn't put the capital behind him soon enough.

Princeton University: June 6, 1967

COMMENCEMENT WAS A DRAG, all pomp and circumstance, but Stephen Barnes was crystal clear on his responsibility to see it through and take the next step toward realization of his father's master plan. He had been born for this. What other reason did he have to even be alive?

Graduation from the Ivy League, as he had learned, wasn't at all the same as passing on from high school, back in Trenton. There was twice the ceremony, and you didn't troop across a stage in alphabetical order, receiving your diploma. Rather, at commencement, seated on the lawn of Nassau Hall, graduates rose *en masse* according to departments—History, in Stephen's case—and heard President Robert Francis Goheen speak the Latin formula translated thus: "By the authority vested in me by the trustees of Princeton University, I admit you to the degree of Bachelor of Arts, with honors as indicated."

Said honor, in Stephen's case, was Magna Cum Laude, one notch below Summa, but it still required a GPA higher than 3.7—and, in fact, his GPA of 3.85 was a near miss to Summa Cum Laude, which began at 3.9.

As the ritual concluded, graduates combined to sing "Old Nassau," then attending guests were told to keep their seats while the procession made its slow retreat. Stephen's adoptive parents, Russian sleeper agents Mark and Isabella Barnes, joined him for the reception afterward, where he finally collected his diploma, posed smiling for photographs, and begged off for a nonexistent date, planning to catch a showing of *The War Wagon*, starring reactionary dinosaur John Wayne and Kirk Douglas, who'd once portrayed a valiant rebel slave in *Spartacus*.

His entry into Yale Law School was already assured, thanks to his Princeton GPA, high LSAT scores, a patriotic essay he'd appended to his application with the proper tone of reverence for human rights, and finally an interview that seemed almost superfluous, considering the wad of laundered cash from Moscow that had smoothed his way.

All Barnes wanted right now was time alone, to think about his future and what had been happening around America. In terms of trivia, his now ex-roommate, Jack Edmonds, was taking off next month to Bakersfield, in California, to join in founding a new far-right vehicle, the American Independent Party. Their hope, apparently, was to elect George Wallace as America's next president in 1968, where Barry Goldwater had failed so miserably back in '64.

Pathetic, but it helped display America's true colors to the world.

Speaking of colors, it was shaping up to be another "long hot summer" in the nation's black ghettoes. Trenton's population—where he'd lived from his arrival in the States till entering Princeton, the capital where Mark and Isabella still resided—was approximately half-black, most of those inhabitants burdened with poverty, organized crime, police brutality, poor schools, and illegitimacy: all the necessary contents of an urban tinderbox.

As for the FBI he planned to join as soon as he was educationally qualified, Barnes kept up with events. On New Year's Day, a new National Crime Information Center had become operational at headquarters, permitting police nationwide to search an electronic database of criminal histories, thereby identifying suspects in custody or still at large, the latter from fingerprints on file.

The Bureau's list of Ten Most Wanted fugitives also remained active, with all but one of those who'd opened 1967 on the list removed by capture or dismissal of outstanding warrants, while another eighteen names were added to the roster. Armed robbers and convicts who'd escaped from prison still predominated, but Barnes reckoned that might change soon, as new militancy among blacks and anti-war protesters escalated nationwide.

He hated missing out on that, while wasting three more years in school, but it was foreordained. Barnes had a job to do, and he was not about to let his absent father down.

———

Harlem: July 10, 1967

PAYTON SAWYER HAD BEEN PROMOTED to the rank of sergeant back in April, having tested well and banked a commendation from Inspector Kevin Shaughnessy at BOSS. He knew a white cop with a good head on his shoulders likely would've earned lieutenant's bars with sixteen years in harness, but the rate of progress for black officers had never been as rapid or predictable. On top of which, he still was saddled with the same assignment he'd been handed when he was recruited for the BOSS squad, after gunning down two cop-killers his rookie year, in 1951.

Little had changed with the Black Muslims, his primary gig, since Malcolm X was publicly assassinated back in '65. His mantle fell to Louis Farrakhan, formerly Louis X, born Louis Walcott thirty-four years earlier. Within three months of Malcolm's murder, Farrakhan had been assigned to lead Mosque No. 7 by "prophet" Elijah Muhammad at Chicago headquarters. This year, he'd been promoted to serve as

Elijah's National Representative, speaking for Muhammad on the radio and TV talk shows, filling in for him at meetings nationwide. Word had it that Elijah's speech in Phoenix, recently, might be his last public address.

Closer to home, the Five-Percenters under "Allah," erstwhile Clarence 13X, were still preaching his gospel about men being divine, creators of their women who couldn't aspire to being goddesses. The patriarchal patter urged fathers to place their daughters in arranged unions, spurning legal marriage while supporting polygamy or what Allah called "serial monogamy," minus the binding vows. Clarence also discouraged use of birth control, apparently convinced that if he couldn't woo more converts from the streets, his flock would breed their own.

The FBI had filled a husky dossier on Clarence 13X by now, sharing some of its dirt with BOSS and branding Allah as a danger to the president, passing his file, or parts of it, on to the U.S. Secret Service. After serving time at Bellevue, following Malcolm's assassination, Allah had been packed off to Matteawan State Hospital for the Criminally Insane, then finally released in March, despite being adjudged as schizophrenic, with delusions of grandeur.

And hey, what other leader of a made-up church could pass that test unscathed?

Now John Lindsay, midway through his second year as New York City's mayor, was putting on a show of forging closer ties to leaders of impoverished neighborhoods. Somehow, he'd tapped Allah as one of them, inviting him to sit-downs with more rational community spokesmen at Gracie Mansion, where Allah seemed sane enough, requesting more bus routes and school funding. Anxious to please, Lindsay provided buses for the Five-Percenters, carrying them out to a Long Island park, and tapped the

National Urban League's war chest to bankroll the "Allah School in Mecca"—an abandoned storefront meant to groom young people for admission to college prep schools. Predictably, Clarence demanded final say over the school's curriculum and struggled to find qualified teachers, while NYPD bluesuits visited to satisfy themselves that Allah wasn't molding children into radicals.

To Payton, it was just another scam, the same kind preachers had been running down in Harlem for as long as he'd been living and, no doubt, for generations before he was born. No crimes had been committed yet, unless you counted skimming money off the top, and what civic improvement group in Gotham wasn't doing that?

But he would keep filing reports to justify his slightly larger paycheck and watch out for anything that might set off alarm bells with the NYPD's brass. There could be danger, after all, waiting to surface the first time that Sawyer dropped his guard.

His father, he supposed, would have expected no less from his eldest living son.

———

Little Italy, Manhattan: November 3, 1967

DOMINIC GIORDANO SIPPED his beer and wondered what the Syndicate was coming to. The bullshit prosecutions were supposed to peter out when JFK went down in Dallas and his brother's days were numbered under LBJ as the Attorney General, but it didn't look that way from where Dom sat.

Take Jimmy Hoffa, for example. He'd faced down both Kennedy's in person, when he'd testified before the Senate, and smart money said he'd likely had a hand in Dallas four years back. Still, he had been convicted twice on federal counts in 1964, and after three years of dead-end appeals, he'd started serving time in March, at Lewisburg, caged in the wing nicknamed "Mafia Manor" for its locked-up wise guys. Before going away, he'd named another crooked operator, Frank Fitzsimmons, to succeed him as the IBT's "caretaker" president until Jimmy was finally paroled, presumably to claim his throne again by acclamation from the Teamster membership.

More recently, just yesterday in Queens, trial had convened for a quartet of hoods accused of killing one-eyed Ernie Rupolo two years ago. Five men had been indicted for the hit, but one of them, Johnny Matera, was already serving time for robbery in Florida and couldn't make it back to Gotham. Those on trial included William Crabbe, Joe "Whitey" Florio, Tom Matteo, and Johnny Franzese, who'd employed Matera as a bodyguard in days gone by. The prosecution's witnesses included four guys from a holdup team that specialized in raiding Queens and Brooklyn banks. One of the four, Johnny Cordero, had been shacking up with Rupolo's widow when the cops arrested him.

The trouble came—no great surprise, in Dom's opinion —from Rupolo's widow, Eleanor. She'd been out boozing with Cordero in July of '65, a month before her hubby's stiff had surfaced in Jamaica Bay. She'd started bad-mouthing Joe Florio, a soldier in Franzese's crew, as poor old Ernie's killer. Someone wound up firing shots at her outside the bar, prompting Franzese to convene the other witnesses and spill his guts about wasting Rupolo. What was the stupid bastard thinking? When they were popped for robbing banks, the squealers instantly rolled over on Franzese and his boys, now facing fifty years apiece if they were finally convicted on the murder count.

The funny part, at least to Dom: Rupolo's death was traceable to 1934, when he'd iced Ferdinand "The Shadow" Boccia for Vito Genovese, then testified against *Don* Vito at his murder trial in 1946. Vito had held a killing grudge since then, though Ernie—moron that he was—told everyone he'd done Vito "a favor," since he'd been acquitted and would never have to face that charge again.

Stupid.

Now, *Don* Carlos Marcello in New Orleans was the next boss on the hot seat, with *Life* magazine reporting that the Syndicate had handed him $2 million on a promise to spring Jimmy Hoffa and he'd fucked that up, but good. On top of that, *Life* blew the whistle on an aide to Governor McKeithen, offering prosecution witness Ed Partin $1 million to recant his testimony from Hoffa's trial in Tennessee. Partin refused and told the feds, which opened up another smelly can or worms.

At least the Giordanos hadn't been sucked into any of that shit, but now, with Papa Carlo standing at death's door, Dom had to wonder if he'd be confirmed to lead the family in turn. If not, who would? And most important, how could they survive at all without taking some risks along the way?

More food for thought, dammit. And what he didn't need right now was one more miserable headache.

SCLC Headquarters, Atlanta: November 8, 1967

ANOTHER "LONG, HOT SUMMER" had begun to fade from memory, but this time, autumn brought no hint of cooling temperatures on the U.S. racial front. Fred Sawyer had his hands full trying to keep Dr. King out of harm's way, particularly when the minister seemed so intent on courting danger.

And danger could be found most anywhere, this year.

The trouble started in Detroit, in June, when a mob of eighty whites smoke-bombed an interracial couple's home in what had previously been an all-white neighborhood, Rouge Park. Ten days later, the mob was smaller but more brutal, shouting threats to rape the wife, killing her husband with gunfire. Police had jailed six suspects, but the D.A. didn't seem to be pursuing charges.

Around the same time, Hough's ghetto flared again in Cleveland, logging several incidents of arson, but then angry blacks rallied behind mayoral candidate Carl Stokes, one of their own, and voted him to victory over a white incumbent in the primary, then trounced the GOP's contender, also white.

Then came the heat wave, with 159 reported ghetto riots nationwide.

The first explosion came from Cincinnati, in mid-June, where jurors had convicted suspect Posteal Laskey Jr. of raping and killing six white women. Family and neighbors claimed he'd been framed, prompting a protest rally that turned violent, blacks looting and torching white-owned stores they accused of "jacking up prices and selling bad products." By the time National Guardsmen restored order, four days later, one white teenager was dead, sixty-three persons hurt, and 404 arrested. The city claimed $2 million in property damage.

Ironically, Fred had been present one day prior to the eruption, when King had preached nonviolence to church-goers in Avondale's ghetto.

Buffalo flared on June 26, with mayhem spanning six long days, nearly paralyzing the city. When it passed, more than forty people had been injured, fourteen suffering from gunshot wounds.

Newark was worse, burning white-hot from July 12 to 17, leaving twenty-six dead—mostly shot by police or Guardsmen—and roughly $10 million in property damage. Amidst that inferno, on July 14 to 16, Plainfield also flared, seventeen miles southwest of Newark. The only death recorded was a cop, shot while he manned a highway barricade.

In Cairo, Illinois, four days of mayhem started with the so-called jailhouse suicide of a black soldier on leave to see his family. Cops said he'd hanged himself with his own t-shirt, prompting furious derision from the inner city's residents. Before the smoke cleared, blacks and self-style "White Hat" vigilantes traded gunfire, with at least six firebombings of stores and a warehouse. After the riot, White Hats met the mayor, complaining of their city's "Negro problem." One black spokesman vowed that if ghetto demands weren't met, next time Cairo would "look like Rome burning down."

North Minneapolis caught fire for three days in the third week of July, recording numerous assaults, arsons and acts of vandalism. No one died that time around, as if Fate was saving its energy for the worst riot of the year.

And that was back in Motor City, starting on July 23 when police raided a "blind pig" after-hours bar. Over the next five days and nights, the storm of pent-up rage claimed forty-three lives: ten white, the rest all black. Among black casualties, cops gunned down fourteen, National Guardsmen nine, store owners or security officers six, a U.S. soldier one. Two more were suffocated in a building fire, and one stepped on a downed high-voltage line. Another 1,189 people were injured and 7,231 arrested. A total of 2,509 stores and 388 dwellings burned, for a cumulative loss of $45 million. Afterward, official analysts accused police of "uncontrolled and unnecessary firing" that endangered civilians and fellow lawmen. A case in point was the Guard's machine-gunning of an innocent tenement family, killing a four-year-old girl.

The violence in Cambridge, Maryland, was almost minor by comparison, sporadic arson that destroyed seventeen ghetto buildings. Alleged instigator H. Rap Brown from SNCC had managed to survive a shotgun blast from the police and slipped away, provoking Governor Spiro Agnew to demand a full-scale FBI manhunt.

Meanwhile, in Saginaw, Michigan, the white mayor limited meetings with civil rights spokesmen to close-door sessions and angry protests boiled over, fanned by the flames from Detroit. Despite hit-and-run battles with riot police, the final list of injuries included only seven individuals.

Milwaukee's riot started on the next-to-last day of July and carried on till August 3, starting with a fight between teenagers, aggravated by club-swinging cops. Four people died, 100 suffered injuries, and jails were crammed with 1,740 more.

For all the random bloodshed, Fred Sawyer was more worried about militant groups denouncing Dr. King and Gandhian nonviolence in general. With fugitive Rap Brown succeeding Stokely Carmichael as chairman, SNCC had formally dropped the adjective "Nonviolent" from its title, while Brown told his cheering audiences, "Violence is as American as cherry pie. If American don't come around, we're gonna burn it down." The Justice Department charged Brown with riot and arson, plus "counseling to arson." G-men nabbed him first in Virginia, released him on $10,000 bond, then busted him again in Ohio, claiming he "advocated criminal syndicalism," then dropping that charge. A third arrest, in Baton Rouge, charged him with failure to register a rifle he carried while boarding an aircraft. Chalk up another $25,000 bail, later reduced to $15,000

Meanwhile, Brown was steering the former SNCC toward alliance with the Black Panther Party in Oakland, briefly serving as the BPP's "Defense Minister." Cops had the Panthers in their sights, particularly after the Party's newspaper questioned the death of Denzil Dowell in Richmond, California, shot through the armpit while he stood with hands raised in surrender.

On October 28, in Oakland, Patrolman John Frey— whose personnel file contained multiple citizens' complaints—radioed headquarters that he had "stopped a Panther car." In the altercation that followed, motorist Huey Newton—co-founder of the BPP—suffered a gunshot wound to the stomach, while Frey was shot dead and his partner wounded. Strangely, the bullets all came from police-issued weapons. Handcuffed to a hospital bed, as nurses later testified, Newton was clubbed repeatedly by other cops across his wounded abdomen. His murder trial was coming up next year, with leaks from the defense promising bombshell testimony from a "surprise eyewitness" to the one-sided shootout.

With every day that passed, each time another body dropped, Fred Sawyer worried more about his task of guarding Dr. King. Threats to his life had multiplied since April 4, with his first speech against the war in Vietnam, and Fred knew from experience that no one who was interested in longevity had ever prospered from lobbing stones into the military-industrial quagmire.

Still, he was resolved to do his best, and give his life if

necessary to defend the longtime target of the Klan, the FBI —and now, it seemed, the CIA as well.

————

FBI Field Office, Jackson, Mississippi: November 16, 1967

THE MISSISSIPPI KLAN was edging into politics, and if he had to guess, Nolan O'Hara thought they couldn't choose worse candidates than those who'd tossed their pointy hoods into the ring.

Byron De La Beckwith had entered the Democratic primary for lieutenant governor, campaigning on the slogan "He's a straight shooter," but lost out to Charley Sullivan, a lawyer from Clarksdale.

More sinister was James Seale, suspect in at least three murders and a fourth "suspicious death" police had managed to ignore. His goal was to become sheriff of Franklin County, with its seat at Meadville, Silver Dollar campaign backer Red Glover declaring that if Seale carried the day, their celebration would include "hanging a nigger." Thankfully, most of the voters couldn't stomach Seale and finally rejected him, though he remained exempt from trial on any of his crimes.

And human sacrifices still continued at the hands of Mississippi bigots. February's victim, Wharlest Jackson, was a coworker of near-miss murder victim George Metcalfe in Natchez, and treasurer of the town's NAACP chapter. Like Metcalfe, he'd worked at the Armstrong Tire and Rubber Company, surrounded by Klansmen who loathed him for his politics and for accepting a promotion that raised his pay by seventeen center per hour. That was "uppity," and it had claimed his life on February 27, when a bomb exploded in his pickup truck while he was driving home. A veteran of Korea, Jackson left a widow and five children. The lead suspect in Jackson's murder—fingered by informers, but so far untouchable—was Red Glover.

Ironically, the Jackson bombing bared fault lines within the Klan. James Seale blamed Jackson's death for his poor showing in the sheriff's race, declaring that his slayers "should be killed themselves." Another Klansman who proclaimed himself a "friend" of Jackson put word out that he was personally hunting down the slayers, but it came to nothing in the end.

In May, local police had opened fire on Negro students demonstrating peacefully at Jackson State College. Inept as usual, they'd only killed Benjamin Brown, an uninvolved truck driver who'd been watching from the sidelines. Still, his dark skin signed his death warrant, and a grand jury deemed the killing "justified."

Another disappointment for O'Hara was the Ben White murder case from 1966. It was resolved—by Mississippi standards—during April 1967, when jurors couldn't reach a verdict on confessed killer James Jones. The D.A.'s office, easily discouraged when victims were black, decided not to put Jones through a second trial. Another jury had acquitted Ernest Avants, based upon his claim that White was dead before Avants shot him, and prosecutors simply dropped their case against Claude Fuller.

Nolan thought he'd found another angle on that case, discovering that White had died on federal land in the Homochitto National Forest, but so far, no one in the Bureau cared to hear it. They were too busy investigating civil rights leaders or planning for the trial of Vernon Dahmer's murderers sometime next year.

In what he called spare time, Nolan kept watch on politics and criminal developments next-door, in Alabama. Lurleen Wallace had succeeded husband George as governor in name only, Ace Carter writing all her speeches and supplying Klan votes when it counted. Meanwhile, racist murders in the Cotton State continued as they always had, without letup.

May's victim had been Rodell Williamson, an active member of the Wilcox County NAACP, snagged on a fisherman's line and hauled up from the Alabama River near Camden. A local constable told journalists that he'd found "no signs of foul play."

More recently, a sheriff's deputy had beaten inmate James Motley to death in Elmore County's jail—another homicide deemed "justifiable." And back in bloody Wilcox County, teenage Archie Wooden "either jumped or fell" into a ditch near Camden, bleeding out after a dead branch ruptured his femoral artery. A simple accident? Police thought so and spent no more time on the case.

Sam Bowers and his knights, meanwhile, has launched an autumn reign of terror focusing primarily on Mississippi Jews. The first bomb struck Jackson's Temple Beth Israel, then the nightriders returned to blast the home of its rabbi. In Meridian, another bomb damaged a second synagogue. A Jackson businessman who voiced his disapproval of the bombers also felt their wrath. And just to prove they still despised Negroes as well as Jews, the raiders targeted a dean at Tougaloo College, together with Laurel's NAACP leader.

O'Hara had identified a suspect in the bombings. Thomas Albert Tarrants had been hanging out with Klansmen since he was a troubled high school student in Mobile, submitted to psychiatric examination by his mother for obsessive anti-Semitism. Two years ago, at seventeen, he'd been arrested with a member of the National States

Rights Party while carrying a sawed-off shotgun. One day after his probation lapsed, he'd been nabbed while riding with Sam Bowers, a machine gun on the backseat of their car. Tarrants had posted bail, then dropped from sight, leaving a note behind, telling whoever cared that that he was "going underground and operating guerrilla warfare"— but where in hell was he?

If Nolan cracked that riddle, maybe he could bring the bombings to an end, and get himself promoted out of Mississippi to some other jurisdiction where the laws of civilized society were recognized.

———

FBI Headquarters: December 7, 1967

DEVON O'HARA FELT like celebrating when Chief Hoover's office cleared his transfer application, shifting him from the Louisiana bayou country, with its rednecks and mosquitoes, back to Washington. Along with the dramatic change of scene and culture, he was also pleased to leave behind his COINTELPRO—WHITE HATE chores and focus on subversives who, in his view, were destroying the United States.

His new assignment, supervising elements of both the Bureau's COINTELPRO—BLACK HATE machinations and its counterpart, the COINTELPRO—NEW LEFT drive, was something Gantt could sink his teeth into with relish.

The New Left and its SDS flagship had grown dramatically over the past year, drawing strength from escalating anti-war campaigns on college campuses from coast to coast. At its yearly convention, the SDS had taken an egalitarian turn, abolishing the posts of president and vice president, replacing them with a National Secretary (Harvard's Mike Spiegel), an Education Secretary (Bob Pardun from Texas), and an Inter-organizational Secretary (ex-Vice President Carl Davidson). To peace campaigns, its program added women's liberation, condemnation of male chauvinism, free access to birth control and abortion, plus establishment of communal child care centers.

That all sounded stylish, but it took a backseat to antiwar protest, highlighted by creation of a National Mobilization Committee to End the War in Vietnam, coupled with local operations such as Oakland's "Stop the Draft Week" in October, prompting skirmishes between protesters and police. Much more impressive was a huge March on the Pentagon that same month, drawing an estimated 100,000 participants, 560 of whom were jailed, including best-selling novelist Norman Mailer. Another key participant busted while trying to "measure the Pentagon" was Abbott "Abbie" Hoffman, a Brandeis graduate and founder of the Youth International Party, dubbed "Yippies." Word from FBI informers claimed Hoffman and Berkeley activist Jerry Rubin, father of the Vietnam Day Committee, were planning to disrupt next year's Democratic National Convention in Chicago.

You couldn't spend much time surveilling New Left radicals without stumbling over Negro activists from groups including SNCC, the Revolutionary Action Movement, CORE, and the Black Panther Party. Edgar Hoover viewed them all as equally subversive, lumped together with the venerable NAACP and Martin Luther King's SCLC. An August memo from the Chief stated the goals of COINTELPRO—BLACK HATE loud and clear.

. . .

THE PURPOSE of this new counterintelligence endeavor is to expose, disrupt, misdirect, discredit, or otherwise neutralize the activities of black nationalist, hate-type organizations and groupings, their leadership, spokesmen, membership, and supporters, and to counter their propensity for violence and civil disorder. Intensified action under this program should be afforded to the activities of the Revolutionary Action Movement. Particular emphasis should be given to extremists such as Stokely Carmichael, H. "Rap" Brown, Elijah Muhammad, and [RAM founder] Maxwell Stanford.

RUNNING parallel to that Bureau program, as Devon learned from off-the-record conversations with his brother Colby, was the CIA's strictly illegal "Operation Chaos," targeting black activists with a particular emphasis on Dr. King and his proposed Poor People's March on Washington next spring. The Agency was barred by law from operating inside the United States, but Langley didn't give a damn about such legal niceties, especially since King's first speech against the Asian war on April 4, delivered at Ebenezer Baptist Church and titled "Beyond Vietnam."

Chief Hoover still loathed King, driving his troops to scotch the "rise of a black messiah," but of late he seemed to waffle between targeting the SCLC's president and "Black Power" spokesman Stokely Carmichael, lately resigned from SNCC. Other groups earmarked for ongoing harassment included the National Welfare Rights Organization, the Dodge Revolutionary Union Movement (DRUM), the Congress of Afrikan People, and chapters of the Black Students Union spread from coast to coast.

No matter. Devon knew there were enough bugs, taps, and spies to go around.

Haight-Ashbury District, San Francisco: December 24, 1967

"I TELL YOU, man, you wanna hear the message, it is *in the music,* dig it? Take the Beatles, man. They've got it *going on.* 'I Am the Walrus,' man. 'Strawberry Fields Forever.' Roll out for the mystery tour. Hey, I'm *living* it, man!"

Charley Manson was high as a kite, and why not? Here they were in the Summer of Love, smack-dab at the heart of the "hippie" counterculture. Why shouldn't an ex-con tune into it, and if his age—now thirty-three—spoiled all the talk about not trusting anybody over thirty...well, so what?

To Colby Gantt, this guy seemed tailor-made for future use.

From hefty prison files, Gantt knew that Charles Milles Manson had been born in Cincinnati, first called "no name Maddox," with the "Charles Milles" added later by his jail-bird mother. A 1937 paternity suit, settled out of court, named his biological father as Colonel Walker Scott Sr., a mill worker and con artist. The "Colonel" was his given name, but Scott enjoyed posing as an ex-military man. Between the time he knocked up Kathleen Maddox and their son's birth, she'd married William Manson, sometimes employed at a dry cleaning plant, but he divorced her when Charley was three, for "gross neglect of duty."

As it turned out, Manson's mom neglected most things, often leaving little Charles with his older brother while she went on benders, once swapping him to a barmaid for a pitcher of beer. She got sent up for robbery in 1939, paroled in '42, often dumping her youngest with an uncle who thought sending Charles to school dressed as a girl would somehow "teach him to be a man."

From that insanity came truancy and theft, landing Manson at Indiana's Gibault School for Boys at age thirteen, where he claimed frequent rapes by guards and older boys. A stint at Omaha's Boys Town failed to reform him, as he spun off into burglary and auto theft, plus the armed robbery of a casino. By 1951 the victim had become an abuser, caught raping a fellow inmate at knifepoint, at Virginia's Natural Bridge Honor Camp. That sent him to the to the Federal Reformatory at Petersburg, where he'd logged "eight serious disciplinary offenses, three involving homosexual acts," then on to a Chillicothe, Ohio, maximum security institution, released at age twenty.

The only thing Manson had learned from jail was how to be a better criminal—but never good enough. By 1956, a Dyer Act violation had him caged at Terminal Island in California. Five years later, still in federal custody, he'd learned to play guitar from 1930s bandit Alvin Karpis at McNeil Island, Washington. Bounced back to Terminal Island for forging U.S. Treasury checks, he was finally freed in March 1967, over his own objections, claiming prison was the only home he recognized.

No matter. Big Brother knew best, granting Manson permission to live in San Francisco, cradle of the hippie "counterculture," LSD, free love, and weird occultism. What raving lunatic could ask for more?

As Colby understood it, Manson had begun collecting runaways and waifs, all younger than himself, most of them female, having sex with any of them who'd sit still for it, turning them on to all manner of drugs, preaching a whacked-out blend of rock-and-roll combined with neo-Nazi racism, mingling with motorcycle thugs and members of the new Satanic underground that had been taking root since 1966. Snuff films were rumored, acid trips obligatory, and the Beatles elevated to a status of divinity while Manson tried to make it as the Next Big Thing in music, getting nowhere fast.

No need to mention that while he had been in prison, he'd also been subject to some of the Agency's attempts at mind control through chemistry.

Hey, what could possibly go wrong?

Watching Manson declaim his madness through the one-way mirror in a CIA apartment at the heart of Haight-Ashbury's human zoo, much as George White must once have spied upon his whores and junkies, Colby thought that in the blue Caribbean, for instance, *anything* could happen and it likely would. After bombs exploded outside Haiti's Presidential Palace, Papa Doc Duvalier had executed nineteen of his military officers at Fort Dimanche, then veered off into another purge of communists, sanctioned by Langley and the White House.

DCI John McCone had bigger problems, working overtime to cover the Agency's tracks in Cuba and Florida. Four days after Thanksgiving, James Angleton had met with William Harvey and Johnny Rosselli at Washington's Madison Hotel, still scheming against Castro, trying to make damned sure nobody in Congress knew about it.

Things were cool in Panama, where National Guard officer Manuel Noriega had emerged from psy-war training at Fort Bragg as a contract agent on the CIA's payroll, disrupting union organizers on behalf of the United Fruit Company, while Agency pros coached him on plans for a *coup d'état* should populist presidential candidate Arnulfo Arias unseat incumbent Marco Aurelio Robles.

South America supplied a victory, at last, against Che Guevara's well trained and supplied guerrilla movement, operating as the National Liberation Army of Bolivia.

Langley and the whole of Washington had been pissed off by Che's early victories this year, but the Bolivian military rebounded, thanks to an infusion of Green Berets and U.S. Army Rangers in the vanguard, severing Che's pirate radio link to Havana, plus advice from Félix Rodríguez, a Cuban exile turned agent for the CIA's Special Activities Division. That overwhelming force—1,800 soldiers in all—finally captured Che at a jungle camp in October, caging him in a dilapidated mud schoolhouse at the nearby village of La Higuera.

Even then, Guevara kicked one soldier who'd tried to steal his pipe as a trophy, then spat in the face of a Bolivian rear admiral sent to question him. On October 9, ignoring U.S. pleas that Che be "debriefed" in Panama, he was machine-gunned by alcoholic sergeant Félix Rodríguez, his volunteer executioner. Notations in Che's captured diary made the long manhunt seem doubly incompetent, noting that Bolivian peasants "do not give us any help, and they are turning into informers." As for Bolivia's Communist Party, Che deemed it "distrustful, disloyal and stupid," a tool of Moscow and no friend to Cuba.

The Middle East remained chaotic as ever, rocked in June by the now-famous Six-Day War between Israel and its Arab neighbors, Egypt, Jordan, and Syria. Outnumbered roughly eleven-to-one in the field, Israel killed more than 20,000 enemy troops while losing only 1,000, turning 300,000 Palestinians from the West Bank and 100,000 Syrians from the Golan Heights into permanent, rootless refugees. Egyptian President Nasser severed diplomatic relations with the U.S. and Britain, accusing them both of fighting on Israel's side, which they predictably denied. In feeble retaliation, Moscow and its Warsaw Pact allies, minus Romania, severed relations with Israel.

Nor was that Russia's only upheaval. In early February, Beijing had expelled Soviet diplomats from China, saying it could no longer ensure their safety. Three months later— some three weeks before Israel's battlefield triumph— Vladimir Semichastny handed control of the KGB to Yuri Andropov, scion of a noble Don Cossack family, ambassador to Hungary in 1954-56, and member of the Party's Central Committee since 1962. He'd come to KGB headquarters pledging "the destruction of dissent in all its forms," proclaiming, "The struggle for human rights is part of a wide-ranging imperialist plot to undermine the foundation of the Soviet state."

Those changes brought no cessation of Red support for guerrillas in Southeast Asia. Unknown to most Americans, B-52s tripled their bombing raids in eastern Laos over 1966's record, logging 1,718 destructive sorties. That failed to halt a Red advance across the Plain of Jars or infiltration of support from North Vietnam, leaving King Sisavang Vatthana's Vientiane regime critically endangered.

In South Vietnam, "pacification" campaigns proceeded under a new Civil Operations and Revolutionary Development Support group, ostensibly merging U.S. forces and with Saigon's military and a peasant militia expected to recruit 500,000 fighters. President Nguyễn Văn Thiệu replaced Premier Nguyễn Cao Kỳ, while Kỳ accepted demotion to serve as vice president. As a hedge against future rivalry between them, a Leadership Committee stood between the two men who'd collaborated to assassinate Ngô Đình Diệm in 1963. Meanwhile, under CIA guidance and bankrolled by Agency funds, CORDS' Intelligence Coordination and Exploitation Program secretly launched the "Phoenix Program," intended to capture and covert or kill Việt Cộng leaders.

In practice, Phoenix teams often skipped directly to Plan B, assassinating both VC officers and their alleged peasant supporters. Ostensibly, new laws passed to "avoid abuses" required that each Red suspect must by accused by three separate sources, whereupon he or she might be convicted and imprisoned for a maximum of six years, said sentence reviewed at two-year intervals. MACV Directive 381-41 called Phoenix a "rifle shot rather than a shotgun approach to target key political leaders, command/control elements and activists in the VC infrastructure," but the "rifle shot" euphemism quickly proved to be a literal alternative to trial and prison. Aside from torture of suspects in custody— simulated drowning, gang rape, electric shock dubbed "the Bell Telephone Hour," starvation, mauling by attack dogs, or pounding wooden dowels into ears with a hammer— hundreds of suspects were killed out of hand on a shoot-first basis, sometimes with whole villages razed.

On the zany side, Colby had to laugh when the Agency's Science and Technology Directorate reverted to fanciful schemes on par with some of those the OSS tried and discarded during World War Two. Among the flops: a seismic intruder detection system whose sensors were disguised as heaps of tiger dung.

Through it all, Washington continued its waffling campaign of smoke and mirrors. In March, LBJ secured another $4.5 billion from Congress to prolong the war. A month later, has-been Richard Nixon visited Saigon and blamed stateside protests for the conflict's ongoing duration. May's brilliant solution to that menace was a 70,000-person pro-war march through Manhattan, led by a New York City Fire Department captain. In July, General William West-moreland requested 200,000 reinforcements on top of 475,000 soldiers scheduled for Asian service in 1967. A month later, California Governor Ronald Reagan—former FBI informer "T-10"—said America should leave Vietnam since "too many qualified targets have been put off limits to bombing." Three days after that, Chinese jets shot down two U.S. bombers straying across its border.

And the confusion went on. In September, North Vietnamese Prime Minister Phạm Văn Đồng vowed that his nation would "continue to fight." An October poll found 46 percent of all Americans calling the war a "mistake," and even conservative *Life* magazine withdrew support for LBJ's foreign policy. Stung, Johnson told a national TV audience, "We are inflicting greater losses than we're taking. We are making progress." *Time* quoted General Westmoreland as saying, "I hope they try something because we are looking for a fight." Twelve days later, Defense Secretary Robert McNamara resigned after repeated clashes with Johnson.

As the year closed, anti-war Minnesota Senator Eugene McCarthy announced plans to challenge LBJ for the 1968 presidential nomination, saying, "The entire history of this war in Vietnam, no matter what we call it, has been one of continued error and misjudgment." Five days later, renowned pediatrician Benjamin Spock, author of the best-selling *Common Sense Book of Baby and Child Care*, laid his stethoscope aside to lead the first of several Gotham anti-war rallies. Refusing to concede fallibility, LBJ visited South Vietnam, proclaiming, "All the challenges have been met. The enemy is not beaten, but he knows that he has met his master in the field."

Or maybe not. If he was right, why had U.S. troop levels in Vietnam hit 463,000, with 16,000 soldiers dead and counting? How had an estimated 90,000 North Vietnamese regulars crossed the DMZ, boosting Red strength to 300,000 fighters?

Stateside, New Orleans D.A. Jim Garrison had charged Clay LaVerne Shaw—director of the Crescent City's World Trade Center and a frequent collaborator with the with the CIA's Domestic Contact Service—with conspiracy to murder JFK in 1963. The Agency retaliated by sending Allan Hughes, a longtime agent and early participant in Operation MKULTRA, to burgle Garrison's office and steal any papers related to Shaw. Drug-dealing contract operative Jean-Pierre Lafitte tagged along on that raid, afterward telling ex-agent George Hunter White that the mission was "maybe one of the only jobs I ever did that made me worry any at all."

In the end, Langley need not have worried. Newly appointed Attorney General Ramsey Clark—Bobby Kennedy's successor and son of Mafia deal-maker Tom Clark, now a Supreme Court justice whom Harry Truman dubbed "the dumbest man I think I've ever run across"—stoutly defended the Warren Commission's report, claiming the FBI had cleared Shaw of any suspicion "in November and December of 1963." If so, no evidence remained of that investigation, Shaw's name appearing nowhere in the commission's report or its twenty-six volumes of supporting documents.

Garrison accused Shaw of conspiring with Lee Oswald, David Ferrie, and unnamed others to murder President Kennedy. By then, of course, Oswald was dead, soon followed to the grave by alleged stroke victim Ferrie and "sudden cancer" patient Jack Ruby. Orleans Parish coroner Nicholas Chetta and pathologist Ronald Welsh found "no evidence of homicide or suicide" with Ferrie—this, despite the fact that he'd died less than one week after the *New Orleans States-Item* named him as a Garrison suspect. The next morning, Ferrie told a friend, "You know what this news story does to me, don't you? I'm a dead man. From here on, believe me, I'm a dead man." Also, on the night he died, Ferrie had written, then discarded, not one, but two suicide notes. Incredulous, Garrison mocked the official denials, saying, "I suppose it could just be a weird coincidence."

While Shaw awaited trial at the Criminal Courts Building in Mid-City New Orleans, hostile media sources ranging from professional conspiracy denier Amos Guidry to *Life* magazine piled on, ridiculing Garrison's witnesses as a seamy collection of psychopaths, compulsive liars, and hired perjurers. *Life* delved into Garrison's rumored ties to Carlos Marcello, noting that the *Cosa Nostra* figured nowhere in the D.A.'s allegations. Guidry tried a subtler route, seeking to infiltrate the prosecution team while warning confidential colleagues not to spill the beans that he was "playing both sides." After milking Garrison for details of his case, Guidry produced a string of articles smearing the prosecutor, clearly hoping that prospective future jurors would buy into his biased account.

Along the way, other convenient deaths besides Ferrie's and Ruby's helped maintain a shroud of secrecy surrounding the events in Dallas four years earlier. A single-car pileup killed Leonard Pullin, a civilian navy employee who helped film an assassination documentary titled "The Last Two Days." A Dallas cop killed Harold Russell—a Tippit murder witness who described a gunman other than Lee Oswald—in a February barroom brawl. That same month saw Eladio Del Valle, an anti-Castro ally of Ferrie, sought by Garrison investigators, shot in the head by persons unknown.

More "weird coincidences," and while they continued, Colby thought the Agency could likely rest at ease.

———

Jackson, Mississippi: December 29, 1967

LUCIA RICA STRETCHED, one of her bare legs draped across Ryan O'Hara's groin, and he could feel himself stirring again. He couldn't say exactly what this twenty-year-old girl —young woman—meant to him, but she could get his motor revving like none other he had known.

"I wish that we could stay like this forever," she half-whispered.

Ryan glanced at his bedside clock and gave his hips a lazy roll against her thigh. "Maybe another hour, anyway."

She slapped his shoulder gently. "You're like some kind of machine."

"And you know how to turn it on."

"You wore me out, Hon. Anyway, you know I've got the breakfast shift tomorrow, at the Freedom School."

What would Agent O'Hara's SAC think, much less Bureau headquarters in Washington, if they knew he was literally sleeping with the enemy? Lucia was a civil rights activist who'd come down from New York last summer to join in James Meredith's "March Against Fear" and had found a new calling of sorts. She was taking "a break" from Columbia University's School of Journalism, butting heads with Jim Crow on behalf of black people who'd started as strangers and turned into friends.

"The Freedom School," he said. "I know."

"You still have doubts about it?"

"Nope. Not me."

"But if your bosses knew..."

"They don't. Not yet."

O'Hara hoped not, anyway.

"Look on the bright side, Babe," she said, running a hand over his chest. "You got a big win, anyway."

She meant the so-called "Mississippi Burning" trial of nineteen Klansmen for a conspiracy that claimed the lives of three civil rights activists—two of them northern whites, much like herself—in June of 1964.

"More like a split decision," he replied.

"Don't do that. Selling yourself short again. You're making history."

"Maybe a footnote."

There'd been twenty-one defendants in the case four years ago, when a U.S. commissioner threw out the early charges. Next, Harold Cox—a federal district judge and one of Mississippi's most outspoken bigots—had dismissed a new round of indictments, claiming that the DOJ had no authority to prosecute for local crimes. Rather than argue that till doomsday, prosecutors had secured new indictments in late February, dropping three of the marginal suspects and charging nineteen under provisions of the same 1870 Ku Klux Klan Act that had jailed other killers in Alabama and Georgia.

Judge Cox didn't like it, but the U.S. Supreme Court had upheld the charges in *United States v. Cecil Price*, *et al*. Price was the fat-assed deputy who'd jailed the three victims, then delivered them to a Klan murder squad. Others accused included his boss, Sheriff Lawrence Rainey, Rainey's predecessor in office, the triggermen who'd done the wet work, various accomplices—and the grand prize: White Knights Imperial Wizard Sam Bowers, who'd ordered the killings.

Trial had convened before Judge Cox on October 7, and jurors began deliberating eleven days later. When they first claimed to be deadlocked, Cox had dropped the "dynamite charge," ordering them to go back and try harder. After Price and killer Alton Roberts had mouthed off, saying they had their own dynamite charge for Cox, the judge had blown his top, revoked their bail, and bore down on the jury to complete its work.

It took two days of arguing, but finally the panel had convicted seven of the nineteen men, acquitted nine, and still couldn't decide on three, including former sheriff Ethel "Hop" Barnett and "Preacher" Edgar Killen—a key plotter, self-ordained minister, and friend of Mississippi Senator James Eastland. Afterward, one juror sheepishly admitted she "could never convict a preacher," whatever he'd done. Sheriff Rainey was among those who walked free. At sentencing, Judge Cox delivered prison terms ranging from three years to the statutory maximum of ten for Bowers and Roberts.

When a reporter asked Cox to explain the varied sentencing, he'd said, "They killed one nigger, one Jew, and a white man. I gave them all what I thought they deserved." That was Cox in a nutshell: racist to the core, unable to admit most Jews were white, and too damned dumb to realize that *both* white victims had been Jewish.

"They're going to appeal, you know," he told Lucia.

"And they'll lose, right up to the Supreme Court."

"Maybe."

"Definitely. It may take a while, but their asses are winding up in jail."

"Speaking of asses..."

Ryan let his fingers do the walking, but she pushed his hand away, saying, "There's something else we need to talk about."

"Okay. What's that?" he asked.

Holding his eyes with hers, Lucia answered back, "I'm pregnant."

CHAPTER 4

Meridian, Mississippi: July 2, 1968

RYAN O'HARA SAT IN HIS MOTEL ROOM, HIGHWAY 19 ON THE northwest edge of town, red neon from its street sign glaring through the flimsy curtain on his single window. On a coffee table set before the low-slung couch, he'd placed a fifth of Jim Beam (now half empty), a cheap water glass (half full but quickly dropping), and his Bureau-issue .38 revolver.

Ryan wanted to shoot someone, but he hadn't yet decided whether that should be another goddamned Klansman, or perhaps himself.

It was a toss-up for him, having lost so much in such a damnably short time: the woman he had come to love, their unborn child—and now, perhaps, his will to go on living.

Since Lucia Rica dropped the news on him in bed, changing his life with one short sentence, they had talked about the possibilities, of course. She was a Catholic, so that ruled out abortion, whether she'd remained in Mississippi, working at the Jackson Freedom School, or had returned to liberal New York, where she admitted "family connections" could facilitate the deed.

All right. But if they couldn't terminate the pregnancy— and Ryan had warmed up to that idea before long—then, what? He'd proposed marriage, a typical knee-jerk response, but Lucia had put him off, explaining rationally that she was a strong and independent woman who could make her own way in the world, and wasn't asking him to alter his career in law enforcement, even if a change were feasible.

That led to arguments, then making up, more arguing, and so it went.

Until the night she died.

The White Knights had continued their bombing campaign from last fall into 1968, striking primarily around Meridian. In May, a blast hit Temple Beth Israel, sister synagogue of Jackson's target from September of last year. G-men were on the case and narrowing their focus to a pair of terrorists. Tom Tarrants, still a fugitive, since getting busted with Sam Bowers and a submachine gun in the car, was nowhere to be found, apparently making his money from a string of armed robberies while planning future raids. Twelve idiots in Covington County, serving as jurors, acquitted Bowers on the weapons charge—convinced he "didn't know" the gun was in the car, in plain view on the backseat—but Tarrants wasn't inclined to roll the dice at trial.

His partner in the bombings, based on what informers said, was one Joe Daniel Hawkins—"Danny Joe" to friends— son of a Klansman and his wife, known to the Bureau, with their son, as the meanest Ku Klux family in Mississippi. Father Joe Denver had been charged, with Danny Joe, for assaulting two special agents last year, then acquitted.

Danny Joe, likewise, had ducked charges of firing into Negro homes and beating up at least one voting activist.

When Bowers and his nitwits started hitting targets in Meridian, Police Chief Roy Gunn blew his top, forming a special "blackshirt squad" to give Klansmen a taste of their own medicine. That meant exploding loud but harmless bombs at Kluckers' homes, all hours of the night, and firing shots into a couple of their favored bars. Police manhandled White Knights as their colleagues often did to blacks, and if a couple of the Klansmen came away believing that their lives had been at risk in custody, so much the better.

But the result of that campaign hit Ryan where he lived.

On June 1, nearly seven months along and still with nothing settled on the baby front, Lucia left the Freedom School, turned the ignition key of her Chrysler Valiant, and was consumed by the explosion that demolished it. Analysis showed composition of the bomb matched those set off in Natchez, wounding George Metcalfe and killing Wharlest Jackson, but that didn't mean the Silver Dollar Group had been responsible. Ryan had checked, joining the squad that shook them down, but after all, the SDG members were all defectors from related Klans, and most members had learned the same techniques of demolition, going back to 1964.

Their break came when B'nai B'rith and its Anti-Defamation League posted a reward for capture of the Mississippi synagogue bombers. Regional Director Adolph Botnick raised the money, working from his home base in New Orleans, and it wasn't long before Chief Joyner—now a fixture on the Klan's hit list—called him, asking whether the ADL would pay "to purchase bodies and not testimony." It meant setting up a death trap for the terrorists, and Ryan, grieving privately, was fine with that.

His SAC in Jackson knew nothing of his affair with Lucia —or maybe just *pretended* not to know, sparing the Bureau from embarrassment—but no complaints were raised when Ryan joined in squeezing Klan informers for hot leads on Hawkins and Tarrants. They soon struck gold with Alton Roberts, presently appealing his ten-year sentence in the "Mississippi Burning" case—and brother Raymond. Both were White Knights and recruiters for the National State Rights Party, but they'd agreed to put their brethren on the spot for $30,000. It also might've helped when Joyner's cops cranked off a few rounds into Raymond's house.

So, it was set. Next up on the terrorists' list was Meyer Davidson, Meridian's ADL coordinator. Hawkins and Tarrants would be dropping by his house around the end of June, the Roberts brothers said. Details to follow, as the target date approached. Joyner prepared his blackshirt squad, inviting Ryan for a ride-along.

But there had been a glitch, unknown to law enforcement, when the bombers rolled on June 30. Hawkins bowed out and was replaced by Kathy Ainsworth, fifth-grade teacher at a private school run by the Jackson White Citizens Council. Butter wouldn't melt in her mouth, unless someone mentioned Jews or blacks. Then, they'd discover that she was a die-hard member of the NSRP, three different Klans in two states, and a Bowers front group, Americans for Preservation of the White Race. No one outside the White Knights' inner circle knew that she'd joined Tarrants in at least one other bombing, nor were they expecting her to show up, armed and dangerous, riding with Tarrants on the night he was supposed to die.

Ryan was watching from the shadows when a green Buick Electra pulled up to the curb, the driver exited and started walking toward Davidson's house, holding a parcel in both hands. One of the city cops shouted for him to halt as spotlights blazed, and Tarrants spun around, retreating toward his car. The cops and Ryan all cut loose on him, but even wounded, Tarrants made it, revved his Buick, and took off with bullets ripping through the car.

Fleeing, he'd fired one-handed with a World War-era German submachine gun, emptying one magazine before the Buick crashed and he'd reloaded, then leapt clear, still firing. Ryan blazed away, emptied his .38, but couldn't swear he'd scored a hit before shotgun and rifle fire dropped Tarrants in a neighbor's shrubbery. Cops rushed him, one asking if he was dead, another answering, "Bad luck. The sumbitch is still breathing."

"I'll fix that," Ryan had snarled, his gun reloaded, ready in his fist, but officers had pulled him back, reminding him that witnesses roused by the gunfire were emerging from their nearby homes.

So, Tarrants had survived and would be facing trial before a Mississippi jury, sometime in the fall, with white Meridian belatedly resolved to lock him up. Dead in the Buick's shotgun seat, accomplice Kathy Ainsworth had taken one round to the neck, a rifle slug, without reaching the automatic pistol in her purse. It rested with her I.D. cards from every crackpot racist group in Mississippi and Louisiana, instantly absolving Ryan of whatever qualms he felt about her death.

That is, until an autopsy revealed that she was three months pregnant when she died.

What were the odds: two pregnant teachers, both working in Jackson, both cut down within a single month by Klan-related violence? Of course, they'd been opponents in the state's new Civil War. They'd never met, had likely never heard of one another while Lucia was alive.

And even with them gone, their schools survived, at least for now: one raising black children to vote, strive, and succeed in a society that disrespected them; the other teaching white kids to be bigots like their parents, blindly loathing all the same people their forebears had despised for generations, hopelessly immune to rationality.

And where did that leave Ryan?

Drinking in a cheap motel, wondering whether he should bother to show up for work tomorrow, or just eat his gun right now.

Lucia was beyond his reach, not only dead, but whisked away by family for burial in New York City. Would there be a separate, small casket for her unborn child?

Ryan set down his empty glass, reached out to touch the .38, then drew his hand back, clutched the fifth, and poured himself another round.

———

FBI Field Office, Jackson, Mississippi: August 13, 1968

THE VERNON DAHMER case had gone to trial at last, with mixed results that left Nolan O'Hara less than satisfied. While the Hattiesburg Chamber of Commerce led a community effort to rebuild Dahmer's burnt-out home, only four out of the fourteen Klansmen charged with murder and arson had been convicted.

Billy Pitts, the raider who had dropped his pistol at the murder scene, then turned state's evidence, was spared state prison time for helping the prosecution, but he still faced trial on federal charges somewhere down the line. Charles Clifford Wilson, convicted of murder and sentenced to life, had been honored as "Man of the Year" by Laurel's Junior

Chamber of Commerce three days before the Dahmer raid, defended at trial by William Waller, ex-D.A. of Hinds County and a presumed gubernatorial candidate in 1971. A third defendant stood convicted of arson, but Wizard Sam Bowers escaped by the skin of his teeth, the jury deadlocked eleven-to-one for conviction.

Now, true or not, Bureau informers claimed attorney Waller had been courting Klan votes for his next campaign, promising to free any nightriders jailed on state charges within six months of his inauguration.

In Natchez, the Wharlest Jackson case dragged on with no prediction of arrests so far. Tension within the fractured Mississippi Klans grew worse daily. Grand Dragon Ed McDaniel had already quit the UKA, accused by headquarters of skimming funds, and murderer James Seale had dropped in at the Bureau's field office, denying any knowledge of Jackson's murder, whining that he had been "falsely accused" of mayhem in the past, but now no longer traveled "in the same circles" as other Klansmen—who, of course, included his father and brothers. He was focused now, Seale said, on earning cash and "improving his property," whatever that might be.

In Alabama, George Wallace was running for the White House after severing his old ties to Ace Carter in the hope it would make him—George, not Ace—seem "less extreme." With wife Lurleen just three months in her grave, he'd also started dating one Cornelia Ellis, twenty years Wallace's junior, niece of Wallace mentor Big Jim Folsom. Scuttlebutt suggested they if George failed in his presidential run—a given—they would marry before he rebounded with a second term as governor.

And finally, from Florida, there'd come a flashback to O'Hara's first year in Miami. Walter Irvin, last survivor of the

1949 Groveland rape frame-up, had been paroled this year by Governor Claude Kirk, and then, against all reason, went back to Lake County for a visit. When police found him slumped dead inside his car, they'd blamed "natural causes" at age thirty-five. One of the many public figures challenging that verdict, Thurgood Marshall—now an associate justice of the U.S. Supreme Court—

had defended Irwin and his codefendants in the 1950s.

Some prosper, Nolan thought. *Some die, and some get lost along the way.*

He hoped his son, Ryan, would share whatever had been eating at him for the past couple of months, but given their communication breakdown, Nolan wondered whether he would ever learn the truth of it.

———

Birmingham, Alabama: November 6, 1968

"SO MUCH FOR WALLACE, ANYWAY," Dave Jordan said, first thing at work this Wednesday morning after the election.

"Not so fast," said Fee O'Hara. "We both know he'll be a shoo-in when he runs for governor two years from now."

"And there goes my fragile balloon of happiness," Dave answered back.

"Sorry. I'm still a realist."

Lurleen Wallace had first been "cleared" of cancer when she'd run for governor in 1966, winning the office that she merely held for George, while he sat out a term under provisions of the Alabama constitution. The disease had come back strong in June of '67, and she'd died in May of '68, succeeded by Lieutenant Governor Albert Brewer, a Wallace protégé. Brewer clearly hoped for election in his own right, come November 1970. Currently, he drew cover support from Richard Nixon, now the president-elect, who wanted Wallace neutralized before the next White House campaign.

As for the race this year, Fiona was relieved when Wallace went down to defeat with running mate Curtis LeMay, a former U.S. Air Force general in love with nukes, who'd vowed that if the Wallace ticket won he'd personally bomb North Vietnam "back to the Stone Age." Tough talk and assorted euphemisms for white racism—led by a call for "law 'n' order" in the ghetto—kept rednecks cheering at AIP rallies around the country, but Election Day revealed the movement's weakness. The party gained a few far-right endorsements: Rep. John Rarick of Louisiana (named in FBI files as a "cyclops" of the KKK); Georgia Governor Lester Maddox (also cozy with the Klan); and, allegedly, James Earl Ray, accused slayer of Dr. Martin Luther King. Dave had researched that, found no evidence that Ray, while on the run or since, had plumped for any candidate—although his brother John *was* pushing Wallace literature from his rough St. Louis bar.

And now, the ballots tabulated overnight, Wallace-LeMay had claimed 13.5 percent, less than 10 million votes out of 73.2 million cast. The ticket *had* received 46 votes in the Electoral College, carrying only the Deep South states of Alabama, Arkansas, Georgia, Louisiana and Mississippi—just what you'd expect.

Now, everyone predicted Wallace would be back and running strong for governor in 1970, likely to win his old job back, hands down. At least, when he was sworn in, he would be confronted with another federal Civil Rights Act, signed by LBJ in mid-April. Its main thrust lay in Title VIII, dubbed the Fair Housing Act, imposing civil and criminal penalties for housing discrimination. Another clause prescribed jail time and fines for anyone seeking "by force or by threat of force, to injure, intimidate, or interfere with anyone by reason of their race, color, religion, or national origin."

And of course, since it came out of Washington, the Land of Compromise, there had to be a twist. A last-minute rider tacked onto the bill made it a felony for anyone to "travel in interstate commerce with the intent to incite, promote, encourage, participate in and carry on a riot." Granted, while that might've once applied to racist agitators like Ace Carter and John Kasper, in the present day it clearly targeted black militants whom Edgar Hoover's FBI regarded as the next subversive menace to be neutralized and crushed.

"Let's worry about 1970 some other time," David was saying now, half-smiling at Fiona. "In the meantime, what's up for today?"

———

West Jackson Boulevard, Chicago: November 13, 1968

BLACK PANTHER PARTY headquarters occupied a three-story redbrick building at 2413 West Jackson, its premises also including the Party's Free Breakfast Program for children, a small classroom, and the upstairs living quarters of chapter president Fred Hampton. Its street entrance was situated to the far left—which Fred Sawyer found appropriate—while something like a dozen good-sized windows overlooked the boulevard. Next-door, a parking lot was packed with beat-up cars.

Fred Sawyer had been pacing up and down the sidewalk opposite for nigh on fifteen minutes now, and figured someone must've spotted him, no doubt becoming curious.

Soon, he must either cross the street or get the hell away from there.

Time, as he old man used to say, for him to shit, or else get off the pot.

A long, tortuous road had brought him here, and now Fred felt as if he'd reached a point of no return.

The journey had begun in May 1967, when Dr. King began planning his Poor People's March on Washington, announcing a shift from "reform" to "revolution" when he'd said, "We have moved from the era of civil rights to an era of human rights." Coupled with his April speech on Vietnam, the new approach made enemies for King in Washington and in the white-owned media, including black columnist Carl Rowan, who opposed Jim Crow but panned King's "meddling" in the realm of international affairs. By late December, it was planned for marchers to arrive in D.C. by May 2, 1968, pressing demonstrations that were "nonviolent but militant, and as dramatic, as dislocative, as disruptive, as attention-getting as the riots without destroying property."

The first roadblock appeared on February 8, when state and local police fired on 200 protesters outside a segregated bowling alley in Orangeburg, South Carolina. The cops claimed they'd come under sniper fire, killing three persons and wounding thirty-three more. All they shot were wounded in their backs while fleeing from the gunfire, a few through the soles of their feet. None of them was armed, and no weapons were found, but white reporters persisted in the lie that blacks had fired first, with "at least one automatic, a shotgun and other small caliber weapons." FBI agents had supported that lie at the trial of nine cops named as wrongful shooters, and all were acquitted. Cleveland Sellers—a SNCC member, protest leader, and one of those wounded—was the sole defendant convicted, sentenced to jail for "inciting a riot."

Three days after the Orangeburg massacre, black garbage men in Memphis staged a wildcat strike, complaining of hazardous working conditions that had claimed two lives, plus being forced to slog through rain and snow while their white supervisors sat indoors, playing cards. Dr. King saw the strike as a fitting prelude to his siege of Washington and led a Memphis protest on March 28. Unknown to King, however, FBI *agents provocateurs*, collected in a gang called The Invaders, had been paid to foment violence, brandishing signs that read "MAYOR LOEB EAT SHIT" before they started smashing windows, looting stores along the route of march. Police rolled out and killed one sixteen-year-old boy—not an Invader— claiming that he'd pulled a pocketknife on two cops armed with shotguns.

Dr. King, embarrassed and disconsolate, fled Memphis but promised to come again, telling his closest aides, "If we can't lead a peaceful demonstration there, no Washington!"

Which must've been what Edgar Hoover wanted all along...or was his master plan even more devious?

King and his entourage, including Sawyer, had returned on April 3, after a bomb threat stalled their plane's departure from Atlanta. While they dawdled there—unknown to King and company, although Fred knew it now—a "light-skinned Negro" had appeared at the Lorraine Motel on Mulberry Street, where King's party had booked their rooms. He claimed to be an SCLC "advance man," insisting that Dr. King's reserved room must be switched for a second-floor suite overlooking the motel's swimming pool, facing the backside of various buildings that lined nearby Main Street.

Today, Fred knew there'd been no such "advance man," no request from King to change his room. The Bureau knew it, too, but they were keeping that and many other details under wraps.

That night, once Dr. King had settled into the hotel, he'd led his people to the jam-packed Bishop Charles Mason Temple, delivering a speech titled, "I've Been to the Mountaintop." Inured to threats of death and physical attacks since 1956, King seemed convinced his murder was inevitable. After Dallas, in November 1963, he'd warned wife Coretta, "This is what is going to happen to me also. I keep telling you, this is a sick society."

His message on that last full night of life cautioned his followers to stay the course with Gandhian nonviolence, whatever might befall him as their leader. Wails and moans rose from the audience as he concluded, "I don't know what will happen now. We've got some difficult days ahead. But it doesn't matter with me now, because I've been to the mountaintop. Like anybody, I would like to live a long life. Longevity has its place, but I'm not concerned about that now. I just want to do God's will. And He's allowed me to go up to the mountain. And I've looked over. And I've seen the promised land. I may not get there with you. But I want you to know tonight, that we, as a people will get to the promised land. And I'm happy tonight. I'm not worried about anything. I'm not fearing any man. Mine eyes have seen the glory of the coming of the Lord!"

At 6:00 p.m. on April 4, Fred was among the aides surrounding King, as he stood on the balcony requested by his mythical "advance man" one day earlier. They had another rally to attend, prior to a march—hopefully peaceful—scheduled for Friday morning, April 5. King was chatting with some friends standing below him, telling Ben

Branch, the famed bandleader, "Make sure you play 'Take My Hand, Precious Lord' at the meeting tonight. Play it real pretty."

Branch barely got his promise out before a single shot echoed across the street behind the Lorraine. A rifle bullet slammed into King's face, breaking his jaw and several vertebrae, severing his jugular vein and carotid artery, snipping off his tie below its knot, coming to rest against his shoulder blade. King survived to reach St. Joseph's Hospital but died there, on an operating table, at 7:05 p.m.

Meanwhile, suggestions of conspiracy were piling up. Shortly before the murder, a black cop assigned to spy on King from an adjacent fire station had been removed by white superiors who claimed they had received a threat against his life but had no evidence to prove it. Seconds after King went down, eyewitnesses beheld a man fleeing from bushes on the far side of the street, while yet another rushed out of the Young & Morrow rooming house on Main Street —whose rear windows had an awkward view of the Lorraine through trees and untrimmed shrubbery.

The second man walked to his car, a white Mustang, but paused to drop his personal belongings in the recessed doorway of a pinball shop instead of driving off with them. Most of the items were mundane, but one was a Remington rifle, recently fired. All bore fingerprints, but FBI technicians would require more than two weeks to match them with a fugitive from Missouri. Meanwhile, as vital seconds ticked away, *two* white Mustangs, one of them with a whip antenna for a CB radio, took off from Main Street, merging with traffic. Soon, while cops all over town hunted a Mustang, CB radio reports described said car escaping to the southeast, Mississippi bound, its driver trading shots with officers before it disappeared.

The broadcast was a hoax. The "real" Mustang, in fact, had fled southwest, to Georgia, where it was abandoned at a housing project in Atlanta. When police recovered it, both floor mats in the front bore muddy footprints from two passengers, and the ashtray was overflowing. Those facts—now suppressed, along with so much else—only became important when the FBI claimed King's "lone nut" assassin, a nonsmoker, had escaped alone. Memphis authorities now blamed the CB hoax on an unnamed teenager who'd done it as "a prank" and wasn't prosecuted for his interference with the manhunt.

The Atlanta Mustang's registration bore the name of "Eric Starvo Galt," who'd purchased it in Birmingham last year, a private sale. Since Alabama drivers' licenses required no photograph, the suspect remained faceless until G-men traced his name to bartending school 2,200 miles west, in Los Angeles. There, during 1967, "Eric Galt" had kept his eyes closed for his graduation photo, and it went onto his WANTED poster that way, plus another version with the eyes drawn in. The charge against him was conspiracy to violate King's civil rights—meaning the feds suspected more than one person involved.

Bureau headquarters finally identified "Galt's" finger-prints as those of James Earl Ray, a convict who'd escaped from Missouri's state prison at Jefferson City one year earlier, in April 1967. The scan of prints had taken sixteen days, Chief Hoover said, because Missouri had "the wrong inmate's" prints filed under Ray's name. Ray hit the Bureau's Ten Most Wanted list on April 20, by which time tardy agents had followed his year-old trail through Alabama, into Mexico, then California, then—after King's murder—to Toronto, Canada, before he caught a flight to London and vanished again. At least one visitor, an unidentified "fat man," had come looking for Ray/Galt at his cheap Toronto boarding house—and in another grating irony, agents discovered a real-life Canadian policeman who closely resembled Ray. Three other names he'd used while traveling —Paul Bridgeman, Ramon Sneyd, and John Willard—also were living Canadians who bore a likeness to the fugitive, all living near Eric Galt.

Coincidence? Fred wasn't buying it.

Of course, when Dr. King was slain, ghettoes across America caught fire, 159 cities in all. Before the so-called "Holy Week riots" burned out, at least forty persons died, more than 2,600 suffered injuries, and arrests topped 21,000. Estimates of property damage ran upward from $65 million, with whole blocks reduced to rubble in some cities.

Through it all, the hunt for James Earl Ray continued, leading searchers from London to Portugal and back again, where they finally nabbed Ray at Heathrow Airport on June 8. In Washington, Hoover delayed announcement of the bust so that its news flash interrupted network coverage of Robert Kennedy's funeral—a petty stunt that prompted Attorney General Clark to briefly suspend Cartha DeLoach, while carefully avoiding any punishment of Hoover.

Ray fought extradition to the States, hired Klan attorney Art Hanes Sr. to defend him, and sold Alabama author William Bradford Huie all rights to his story. Huie—who had previously published the confessions of Emmett Till's slayers in *Look* magazine, chose the same venue for a series describing Ray's movements and motives. Its first installment, published only yesterday, was titled "The Story of James Earl Ray and the Conspiracy to Kill Martin Luther King." Huie called Ray a dupe of plotters who intended King to fall in an election year, benefiting racist candidates and stating that the plan's real victim was America.

Fred had remained in service to the SCLC as Ralph Abernathy stepped into the fallen leader's shoes, but each new day intensified Sawyer's misgivings about blind devotion to nonviolence. In Cleveland, for example, he knew FBI agents had primed local police with rumors that a local activist, Fred Allen Evans—now preferring "Ahmed" as his middle name—was plotting rebellion against the city's Negro mayor and mostly-white establishment, led by his tiny group, "New Libya." The Bureau's lead informer was a drug dealer, not part of Evans's clique, but law enforcement swallowed his bullshit and placed Evans under "rolling surveillance," with calamitous results.

On July 23, police received complaints of an abandoned car near New Libya's Lakeview Road headquarters. A tow truck dispatched to remove it came under gunfire from persons unknown—an apparent ambush, but by whom? A muddled DOJ report said the tow truck was "inadvertently trapped in the crossfire between police and snipers," and the shooting swiftly escalated, both sides later claiming that the other started it. The final tally: six dead—three cops, two members of New Libya, and a black bystander police drafted to drive a decoy car—plus fifteen wounded. Ghetto rioting erupted in the wake of that shootout, claiming two more lives, inflicting damages of $2.6 million.

In August, prosecutors charged Evans with four murder counts, later reduced to "killing by shooting," which avoided pesky questions of premeditation. He would face trial in the spring. In the meantime, autopsy reports describing several deaths from "shotgun wounds" were clumsily altered to "gunshot wounds." The reason? When police collected weapons from the handful of New Libyans, their arsenal included only rifles, not a shotgun to be found. The obvious conclusion: cops had shot each other and the unlucky civilian they had forced to help them in the fight.

From that fiasco, Fred Sawyer had watched the year's White House campaign make matters even worse. Former Red-hunter Tricky Dick, picked once again by mostly-white Republicans to run as the "New Nixon," claimed to speak for America's conservative "silent majority" while pursuing a slick "Southern strategy" that wooed ex-Dixiecrats to switch parties for race and nation. It had proved to be a winning combination for the old Party of Lincoln, now apparently controlled by men who might have sided with Confederates during the Civil War.

And finally, Sawyer had seen enough. The SCLC's Poor People's Campaign turned out to be a bust, as far as he could tell, its grim "tent city" made the butt of scornful jokes, its call for an Economic Bill of Rights falling on deaf ears in Congress. So, Fred was giving up, quitting the movement for which he had previously left the FBI. These days, the Panther Party's program seemed to make more sense to him. If that meant "picking up the gun," in Huey Newton's words, so what? He'd carried one throughout his tenure with the Bureau but had yet to fire a shot in anger.

Maybe it was time.

Crossing the street, Fred pushed his way in through the redbrick building's entrance, wincing slightly as the door slammed shut behind him with a sharp note of finality.

———

Harlem: December 13, 1968

ON ODD DAYS, normally when he was waking up or lying down to sleep at some ungodly hour, Payton Sawyer thought of his old man, now five years dead. Ike Sawyer had devoted almost forty years to federal law enforcement—first the Bureau of Investigation, until Edgar Hoover laid him off for being black, then the Narcotics Bureau under Harry Anslinger. Nothing except technology had changed about the FBI, as far as Payton knew, but now the former FBN had been replaced by a new Bureau of Narcotics and Dangerous Drugs, merged with something called the Bureau of Drug Abuse Control, removed from the Treasury Department and shoved into Justice as part of what the feds called Reorganization Plan No. 1.

But what, if anything, had really changed? Payton's twelve years with NYPD, most of that with "BOSS," led him to think that fundamental changes in the hard heart of police work were as rare as hen's teeth in America, or anywhere around the world.

BOSS and the FBI were still pursuing the Nation of Islam, just as they had hounded Marcus Garvey before Payton's birth. In a September statement to the lofty-sounding National Commission on the Causes and Prevention of Violence, spending millions to analyze April's riots, Chief Hoover warned the panel that NOI meetings "are replete with condemnations of the white race and vague references to the physical retribution that will be meted out to oppressors." In fact, spokesmen for the Black Muslims condemned bloodshed, except in self-defense, and their religious trappings hampered Hoover's COINTELPRO jive, restricting some of the illegal dirty tricks he'd used against the CPUSA and Dr. King.

In Payton's own backyard, the Five Percenters led by Clarence 13X—or "Allah," if you pleased—had topped out at 600 members. Harlem had escaped the April fires of rage that blazed across America, at least in part because of

Clarence and his followers walking the streets, urging a calm that other cities couldn't manage. As for Allah, he'd convinced Gloria Steinem that NOI leaders were behind his near-murder in 1964, a story she published in *New York* magazine. On the private side, Clarence had fathered a son this year, *sans* marriage, with a young convert he called Gusavia.

In terms of fear inspired by militants, the Black Panthers were No. 1 on everybody's list today. FBI Special Agent Henry Naehle had shared the Bureau's Panther files with BOSS in August, reporting back to headquarters that Gotham's field office "has been working closely with BOSS in exchanging information of mutual interest and to our mutual advantage." He could easily have said the same for any other sizable police department in the country, all on board the anti-Panther train and yearning for a chance to crack some nappy heads.

In Brooklyn, for example, some off-duty BOSS detectives had attacked Panthers during a court appearance, stealing a briefcase from BPP chapter head David Brothers. Rather than prosecuting the rogue cops involved, Hoover had ordered "a review of these names and telephone numbers so that appropriate action will be taken" against Panther allies.

Another brainstorm from the Gotham field office, approved by Washington, involved printing fliers headed "DANGER," spelling out the so-called menace posed by Brothers and his followers. The New York SAC proposed that fliers "should be left in restaurants where Negroes are known to frequent (Chock Full of Nuts, etc.)." After that was done, another memo from the field to Hoover gloated that blacks now suspected Brothers of betraying them somehow.

Another local Panther on the firing line was Richard Moore, aka "Dhoruba al-Mujahid bin Wahad," who'd been labeled a "key agitator" and placed in the Bureau's "Security Index" for future detention. His face also adorned the FBI's Black Nationalist Photograph Album, coupled with orders to "develop better liaison and closer working relationship with the NYCPD" to make Moore's life miserable.

Sometimes, Payton wondered how long people of color would endure such oppressive tactics, then he'd recognize anew that he was part of it, just as his father had been, and he'd pour himself another double whisky. Only younger brother Fred had broken with the family tradition, first defecting from the Bureau to the SCLC, and now to the Panthers, with their black berets and leather coats.

Payton was keeping *that* news out of his reports. If someone called him on it later, he could always claim that he and Fred weren't speaking—very nearly true these days —and that he hadn't known about the youngest Sawyer's heresy.

Hell, what was one more personal betrayal, after all?

———

FBI Headquarters: December 17, 1968

OCCASIONALLY, Devon Gantt suspected that the walls were closing in on Chief Hoover, with fifty-one years at Justice, forty-four of those as the FBI's director. His age was showing —although not as badly as Clyde Tolson's—and it was an open secret that his daily shots of "vitamins" from a particular physician who made office calls were something more akin to speed.

Congress had made a not-so-subtle move against him on June 1, enacting Public Law 90351, which required the next Bureau director and all those who followed him to serve a ten-year maximum in office, following approval from the Senate for whoever got the presidential nod. Alas, the law's wording ensured that it would only take effect after Hoover retired—and President-elect Nixon had already announced that he was keeping Hoover on the job.

Until the Old Man died, or went stark raving batshit crazy, it would be business as usual—and that meant constantly improving COINTELPRO, making the illegal program ever more intrusive and disruptive to selected segments of American society.

Already, the New Left had suffered rifts that Devon viewed as critical, perhaps fatal. For one thing, presidential candidates Eugene McCarthy and Bob Kennedy had carried anti-war rhetoric into the mainstream, splitting New Left activists who still believed the system might be salvaged from their revolutionary counterparts who longed to burn the whole thing down. Clamor against the war in Vietnam had driven LBJ from office, going on TV in March to say he wouldn't run again. Meanwhile, agents and their informers chipped away at activism wherever it dared arise, whether in neighborhood associations or mass movements, revolutionary cells or staid religious groups.

While SDS waffled, promoting "Ten Days of Resistance" in the spring, backing a "Third World Student Strike" at San Francisco State College, while part of the New Left movement had veered off into a comic vein. Abbie Hoffman's Yippies—christened "Groucho Marxists" by one mocking journalist—had nominated a hog named "Pigasus the Immortal" as their White House candidate, and packed Grand Central Terminal with some 3,000 demonstrators celebrating the spring equinox. They'd brought Pigasus to Chicago for the Democratic National Convention in August, and the whole world watched as that devolved into a scene of bloody chaos, described by federal investigators as a "police riot."

On top of all that, if you could believe it, the Bureau now had to grapple with an Indian uprising, of all things. In March, shortly before he pulled the plug, LBJ had signed an executive order creating a National Council on Indian Opportunity, declaring that "the time has come to focus our efforts on the plight of the American Indian." So what if he was 350 years late? Johnson claimed the new NCIO would "launch an undivided, government-wide effort in this area." Of course, it wasn't really "undivided." Florida's James Haley, Democratic chairman of the House Subcommittee on Indian Affairs, agreed in principle that Indians "should participate more in policy matters," but then reassured white folks that "the right of self-determination is in the Congress as a representative of all the people."

Since when had Congress ever represented Indians? Gantt wondered. Hell, Indians were here before the white man, but they hadn't been granted U.S. citizenship until June 1924 —and even then, they couldn't vote unless their individual state laws allowed it. A majority still lived on squalid reservations, plagued by alcoholism and epidemics long since vanquished in the white world, First Amendment freedom of religion denied if native customs called for use of peyote or other drugs.

So far, the only actual result Devon had seen from Johnson's "generosity" was July's foundation of an American Indian Movement in Minneapolis. Created to address issues of sovereignty, treaty rights, racism and police oppression, AIM was instantly appended to the Bureau's list of "radical" groups marked for COINTELPRO disruption.

And why not? Devon asked himself. If Indians wanted equality, why shouldn't they be equally subverted, spied on, and harassed by the same government that pledged to offer them relief?

The presidential race this year had been explosive, fraught with riots and assassinations, each new headline more alarming and bizarre than those preceding it. Nixon was back—or would be, as of January—finally claiming the Oval Office that he'd lusted for since he first entered politics in 1946. His top aides made no secret of that fact that Tricky Dick would be inaugurated with a list of "enemies" in mind. The roster was extensive, ranging from the broad strokes—blacks and antiwar leftists—to rival politicians and which-ever media outlets he felt had slighted him over the years. In 1962, after a losing run for governor of California, he'd chas-tised reporters, telling them, "You don't have Nixon to kick around anymore, because, this is my last press conference."

That, of course, was simply one of countless lies from Tricky Dick. He'd be in power soon, and when the kicking started, he'd be doing it.

Strange days, and Gantt knew they'd be getting even stranger soon enough.

In line with Nixon's planning of the war at home, Chief Hoover's COINTELPRO—BLACK HATE schemes were barreling along, full speed ahead. Aside from frustrating "the rise of a messiah," Hoover's memos ordered all field offices to "prevent militant black nationalist groups and leaders from gaining RESPECTABILITY, by discrediting them to both the responsible community and to liberals who have vestiges of sympathy." At the same time, all G-men assigned to COINTELPRO should also "prevent the long-range GROWTH of militant black organizations, especially among youth." The erratic capitals were Hoover's, just in case his minions missed the point.

And the Bureau had no shortage of black targets lately.

Rap Brown, facing prison in Louisiana for a violation of the Federal Anti-Riot Act, kept huddling with the Panthers when he wasn't stuck in court or busy raising bail. One of his sometime cohorts, Stokely Carmichael, seemed to be stepping back a bit from activism, having wed exiled South African singer Miriam Makeba, reportedly planning a life together in Guinea.

Group-wise, G-men were tracking and disrupting the Revolutionary Action Movement; the Republic of New Afrika, led by brothers Milton and Richard Henry, aka Gaidi and Imari Obadele ("obey them," in Swahili); and George Jackson's mostly prison-bound Black Guerrilla Family. Admittedly, the Bureau couldn't do much to incarcerated inmates, beyond urging wardens to suspend whatever piddling privileges they had, but neo-Nazis on the inside made life dangerous for militants, as with the April stabbing murder of BGF member Clarence Causey in California, touching off a string of bloody incidents that claimed the lives of more inmates and prison guards.

Meanwhile, above all other brooding ghetto threats, there were the Panthers, whom Edgar Hoover told Congress "without question, represent the greatest threat to the internal security of the country." Apparently, their party had outstripped the feeble CPUSA, merging Red and black to embody the Chief's worst nightmare.

While Panther membership was sparse, they were on the march from coast to coast, scowling and clutching guns on TV nightly news, "patrolling pigs" and spoiling for a fight, mourning Huey Newton's manslaughter conviction, but still refusing to back down.

Arthur Morris was the first Panther to fall, shot by persons unknown at an L.A. neighbor's house, while free on bail from conspiracy charges. Oakland police killed member

Bobby Hutton in May, LAPD killed three Panthers while they were gassing up their car in August, and someone twice firebombed the Party's Newark office in November and December.

Anywhere that Panthers organized, police harassment followed as a matter of routine. Cops raided Party offices and homes in Denver, San Francisco, Oakland, Berkeley, Kansas City, Seattle, Chicago, Des Moines, and Indianapolis. Most of those arrested were acquitted after costly trials designed to sap the Party's treasury, but one—Elmer "Geronimo" Pratt—was framed for murder in Los Angeles and jailed for life. George Murray lost his job at San Francisco State University after a local paper blew the whistle on his Party membership. Eldridge Cleaver, the Peace and Freedom Party's presidential nominee, suddenly found his parole revoked and was returned to prison, but he'd still received some 36,000 votes. Two Oakland cops, both drunk on duty, celebrated Huey Newton's conviction by firing carbines into the local Party office. In Chicago, where leader Fred Hampton rated inclusion in the "Agitator Annex," G-men tapped his mother's phone in search of nonexistent evidence.

How many would survive the COINTELPRO—BLACK HATE purge? Gantt was no prophet, but he would've bet his past year's salary that most of the survivors would be white.

———

CIA Headquarters: December 20, 1968

COLBY GANTT WAS TRYING to decide exactly how he felt about his son joining the Agency. As Hardy's father, should he feel a certain pardonable pride? Or would approval of the twenty-one-year-old's ambition mean perpetuation of a curse that hung over their family?

Either way, he had decided that the choice couldn't be his to make.

If no part of the past chaotic, bloody year dissuaded Hardy from retracing Colby's footsteps, how could mere words change his mind? And did mother Eileen, also serving the Agency, bear any part of the responsibility involved?

In Washington, ten miles away from Colby's small office, Air America had made its latest move, this time to 815 Connecticut Avenue, within a stone's throw of the White House. The airline was going strong, although its planes were barred—at least officially—from touching down at CIA airfields abroad. That petty furor had arisen over "rumors" of drug smuggling from Vietnam, and while a couple of the Agency's case officers had staged impromptu raids on Asian heroin refineries, such unapproved action had swiftly been reined in by the CIA's Office of General Counsel.

One thing that Langley had in common with the rival FBI was pathological aversion to embarrassment.

In Uruguay, for instance, any active role in government suppression of the radical Tupamaros National Liberation Movement—named for 18th-century rebel Túpac Amaru II —was cloaked in anonymity. Langley approved of President Jorge Pacheco's attempts to crush labor unions, thereby keeping workers' wages low, and it was pleased to have oper- ative Daniel Mitrione train members of Pacheco's Anti- Subversive Activities Co-ordination Organization in fine points of torture, but press leaks were strictly *verboten*.

Eastern Europe was another problem altogether, agitated by Czech Communist Party leader Alexander

Dubček's "Prague Spring." After replacing Antonín Novotný, Dubček had gone off the rails, in Moscow's view, promoting a new Action Program that assured Czech citizens of new freedom to speak freely, organize associations, and travel as they liked. That movement toward reform lasted five months, from April to August, when some 200,000 Warsaw Pact soldiers invaded with 2,000 tanks, capturing Dubček and other leading liberals. Flown out to Moscow, Dubček was compelled to rescind all reforms, while that, in turn, set off resistance reminiscent of Hungary's uprising twelve years earlier. Some Czechs protested by self-immolation; others took up arms to wage guerilla war against the occupying forces. They were doomed to fail, of course, but with 300,000 refugees in transit, while the Free World's media condemned Russia, Gantt thought the exercise might still be counted as a win of sorts.

The same couldn't be said for North Korea, which in January seized the environmental research vessel USS *Pueblo*, serving as an undercover spy ship. One crew member died in the attack, with eighty-two held hostage for eleven months. During that diplomatic standoff, North Korean soldiers also crossed the DMZ and killed twenty-six South Koreans in a failed attempt to raid President Park Chung-hee's mansion in Seoul. Of thirty-one invaders, twenty-nine were slain, one captured, and a lone escapee made it home. Pyongyang still retained the *Pueblo*, though its crewmen had been freed, and mocked the West by turning it into a tourist draw.

In Laos, Air America had lost a Huey helicopter and two pilots, shot down during the Battle of Phou Pha Thi, a March engagement pitting the Royal Lao Army and the U.S. Air Force 1st Combat Evaluation Group against Pathet Lao guerrillas and North Vietnamese regulars. Even the

Agency's Hmong Clandestine Army couldn't save the day in that clash, fought to save an airstrip used for raids against North Vietnam. Before that fight wound down, a full one-third of RLA soldiers—more than 3,200 men in all—were killed in action or reported missing from the battleground.

But that was nothing, next to Vietnam. The nine-month Tet Offensive, carried off by Việt Cộng and NVA soldiers claimed more than 54,000 lives, wounded some 96,000, and saw more than 6,600 logged as missing. Huế, 940 miles north of Saigon, was virtually bombed and shelled out of existence, an American officer famously telling reporters, "We had to destroy Huế in order to save it." The CIA's "Operation Shock" proved a feeble rejoinder, although most Americans would never hear of it. What stuck with them was a freeze-frame snapped by Associated Press photographer Eddie Adams, catching Brigadier General Nguyễn Ngọc Loan, chief of South Vietnam's National Police, executing handcuffed VC member Nguyễn Văn Lém with a point-blank pistol shot to the head.

From that Pulitzer Prize-winning take, millions of Americans who'd supported military force in Vietnam thus far abruptly changed their minds. The saw exactly what their sons and grandsons had been dying for and understood that Washington's predictions of impending victory were lies.

Which didn't mean the war would end, of course; not when the Phoenix Program was involved in "neutralizing" more than 80 million South Vietnamese, at least one-third of whom were executed without trial. Khe Sanh was under siege, 5,000 U.S. Marines outnumbered four-to-one. LBJ might call the Tet Offensive "a complete failure," but TV news footage contradicted him, exacerbated by the U.S. Army's massacre of 300 Vietnamese civilians at My Lai. Less than two weeks after those photos aired, Johnson dropped out of the presidential race and thus become the highest-ranking casualty of Vietnam to date. In April, Defense Secretary Clark Clifford rejected General Westmoreland's request for 206,000 additional warriors, while SDS protesters seized five buildings at Columbia University. By July, Westmoreland was out, replaced by General Creighton Abrams. September logged the 900th U.S. aircraft shot down over North Vietnam.

No one on "freedom's" side was winning, but so what? The object, now, was not to be seen *losing*.

Stateside, the Agency's illicit Project MKCHICKWIT forged ahead, ostensibly studying "new drug developments in Europe and Asia," but in fact conducting many of the same experiments that had distinguished MKULTRA. One subject of said research was the growing "Manson Family," led by the drugged-out ex-convict and drifter Colby had encountered last year, in Haight-Ashbury.

Charley Manson, these days, had moved from admiration of the Beatles to obsession with the "hidden meanings" of their latest tunes. Their new *White Album* told Manson that "Happiness is a Warm Gun," reviled rich "Piggies" (which apparently excluded millionaire rock stars) and raved about chaos in "Helter Skelter." Manson had adopted its title as the codename for impending racial warfare in America, wherein Manson would lead "Blackie" to slaughter whites, then turn around and rule his dusky troops as slaves. For anyone who missed his point, the pint-sized failed musician praised failed painter Adolf Hitler as "a tuned-in guy who leveled the karma of the Jews."

Between sex orgies fueled by any drugs available, Manson stalked Denis Wilson of the Beach Boys, desperately seeking a recording contract, once invading Wilson's home with twelve of his disciples, prostrating himself and kissing Wilson's feet. Over the next few months, the tribe moved in with Wilson running up a fat $100,000 tab, including $20,000 spent to treat their rampant gonorrhea. By the time Wilson got bored and tossed them out, Manson had fixed his sights on an abandoned movie ranch in Death Valley's wasteland, hyping the desert as his "Helter Skelter" training ground.

Crazy, but Gantt was curious to see what would become of the pathetic gypsies as they traveled in a madman's wake.

Meanwhile, Clay Shaw was still winning postponements of his trial date in New Orleans, for conspiring to assassinate President Kennedy. Anxious to nip that controversy in the bud, Attorney General Clark hand-picked four medical experts to reexamine X-rays, photographs, and any other evidence that might debunk Dallas conspiracy theories. Gantt hadn't been surprised when that panel affirmed Warren Commission findings that all shots fired at JFK came from behind, and that the pristine "magic bullet" had, in fact, caused half a dozen major wounds to Kennedy and Connally without being deformed in any way.

And as that august quartet labored, the convenient deaths continued. "Sudden cancer" claimed the lives of Deputy Sheriff Hiram Ingram, who claimed knowledge of a plot to murder JFK, and Dallas prosecutor A. D. "Jim" Bowie, who'd tried Jack Ruby's case. A supposed heart attack dropped Dr. Nicholas Chetta, the New Orleans coroner who presided at Dave Ferrie's autopsy. Somewhat harder to explain, the "accidental" electrocution of Philip Geraci III silenced a friend of Perry Russo, a Garrison witness who told of Clay Shaw's meetings with Lee Oswald.

At the same time, new assassinations managed to divert public attention from the JFK investigation. Weeks before London police arrested James Earl Ray, Attorney General

Clark parroted Edgar Hoover's line that there was "no sign of conspiracy" behind the death of Martin Luther King. That was a patent lie, Gantt knew, and should have instantly invalidated the conspiracy warrant demanding Ray's arrest. Gantt also knew what most Americans did not: that Dr. King's involvement in the Memphis garbage strike placed him at odds with *Don* Carlos Marcello, who controlled garbage collection and dozens of other rackets ranging from the Crescent City to Memphis and Dallas. On the side, Marcello was a bitter racist who employed Klansmen as muscle when it suited him, and donated drug money to the KKK because he simply hated blacks.

King's death had set America on fire and swung white voters farther to the right, casting their ballots for Dick Nixon after Wallace quit the three-way race, but more important to the campaign's outcome was the bloody death of Robert Kennedy. No longer the Attorney General, serving as one of New York's U.S. Senators, Bobby was late joining the race but did so with élan, casting himself as a die-hard opponent of the war in Vietnam. On June 5, he had won the crucial California Democratic primary, then suffered point-blank gunshot wounds while trying to depart from L.A.'s posh Ambassador Hotel, dying from his injuries less than two hours later.

At first, unlike Dallas and Memphis, Bobby's murder seemed to be open-and-shot. His bodyguards captured Palestinian refugee Sirhan Bishara Sirhan at the scene, smoking revolver in his hand, and held him for police. LAPD swept in, secured spent slugs and shell casings, took countless photographs, and told the press that Sirhan's diary ranted about killing Kennedy over the candidate's support for Israel.

Simple...or at least it was, until more details started leaking out.

For starters, Sirhan's .22 revolver held eight rounds, but when you added up the eight wounds—seven slugs retrieved from human bodies—plus more bullet holes from walls, doorframes, and ceiling tiles, the total hit thirteen. Police made matters worse, removing and destroying bullet-scarred doorframes. Worse still, eyewitnesses—including some who'd suffered wounds themselves—insisted that Sirhan had come no closer than three feet to Kennedy while firing from in front of him. The problem: Coroner Thomas Noguchi swore the fatal headshot had been fired from less than two inches away, with powder stippling clearly visible *behind* Kennedy's ear.

That proved there were at least two shooters, then, beyond the shadow of a doubt.

On top of those discrepancies, when LAPD test-fired Sirhan's gun, their firearms expert jotted down the registration number of another .22, logged into evidence, then melted down to nothing as a matter of "routine." Headquarters called the erroneous number a "clerical error," but who'd ever know?

Something Gantt did know for a fact: one armed man stood within a foot or less of Kennedy the night he died, a uniformed commercial rent-a-cop with rumored Mob connections. Under questioning the guard claimed that he'd worn a .38 revolver on that fatal night and drew it from his holster when the shooting started but had never fired, a claim disputed by eyewitnesses. He'd also owned a .22 resembling Sirhan's, but he swore he'd sold that gun several weeks before the murder. Oddly, when the bill of sale finally surfaced, it was dated from September, three months *after* the assassination—and that gun, of course, was nowhere to be found these days.

Another indication of conspiracy arose within mere seconds of the shooting, when a blonde young woman in a polka-dotted dress ran through the hotel's milling crowd, shouting, "We've killed the senator!" No one who saw her knew the woman's name, and hard-eyed cops from LAPD's "Special Unit Senator"—led by a part-time contract operative with the CIA—strong-armed them into recantation of their claims. One witness who'd refused to lie later perused "her" statement and found someone else had changed her words, specifically denying she'd seen anything suspicious happening at the Ambassador. At least one other witness swore he'd seen the same blonde girl before the shooting, huddled with two "Arab-looking men."

Another glaring problem was alleged lone-nut assassin Sirhan Sirhan himself. At his arrest, multiple witnesses described him acting "dazed" or "drugged." That might result from being tackled and disarmed by two ex-pro linebackers who were part of Kennedy's entourage, but a perusal of Sirhan's diary, written over a span of weeks before the murder, showed disjointed, rambling phrases that a subject of intense hypnosis might've scrawled. One oft-repeated line read "RFK Must Die!" Another, which required more thought, read like an invoice: "Pay to the order of Sirhan Sirhan!"

What did any of it mean? Why did Sirhan, in custody, deny all memory of shooting Kennedy or even giving him much waking thought? Why did he claim, under interrogation, that he had no animosity over the victim's stance on Israel? Would a dedicated terrorist not proudly claim his crime?

Another clinker: months before the shooting, Sirhan

was employed as a horse-walker at a stable owned by men with Mob connections. And who else turned up in L.A. on June 5, except the same "Jim Braden" Dallas cops had fleetingly detained at Dealey Plaza in November 1963.

From scuttlebutt at Langley, Colby also knew that two agents who'd worked on Operation JMWAVE five years ago were also seen at the Ambassador when Kennedy was slain. In fact, their faces had been caught on film, which might've caused the Agency fatal embarrassment if that footage had not been stolen and destroyed. One of those agents kept a lawyer on retainer, who was prone to talking out of turn. Another problem to be dealt with, he quoted the agent in question as boasting to him, "I was in Dallas when we got the son of a bitch and I was in Los Angeles when we got the little bastard."

Never mind.

What mattered now was President-elect Nixon's announcement that along with Edgar Hoover at the FBI, he'd also be retaining Richard Helms to head the CIA. Whatever storms might lie ahead, Colby believed he could trust Helms to keep critical secrets safe and sound until his dying day.

———

Little Italy, Manhattan: December 23, 1968

"CHRISTMAS WITHOUT THE OLD MAN, I don't know," Angelo Giordano said. "It just don't feel the same."

"It ain't the same," said brother Dominic. "That doesn't mean we all lay down and die, though, right?"

"I didn't say—"

"Forget it, Ange. We gotta stay sharp, keep our eyes right on the ball."

"What ball is that, Dom?"

Jesus Christ, Dominic thought. It was two months since Papa Carlo passed away—natural causes, which was rare in their business—and Angelo still hadn't come to grips with it. If—*when*—Dom was confirmed to lead the family in his father's place, he'd have to think about how valuable Ange was. Dom wouldn't have called him underboss material, by any means. Sometimes he had to wonder if his younger sibling even had the makings of a decent button man. Frankly, he didn't earn for shit and had been coasting on their father's name so long, Dom wasn't sure he'd ever make the grade.

"Which ball? You may have noticed guys are gettin' killed all over town," Dom said.

No doubt about it, the so-called "Banana War" was shaping up to be a pisser, maybe the worst civil war inside of *Cosa Nostra* since the Thirties, when Dom was just a kid.

First up, Santo Perrone, a bodyguard for Bill Bonanno and the owner of a Brooklyn trucking company, had been gunned down by one of Gaspar DiGregorio's guys, Frank Mari. Three weeks later, a Bonanno family defector, Mike Consolo, got knocked off by his own men for speaking cordially to Bill Bonanno outside the Manhattan court-house, taken as a sign that Consolo was planning to switch sides again. Frank Mari and *consigliere* Michael Adamo had disappeared together in September, and their bodies hadn't surfaced yet, though anybody with a lick of common sense knew they were dead as dirt.

Still, Dom figured it could still be worse.

Look at the Mafia in Sicily, for instance. Only yesterday, the year-long trial of 114 members had concluded in Catanzaro. All were charged with crimes related to the so-called "First Mafia War," fought during 1962 and '63. Jurors only convicted ten of those accused, but the publicity was bad for business, most particularly their alleged connection to a Ciaculli car-bombing that killed five cops and two soldiers in June of 1963.

What were the bosses thinking, when they pulled off shit like that? Were they so arrogant and stupid that they thought no one would notice, or else simply wouldn't care?

Snafus like that were lessons Dom tried to absorb and learn from, making sure he didn't fall into the same traps on his own home turf. In days like these, staying alive was hard enough, much less trying to lead a family into the future, as a major player in New York.

———

Trenton, New Jersey: December 23, 1968

STEPHEN BARNES WAS home for Christmas with adoptive parents Mark and Isabella, going through the motions of a celebration they regarded as commercialized and fraudulent, another steaming pail of capitalist crap. Appearances were vital, though, particularly now that Stephen was a law student at Yale, committed to enlistment with the FBI and serving as a mole to gut it from within.

Yale Law School was the perfect launching pad for that ambition, founded in 1824, boasting the most selective admissions process of any American graduate school. Stephen's Magna Cum Laude from Princeton, coupled with his high LSAT scores, got him past the entry hurdles, while tuition and his other costs were bankrolled by the secret bank account replenished periodically with laundered Moscow gold.

Upon receipt of his J.D. at graduation, Barnes would join an illustrious list of alumni. Their number included ex-President William Howard Taft (who'd taught constitutional law at Yale from 1913-21, before joining the Supreme Court), seven U.S. Attorneys General, five other cabinet-level officials, twelve senators, twenty-eight congressmen, eight Supreme Court justices, nine federal appellate court judges, twelve U.S. district court judges, and six state governors. With Yale Law behind him, no one on Earth could logically challenge Barnes's credentials.

And his Russian past was strictly off the books.

The year just past had brought riots to Trenton after Dr. King was slain, with more than 200 downtown stores looted and burned, at least 300 young black men jailed on charges ranging from arson, assault, and looting to curfew violations. Surprisingly, no one had died, but thirty-one cops and firefighters were injured, most of the latter from smoke inhalation.

The April riots had encouraged Barnes. If 159 cities could burn over one man's murder, what might happen when, as the Americans might say, shit really hit the fan?

When not immersed in studies or the sporadic pursuit of coeds, Barnes kept track of the FBI he planned to wreck. In April, at El Paso, fugitive killer and car thief David Chubb had murdered Special Agent Douglas Price, concealed the victim's corpse in shrubbery, then showed his yellow streak when he committed suicide in a suburban parking lot.

The year's big case was the recent kidnapping of Emory University coed Barbara Mackle from an Atlanta hotel, where she'd been recuperating from illness with her doting mother. Mackle's parents were wealthy and ripe for picking, her father a close friend of President-elect Nixon. Given Nixon's sway over the FBI, it hadn't taken long to name the kidnappers as Gary Krist and Ruth Eisemann-Schier, a Honduran native who'd dressed as a man to snatch Mackle. They'd buried their victim in a wooden box, doped with sedatives, and tipped G-men to her location after payment of $500,000 ransom. Krist was already in custody, trapped in a Florida swamp, but Eisemann-Schier was still at large, honored as the first woman ever posted to the Bureau's Ten Most Wanted list.

Cases like that made news, but Barnes had other plans, once he had served the standard FBI apprenticeship. He craved assignment to the Espionage Division, where he could feed critical information back to Russia and subvert the Bureau's quest for foreign spies.

And by achieving that, he'd make his father's lifelong dream come true.

CHAPTER 5

Little Italy, Manhattan: February 15, 1969

"ME, FOR ONE, I AIN'T SORRY HE'S GONE," ANGELO GIORDANO said.

His brother Dominic cast wary eyes around their new hangout, DeCicco's Social Club at Mulberry and Baxter Streets, before he said, "Ya wanna talk a little louder, Ange? I think one a the busboys missed that in the kitchen."

"*Fanculo*, eh? You think I care?"

"I think a lotta people from *Don* Vito's crew hear that, they'll hold a grudge until they get a chance to pay ya back. Them *stronzi* don't forget nothin'."

But Dom, for his part, also felt relief over the news that Vito Genovese was dead. Plagued by heart trouble, he'd been transferred from the prison in Atlanta to a hospital for federal prisoners at Springfield, Missouri, where his ticker finally gave out and that was that. Replacing him as boss, age sixty-one, was Phil Lombardo, whose weird eyes explained the nicknames "Benny Squint" and "Cockeyed Phil."

A friend of Vito's and the *Cosa Nostra*, Jimmy Hoffa, still locked up at Lewisburg, had lately come to blows with Tony Provenzano, a Genvese *capo* who would likely have succeeded Vito if he hadn't been confined for looting Teamster funds as vice president of Local 560 in Jersey. Their beef, apparently, was over Hoffa still receiving union benefits inside while Tony's were cut off.

Another wiseguy on the rocks was John Rosselli, marked for deportation back in '68, but that was scotched when Italy refused to take him. Pissed by that, the feds had tied Rosselli to a scandal at the Friars Club out west, Beverly Hills, where Frank Sinatra and Dean Martin sponsored him for membership. His latest crime: since 1962 he had participated in card-cheating at the club—gin rummy, of all things—using peepholes in a scheme to swindle various celebrities. Indictments named six cheaters, one pled guilty, and jurors convicted four including Johnny, slapped with five years at McNeil Island in Washington. Word had it that he'd tried to borrow fifty grand for legal fees from Howard Hughes—who owed Rosselli big time for his entrée to Las Vegas, where he'd been intent on buying up the town these past two years—but Hughes had turned him down.

Closer to home, Dom had his hands full guarding the restricted borders of his family's turf in Gotham, feeling weak compared to New York's other familes, but nobody had made a move against him yet.

Missing his father worse than usual these days, he guessed tomorrow would just have to take care of itself.

———

One Police Plaza, Manhattan: June 14, 1969

PAYTON SAWYER—SERGEANT Sawyer of the NYPD since the end of February—finished sorting files in his small office cubicle, checking the wall clock, wishing that its hour hand would pick up speed. Promotion had increased his monthly pay, and he was now entitled to wear chevrons on his sleeve, but only when attired in uniform—which meant approximately never.

The department's manual called sergeants "field supervisors usually responsible for patrol officers," which included issuing duty instructions, investigating police misconduct, and evaluating personnel. The key word there was "usually," and Payton knew even before he got his stripes that nothing *usual* occurred with BOSS.

His job remained essentially the same as it had been when he'd joined the Bureau of Special Services: infiltrating and reporting back on agitators of the black persuasion, logging new names into dossiers, and following the progress of known militants now serving time. Harlem was still his beat, and in some ways—despite the ten-mile distance from police headquarters to the ghetto—Sawyer felt as if he hadn't moved an inch in eighteen years.

Muslim Mosque No. 7 was still in business and under surveillance, but Clarence 13X's spin-off Five Percenters had attracted more police attention lately, harboring one white convert Clarence had met while sharing time in prison. Once paroled, Clarence had started fiddling with his former policies: announcing that he now supported Richard Nixon's war in Vietnam, addressed black Marxists on the art of numerology, and urged his followers to celebrate Christmas. At the same time, Clarence often appeared rundown, worn out from lack of sleep, oppressed by fears that he would be assassinated.

And just two days earlier, his nightmare had come true,

when three unknown assailants shot him in the lobby of a friend's apartment building. The *New York Daily News* claimed Clarence had been feuding over doctrine with the leaders of Mosque No. 7, calling it another "Muslim War." Louis X Farrakhan, now leader of Black Muslims in Gotham, denied responsibility, supported in that claim by Mayor Lindsay. Sawyer's evidence suggested an extortion ring at work, but he might never get enough to charge the leeches he suspected.

Meanwhile, BOSS and NYPD generally focused more on the Black Panther Party these days, with its black berets and leather, not-so-secret arsenals, and hatred of the cops its newspaper reviled as "pigs." Bronx Party leader Nathanial Burns, aka "Sekou Odinga," was among twenty Panthers indicted in April for conspiring to assassinate police and blow up public buildings including two NYPD precinct houses and the Queens Board of Education's office. Held in lieu of $100,000 bail apiece, the Panthers didn't know that BOSS had worked in concert with the FBI for nearly three years prior to filing charges. Only one of their supposed bombs had detonated, out in Queens, where officers had nabbed a teenaged Panther in the general vicinity.

Payton had doubts about the case landing convictions, but that was the D.A.'s call, not his. The longer it dragged on, the more Sawyer felt he was plodding in his father's footsteps, just as Papa Ike had helped to jail black nationalists of another time, during and after World War One.

And every day, over his solitary breakfast, Sawyer pondered how much longer he could keep up that campaign. His younger brother Fred had quit the FBI, joined Dr. King's SCLC, then veered hard left into the Panthers after King was killed. They'd rarely spoken since that time, divided like some families he'd read about who'd fallen out during the Civil War.

But this time, Payton wondered, which one of them was defending modern slavery?

———

FBI Field Office, Jackson, Mississippi: July 25, 1969

NOLAN O'HARA HAD DECIDED that the Klan would never be wiped out within his lifetime, and that prospect sickened him. In March, on the same day that James Earl Ray pled guilty to assassinating Dr. King in Memphis, three judges of the U.S. Seventh Circuit Court had nolle prossed Byron De La Beckwith's murder charge for killing Medgar Evers back in 1963. Two white juries had failed to reach a verdict in that case, and now the federal appellate court ruled that a third trial would be futile.

Sam Bowers of the White Knights was doubtless cheered by that news. He was still serving time on his conviction in the "Mississippi Burning" case, but on the Vernon Dahmer slaying, yet another hung jury had sent him home. In fact, his numbers had improved slightly: eleven jurors wanted to convict him at his trial in 1968, but only ten had voted guilty on the latest round.

Next door to the Magnolia State, notorious Louisiana Klansman Robert Fuller was supporting two "freedom of choice" candidates for election to Ouachita Parish's school board. In 1960, Fuller had killed four of his black field hands, but a grand jury believed his tale that it was "self-defense." More recently, his name has surfaced in relation to a pair of Mississippi bombings by the Silver Dollar Group, but prosecutors filed no charges there. Today, the men whose school board race he'd bankrolled were denouncing "rumors" that they were supported by the Klan. Their only cause, they claimed—and Fuller had endorsed the lie—was making sure white parents had the freedom to enroll their little darlings at illegal segregated schools. Oddly, they balked at talking about Fuller's sideline as a pimp.

The greatest shock to Nolan, this year, was his son Ryan's announcement of his resignation from the Bureau. After barely three years on the job, Ryan had packed it in, refusing to explain his reasons beyond telling Nolan that he "couldn't take it anymore." Nolan smelled liquor on his son's breath during that discussion—not the first time—and while Ryan wouldn't spill the details, Nolan guessed his son had been romantically involved with someone whom he didn't think the Bureau would approve of. There was "nothing going on now," he insisted, but he had to get away —from Mississippi, from the FBI, from all of it.

His new plan was to practice law, and Nolan wished him well, but wondered whether one of Edgar Hoover's well-known grudges would pursue Ryan during the years ahead.

Spahn Movie Ranch, Death Valley: August 13, 1969

"LOOKS LIKE A DUMP TO ME," said Colby Gantt, peering downrange through field glasses, two hundred yards away from the ramshackle village spread before him. It was hot as hell, pushing 115 degrees in the shade if you could find any, with zero days of rain since March to break the desert heat. Conversely, if he stuck around too long, he knew the temperature would drop thirty degrees or more after the sun went down.

"They used it for old Western movies years ago," Agent Beau Stancil said. "I tell you that already?"

"Only three, four times," Gantt said. "Why would they move out here?"

"You know Charley," said Stancil. He was from the Agency's Los Angeles office and Colby didn't like his easy manner of assuming things.

"I'm going to forget you said that," Gantt replied. "And you should, too."

"My bad."

The fellow Stancil had in mind was Charles Manson, ex-con and once a subject of the CIA's experiments with drugs before he hit the street last time. He wasn't visible just now, from where they lay beside a massive boulder on a wrinkle in the arid landscape, but some of his girls were moseying around the place down there, one topless, seeming three sheets to the wind.

"Okay," Beau said. "It's all about his 'Helter Skelter' rap. The coming race war, yeah? He and his people plan to sit it out here, while the blacks are killing off rich whites from coast to coast, then Charley and his tribe pop out and magically convince the winners that they need a thirty-something honky jailbird to show them what's what."

"I mean this place, specifically," Gantt prodded him.

"Oh, well...it used to be a regular location for the Westerns, like I said. Five hundred acres and the scenery speaks for itself. The cameras love it. Old George Spahn—he's eighty, nearly blind now—lets the tribe live here rent-free, doing his chores and taking care of horses that he rents to tourists now and then."

"The girls take care of him?" asked Gantt.

"Depends on what you mean by that. I doubt he has

much use for pussy, but they cook his food and play guitars for him, whatever."

It was the *whatever* that had brought Gantt here, lying behind a rock and watching unkempt hippies roam around the place.

The CIA was cutting back on its experiments with drugs these days, after the Sirhan deal with Bobby Kennedy, but there were still loose ends that could rebound to haunt Langley. The Agency had scrapped Project MKNAOMI earlier this year, but Gantt knew they'd be dealing with the fallout from that operation and from MKULTRA well into the future.

Back in January, Manson and his doped-up creeps had occupied a small house in Canoga Park, 250 miles southwest from their Death Valley digs, a suburb of Los Angeles. While there, they'd hung out with more Satanists and outlaw bikers, Manson constantly replaying Beatles' songs that "told" him he would find a secret city in "the bottomless pit," somewhere beneath Death Valley's sunbaked sands. That was the place he planned to huddle with his brood during the race war christened "Helter Skelter," but they hadn't found it yet, despite continuous forays in beat-up dune buggies.

In March, Mason tried reconnecting with musician Terry Melcher, whom he'd met in '68 through Bryan Wilson of the Beach Boys, but Melcher had sold his mansion on Cielo Drive to film director Roman Polanski and his actress-wife Sharon Tate. At that point, Charley must have made a mental note before proceeding down his lifelong road of crime.

In May, Manson informed his acolytes that he might have to jump-start Helter Skelter to help "Blackie" get the right idea. To that end, he'd gut-shot Bernard Crowe, a Black

Panther Party member, at his Hollywood apartment, but Crowe had surprised Manson by living through it and refusing to involve LAPD.

The next run, in July, was more successful. Manson, Bobby Beausoleil, and two of Charley's girls had shot and stabbed a music teacher, Gary Hinman, who'd declined to join the family and give them all his worldly goods. Hinman was dead when they departed his Topanga Canyon home, after scrawling "Political Piggy" on a wall beside a crude sketch of a panther's paw.

Still, no race war erupted, and the cops caught Beausoleil cruising in Hinman's stolen car on August 6. Manson considered that development for two days, dropping any pills that he could lay hands on, then told his people, "Now's the time for Helter Skelter."

During the night of August 8 they'd struck again, at the Polanski mansion on Cielo Drive. Polanski wasn't home when Charles "Tex" Watson and a couple of the girls showed up, but they went right ahead, killing and mutilating five victims including Sharon Tate and coffee heiress Abigail Folger. Tate was eight months pregnant, and her baby also died, speared with a barbecue fork in its mother's womb. Before they split, a waste of space named Susan Atkins scrawled "Pig" on the home's front door in blood.

That news had stunned L.A.'s legion of rich and famous folks like nothing coming out of Vietnam so far. It went from bad to worse on August 10, when Manson led Watson and four more of his tribe to a house on Waverly Drive, eleven miles due east of the Polanski digs. There, Charley watched while his disciples shot and stabbed a married couple, Leno and Rosemary LaBianca, after scouring their home for a mythical fortune in silver dollars. As they exited, the killers left graffiti reading "Death to Pigs," "Rise," and

"Healter Skelter," clumsily misspelling their guru's catchphrase.

The flaw in Manson's plan—besides total insanity—turned out to be an act of simple vandalism. While they roamed around Death Valley looking for a hidden city that didn't exist, his idiots had been offended by an earthmover standing idle and gathering dust, so they'd torched it, leaving no shortage of clues at the scene. That foolishness resulted in a call to Gantt at Langley from the L.A. office, which was keeping tabs on Manson's misfits, and Colby had flown west, cooking up a plan en route.

"Okay, I've seen enough," he told Stancil. "As soon as we get back to town, have someone call the county sheriff's office, keeping it deniable, and have them send their men out here."

"Is that...um...wise, Sir?"

"You mean, as opposed to letting these dipshits keep wandering around and cutting people up till they get caught red-handed? Let me do the thinking on this, will you?"

"Yes, Sir. Absolutely."

"Good. Now let's get out of here before they notice us and chase us through the goddamned cactus."

Driving back to L.A. with the air-conditioning turned up full-blast, Colby tried to erase the Manson problem from his mind. His thoughts turned toward his son Hardy, who had enlisted with the Agency and breezed through training at The Farm in York County, Virginia, before shipping out with orders for a rookie tour in Southeast Asia. It wasn't a great time to be over there, but what *had* been, during the span of Colby's life? He had to trust that Hardy would come through it in one piece and find his niche within the CIA, the basis for a long career.

Closer to home, President Nixon hadn't even been inaugurated yet, when he began to lose his shit over impending publication of the so-called "Pentagon Papers"—3,000 pages of historical analysis on Vietnam, plus 4,000 original documents bound in forty-seven volume stamped "Top Secret." A think tank based in southern California, the RAND Corporation—short for "Research and Development"—had pulled it all together, fifteen copies printed for dissemination under wraps throughout the upper echelons of government. Of course, that guaranteed a copy would be leaked and wind up at the *New York Times,* whose lawyers were in court, demanding that "the people have a right to know" and all that crap.

The upshot: Tricky Dick, already paranoid before he hit the campaign trail last year, had lost it, clamoring for Edgar Hoover to locate and plug the leaks in government. It shocked the Nixon crowd when Hoover stalled, dragging his feet, likely from fear the White House would find some way to absorb the FBI and have no further need of him. Colby knew for a fact that William Sullivan, the Bureau's number three, was playing games with Langley in defiance of his Chief's orders and likely didn't have much time remaining on the federal payroll. Colby was surprised that Hoover hadn't dusted off his file on Nixon's 1967 fling with a Chinese woman believed to be a spy for Mao Zedong, but if the Old Man dropped that bomb, it might take everybody down.

And then, in May, the *Times* reported U.S. bombers hitting targets in Cambodia, a neutral country. More leaks spurting, and the president apparently had no idea of who might be behind them or their motives.

In Haiti, land of poverty and voodoo, Papa Doc Duvalier had launched one of his periodic efforts to eliminate all "communists," defined as anyone who questioned his regime. Another benefit of killing phony Reds was confisca-

MICHAEL NEWTON

tion of their property to benefit Duvalier. Meanwhile, Doc's propagandists claimed he was "one with the *loa*, Jesus Christ and God himself." To prove it, they produced a poster showing Jesus with his hand on Duvalier's shoulder above a caption reading, "I have chosen him." Apparently caught up in the insanity, Duvalier declared himself an "immaterial being" and "the Haitian flag," whatever in hell that meant.

In nearby Central America, leaders of the Farabundo Martí National Liberation Front—real Reds this time, not make-believe—had sparked a border clash between Honduras and El Salvador, nicknamed "the Soccer War" because it coincided with traditional riots over a World Cup match. While the dust-up only lasted for 100 hours, give or take, Colby suspected it would have long-term effects on both countries, requiring intercession from Langley.

Czechoslovakia still roiled with chaos from last year's "Prague Spring." One student torched himself in Prague's Wenceslas Square, protesting communist suppression of free speech, and things like that were always helpful to the CIA. Eight months later, seven demonstrators were imprisoned for their "anti-Soviet" activities, while in Romania, Prime Secretary Nicolae Ceauşescu advertised his friendship with Alexander Dubček. Hospitalized with suspected radiation poisoning in January, Dubček resigned in August, and Moscow-style "normalization" began.

In the Middle East, a blip occurred in June, when President Qahtan al-Shabi was deposed in the People's Republic of South Yemen, replaced by Salim Rubayi Ali of the Marxist National Liberation Front. Just what the Arab world needed: another Red stirring the shit.

Africa wasn't much better. In Somalia, cops and soldiers occupied the capital at Mogadishu, establishing a Red government led by Major General Siad Barre, a Marxist revolutionary who'd coordinated the assassination of his predecessor, President Abdirashid Ali Shermarke. Barre called his new military junta the Supreme Revolutionary Council, striving to dismantle the Somali clan system.

That paled in Colby's mind beside events at home, the Manson cock-up and the Clay Shaw trial on charges of conspiracy to murder JFK. The latter got off to a rocky start in January, when Attorney General Clark—on his last day in office—ordered Justice to withhold from D.A. Jim Garrison all photographs and X-rays from the Kennedy autopsy. All the same, Shaw's trial convened just four days later in New Orleans, lasting five weeks while the media kept roasting Garrison daily. On March 1, jurors took less than an hour to acquit Clay Shaw, who then denied his guilt once more via an interview with *Playboy* magazine.

Coincidentally or otherwise, Dr. Sidney Gottlieb, late of MKULTRA, notified Langley that G-men had arrested Jean-Pierre Lafitte, whose links to Agency drug-dealing and the hit on JFK were well-nigh legendary. At the time of his arrest, Lafitte was working as top chef at the Plimsoll Club, a hotspot of the New Orleans International Trade Mart, where friend and ITM founder Clay Shaw was proud to tout him as "the best chef in New Orleans." Lafitte's latest charge: swindling a wealthy businessman out of $400,000 in a scam involving South African diamond mines.

Meanwhile, deaths perhaps related to the Dallas crimes of 1963 kept happening. Deputy Sheriff E. R. "Buddy" Waters, who'd searched the book depository and reported finding a .45 slug, died in a January shootout with a fugitive from Georgia. A "heart attack" killed Charles Mentesana, a photographer who snapped police removing a rifle from the depository that didn't resemble Lee Oswald's Mannlicher-Carcano. "Natural causes" claimed Mary Bledsoe, a neighbor of Oswald's who also knew David Ferrie. John Crawford, a friend of Jack Ruby who gave Oswald a lift on assassination day, died in a private plane crash. Unknown persons shot Reverend Clyde Johnson, scheduled to testify about Shaw's links to Oswald, but cut from the witness list before trial.

In other assassination news, James Earl Ray fired first attorney Arthur Hanes, then hired Percy Foreman, whose legal defense sent Jack Ruby to death row. Foreman slapped a lien on Ray's Mustang and loaned cash to Ray's relatives, with no repayment called for if James would just plead guilty. Otherwise, said Percy, Ray was guaranteed a date with the gas chamber. Ray agreed, but even then, when prosecutors rose in court to claim that there was no conspiracy, he'd objected, saying, "I don't agree with that. I don't say there was no conspiracy."

No sweat. The judge gave Ray a 99-year sentence, sent him on his way, and that was that.

In L.A., at the Sirhan trial, psychiatrists for both sides readily agreed the lone defendant was "out of touch with reality" at his arrest and claimed amnesia afterward. No one had tested him for drugs or alcohol, of course; he was supposed to be a Muslim, after all. Attorneys for both sides called for a guilty plea and life imprisonment, but Judge Herbert Walker refused, and the case went to trial—where no one mentioned pesky problems like five extra bullets Sirhan's gun couldn't have fired without reloading first. After two months, jurors convicted him and sentenced him to death. No one outside LAPD new anything about the ballistic anomalies until May, when the *Los Angeles Free Press* belatedly reported on the extra bullet holes, still unexplained. The answer: one month later, almost to the day from publication of that article, LAPD "routinely" burned the ceiling panels and doorframes from the Ambassador

Hotel. When questioned, D.A. Evelle Younger claimed "there was nowhere to keep them," even though police commonly warehoused confiscated weapons, cars, and tons of drugs without complaint.

All good, thought Colby, *just as long as John Q. Public never learns the truth.*

———

Birmingham, Alabama: October 30, 1969

"AREN'T YOU EXCITED, Dave? I mean, this is *good* news!"

"Agreed," Dave Jordan answered. They were sipping wine and sitting on Fiona's sofa in her small apartment, but his mind was elsewhere. Part of it wished they were already in bed. As for the rest...he wasn't sure.

Fiona was correct, of course. The news from Washington so far this year *was* good for blacks and human rights in general. In August, Richard Nixon had surprised most anyone who'd ever known him, signing an executive order that required all federal agencies to adopt "affirmative programs for equal employment opportunity." More recently—just yesterday, in fact—the Supreme Court had unanimously ordered immediate integration of thirty-three Mississippi school districts in the case of *Alexander v. Holmes County Board of Education.*

Good news, and yet...

What if the Magnolia State's elected leaders just ignored the latest ruling, as they had so many others in the past? Who would restrain police from killing black victims whenever they chose to, whether it happened in the South or North?

Bombings and racist murders had subsided, for the

moment anyway, in Alabama, but too many killers still walked free, confident that they'd never come to trial. The worst crime Jordan could remember—four young girls blown up in church six years ago—had been forgotten after three Klansmen faced misdemeanor charges that were later dropped. What did that say about America, about its vaunted "rule of law"?

This very minute, George Wallace was plotting his return as Alabama's governor, still pledged to "segregation forever," and beyond that, no one seriously doubted that he planned another White House run. The American Independent Party couldn't wait to back him, lately dropping "Independent" from its title, even while recycling 1968's "Stand Up for America" posters. Wallace might have burned his bridge with Asa Carter, but he still stayed close to Robert Shelton and the violent United Klans.

"Don't mind me," Jordan said, trying a smile for size. "I specialize in looking at a glass and seeing it half-empty."

"Well, then," said Fiona, "what you need it more of *this*." She filled his wine glass almost to the brim, adding, "The sooner you get done with that, the sooner we can go to bed."

———

FBI Headquarters: November 21, 1969

ONLY FIVE DAYS remained until Thanksgiving, but there seemed to be no chance that Devon and Camille Gantt would be seeing their son Hardy for the holidays. Since he had joined the Bureau, Hardy was assigned to work the COINTELPRO—NEW LEFT beat. Not only that, but after years of rigid grooming and dress codes, Chief Hoover had approved creation of an undercover unit dubbed "The

Beards," agents both white and black assigned to infiltrate the nation's prominent left-wing subversive groups, and Hardy had been chosen for that scruffy team.

At headquarters, it seemed Chief Hoover was attempting to accommodate President Nixon, within limits, via INLET, periodic "intelligence letters" advising Nixon on matters of national security, also including—Hoover's words—"items with an unusual twist or concerning prominent personalities which may be of special interest to the President." That list included numerous celebrities, praised or reviled on the basis of rumors, back-fence gossip, and the Chief's own suppositions, but it seemed to keep the White House off of Hoover's back, as he turned seventy-four amid numerous calls for retirement.

On the COINTELPRO—BLACK HATE front, the FBI kept hounding Martin Luther King, nineteen months in his grave by now, with press releases and a whispering campaign against any attempt to cast King as a posthumous hero.

Stokely Carmichael, residing with his bride in Guinea as "Kwame Ture," had denounced the Black Panthers for their "dogmatic party line favoring alliances with white radicals." The CIA was keeping tabs on him, but Gantt suspected that he wouldn't be returning to the States anytime soon.

Rap Brown was still in Devon's crosshairs, but he kept ducking and weaving out of focus. In April, the Fifth Circuit Court of Appeals voided his "technical" firearms indictment and remanded it to a Louisiana District Court for consideration of electronic surveillance in lieu of trial.

Results in Cleveland proved more satisfactory, where Fred "Ahmed" Evans stood convicted of multiple murders and sentenced to die. Four teenagers were also indicted for the Glenville shootout, one of them declared unfit for trial and packed off to Lima State Hospital for the Criminally Insane while another, convicted and granted judicial "mercy," was sentenced to 110 years in prison without parole.

Among the black organizations targeted by COINTEL-PRO, the Revolutionary Action Movement had disbanded, changing its name to the Black Liberation Party and dropping overt militancy as prominent members devoted their time to alternative groups.

The Republic of New Afrika had gone the other way, founding a paramilitary unit called the Black Legion. In Detroit, its members got into a shootout with police that killed Officer Michael Czapsk while leaving four blacks wounded and 142 jailed on various charges. Twelve hours later, a judge in Recorder's Court freed all but two suspects, and the D.A. was scrambling to make charges stick against them.

George Jackson's Black Guerrilla Family kept making news at California's Folsom Prison, where Jackson lost his latest parole bid and Aryan Brotherhood Nazis knifed BGF member Leonard "Sheik" Thompson. Four BGF survivors filed a petition seeking review of conditions on O-Wing, where they claimed guards had encouraged white and Hispanic inmates to attack them, sometimes leaving cells unlocked to make them vulnerable, otherwise engaging in "direct harassment and in ways not actionable in court." So far, that suit was going nowhere, but it made headlines.

And then, there was AIM. In October, after fire destroyed offices of something called the United Council of the Bay Area Indian Community spokesmen proposed turning Alcatraz into a "cultural center." Rebuffed on that front, four Council members made the trip to Alcatraz and claimed the island "by right of discovery," as if they were the first to find it. Ten days later, AIM leaders got involved, dispatching 89 Indians to occupy the abandoned prison, that number soon increasing to 400. They had settled in to stay a while, from all appearances, and no one in authority seemed anxious to expel them with the TV cameras rolling. Hundreds more supporters were expected for Thanksgiving dinner on The Rock, while White House Special Counsel Leonard Garment took over ongoing negotiations.

If they want The Rock so badly, Devon thought, *just let them have it. Better out of sight and out of mind than marching in the streets.*

––––––

Trenton, New Jersey: November 27, 1969

MARK AND ISABELLA BARNES were putting on the usual Thanksgiving show to satisfy their so-called Christian neighbors, keeping up appearances with their adopted son Stephen. As loyal Communists, they cared nothing about the holiday per se, but it was an excuse to gather, glut themselves on carbohydrates, and discuss their future goals.

As Russian "sleepers" in America, Mark and Isabella continued traveling as time allowed, observing, photographing, and reporting on activities at various military installations around the tri-state region of New Jersey, New York, and Pennsylvania. Stephen—born Stefan Babin, bastard son of a now-deceased KGB officer and prostitute hand-picked according to her health, was in his second year at Yale Law School, his first goal a degree of Juris Doctor, followed by enlistment with the FBI to crack it from within.

That was—*had been*—his father's dream, vengeance for deportation from the States in 1917, which had transformed him from a lowly urban radical into an operative who had scaled the ladder of command with Russia's dread secret police.

Law school was going well, sometimes a challenge, but nothing his agile mind wasn't equipped to handle. In his spare time, Stephen kept a close eye on the Bureau, starting with this year's release of Edgar Hoover's third ghostwritten book, immodestly titled *J. Edgar Hoover On Communism*. It was entirely typical of Hoover, Stephen thought, that the Director made his staff research and write "his" books, then banked the proceeds for himself, while falsely claiming they were used to bankroll the Society of Former Special Agents of the FBI.

A fraud from start to finish, but his day was coming, finally—assuming he survived that long. If not, the institution he had built would have to suffer in his stead.

Two G-men had already gone to their reward this year, Special Agents Anthony Palmisano and Edwin Woodriffe slain in Washington, D.C. while trying to arrest fugitive bank robber Billie Austin Bryant. Captured at the shooting scene, Bryant had been convicted of murder in October and sentenced one week later to a double term of life imprisonment without parole.

In other news, Ruth Eisemann-Schier—the first woman added to the Bureau's Ten Most Wanted List last year, was caught in March and sent to prison, deportation to Honduras waiting for her if and when she made parole. Aside from Eisemann-Schier, 1969 began with nine other "Top Tenners" listed between 1965 and '68, five of them captured by June, the rest still at large. Another female fugitive replaced Eisemann-Schier on the roster: Marie Dean Arrington, a fugitive from Florida who'd broken out of death row after murdering the legal secretary of a public defender who'd failed to spring her two children on felony charges.

Every day, it seemed, headlines and television news revealed more decadence in the United States.

As for the nation of his birth, Stephen had watched developments within the USSR from afar. In March, Soviet Border Service troops clashed with Chinese soldiers on Zhenbao ("Rare Treasure") Island, a quarter-square-mile spit of land in the Ussuri River, between Primorsky Krai and Heilongjiang Province. The seesaw skirmishing went on for seven months, each side blaming the other for aggression, leaving eighty-seven fighters dead, 156 wounded, and one Chinaman missing.

On the more peaceful side, just ten days earlier, Soviet and American diplomats had launched Strategic Arms Limitation Talks in Helsinki, Finland. Their goal: a treaty mandating that addition of new submarine-launched ballistic missiles might proceed only after the same number of older intercontinental ballistic missiles were dismantled.

But there would be no peace, as far as Stephen was concerned, no détente or rapprochement. There could only be vengeance for ancient wrongs—a concept of vendetta any student of the Mafia would recognize and understand.

Barnes was his father's son, and anxious to proceed with his appointed task.

———

West Jackson Boulevard, Chicago: December 4, 1969

FRED SAWYER HAD BEGUN to think of his life as a roller-coaster ride from Hell. Since joining the Black Panther Party one year earlier, he'd seen it reeling from attacks by so-called "law enforcement" officers and their *agents provocateurs* across the country, people dying faster than the media could learn their names—assuming that they even cared.

He'd also called his brother Payton twice, at home in Harlem, hoping to explain the turn his life had taken after Dr. King was killed. The first time, Fred had lost his nerve and hung up after Payton twice asked, "Who is this?" He'd tried again one week ago, the day after Thanksgiving, and identified himself but wouldn't say where he was calling from. Fred knew BOSS might attempt to trace the call, but it would only lead them to a drugstore phone booth close to Wicker Park, some two miles distant from the Party's head-quarters.

Besides, Fred's fall from grace was Payton's greatest shame. He would take pains to hide it from his fellow NYPD officers. Their conversation had been stiff, unnatural, Fred hanging up when Payton shouted at him, "Have you lost your fucking mind? Joining the Panthers, man?"

Fred knew his older brother didn't understand and wouldn't try. They'd both witnessed their father's inner turmoil from the years he'd spent betraying other blacks. Payton had chosen to pursue the traitor's course, following in Papa Ike's footsteps, and Fred had started down that path himself, until the murders of two proud black leaders changed his mind.

But what had he accomplished for the Party, when the Bureau's COINTELPRO crimes still haunted them at every turn, mimicked by cops in every city, coast to coast?

Fred knew that when an FBI agent in San Francisco told headquarters that the local BPP did little beyond feeding ghetto children breakfast, Hoover wrote back personally, warning that the G-man faced suspension or dismissal if he didn't toe the Bureau line, inventing "evidence" to prove the Party was "a violence-prone organization seeking to overthrow the Government by revolutionary means." Said agent, with an eye fixed on his pension, had complied.

In January, members of FBI informer Ron Karenga's US Organization murdered two Panthers—John Huggins and Alprentice Carter—on the UCLA campus, touching off a feud that saw two more Panthers slain in San Diego and another wounded in L.A.—the latter shot while cops sat watching from their cruiser and did nothing. Next, Hoover had approved a series of malicious letters, penned by his own agents, seeking to incite mayhem between Chicago Panthers and mayhem-minded Blackstone Rangers street gang, but that plot had fizzled out.

Police raids against Panther offices became incessant: in Richmond, California, San Francisco, San Diego, Indianapolis, Philadelphia, Chicago (three times), and Detroit, where cops caused $25,000 damage in a search for nonexistent fugitives. The office in Des Moines was hit four times, twice by police and twice by bombs, the first employing military grade C4 plastic explosives. False arrests during those raids and other incidents hit triple digits, with charges ranging from the trivial—jaywalking, blocking sidewalks, or "obstructing vision" with too many Party members in a single car—to murder and vague allegations of "conspiracy." Most of those charges were dismissed, but only after Panthers drained their local treasuries for bail.

Of course, some cases would proceed to trial. The "Panther 21" in Gotham stood accused of plotting to bomb precinct houses and a school board office; Bobby Seale and eight others faced murder charges after paid police informer George Sams fingered Panther Alex Rackley as a rat and slaughtered him in New Haven, Connecticut.

And there were other deaths along the way. LAPD's Metro Squad ambushed Walter Pope as he delivered Party newspapers to a ghetto store, leaving him dead on the sidewalk, unarmed. On the police side of the ledger, Panthers allegedly killed two officers in Chicago and one in Santa Ana, California. Tension red-lined in the Windy City, leaving Fred on guard duty tonight with friend Mark Clark, while chapter leader Hampton and his nine-months-pregnant girlfriend tried to catch up on their sleep.

Sawyer had been rousted with his fellow Panthers when the cops hit Party headquarters, hauled in for questioning about some missing suspects from the bomb trial shaping up in New York City, but the two detectives grilling him turned shifty when he'd mentioned previously working for the FBI. They'd left him on his own in the interrogation room, then came back later to release him, one saying, "We didn't know the Bureau had two men inside the Panthers here. No sweat, though. The roust should help your cover, if you think about it."

Fred had played along with them and spilled the story to Fred Hampton, first thing after they were all released. The news of infiltration hadn't come as a surprise to Hampton, but he'd thanked Fred for the confirmation, adding, "We still have to find the Uncle Tom and deal with him."

They hadn't found him yet, but Fred now viewed the other Panthers with suspicion, wondering which one of them it was and what Hampton had meant by dealing with the traitor when he was identified.

Tonight, on guard duty, Fred wore a .45 Colt in a shoulder holster, no coat hiding it in case the cops came back and tried to slap him with a charge of having it concealed. That shouldn't matter in a private residence, but with Chicago cops, you never knew.

Hampton was snoring on his mattress in the next room when Sawyer heard people, plenty of them, crashing through the street door and rushing upstairs. He didn't need a crystal ball to know who it must be. He pulled his .45 just as Mark Clark, also on watch tonight, came down the hallway, shouting into Hampton's room, "The pigs are vamping! Wake up, man!"

If Hampton heard the warning, he made no response. In fact, it sounded like he kept on snoring, stuck in some deep dream.

"You with me, Bro'?" Clark asked Sawyer. Damned if he wasn't grinning, with the twelve-gauge shotgun in his hands.

"I'm with you," Fred confirmed.

"Awright. Let's make some bacon."

As it was, he never got the chance. The cops started shooting the moment they'd reached the second-story landing, pumping semiautomatic rounds into the door that sealed off Hampton's sleeping quarters from the other rooms upstairs. Sawyer heard bullets striking Clark and saw him going down, a muscular reflex firing a shotgun blast up toward the ceiling, hitting no one on the other side.

Fred scuttled backward, looking for someplace to hide, pitching his Colt away, giving them no excuse to murder him on sight. Not that they needed one.

The bullet-riddled door slammed inward, bluesuits following with carbines, shotguns, pistols drawn, and someone in the gang shot Fred as he was turning, empty hands raised, dropping him face-down on threadbare carpeting. Behind him, Sawyer heard more gunfire, bullets ripping through drywall and striking other walls beyond. That would be Hampton's room, and from the sound of it, he'd never had a chance to rise from bed, no opportunity to fight.

At last, silence descended on the scene, Fred lying still as he could manage, breathing in a mix of plaster dust and gunsmoke. From the chairman's room, he heard a man say, "That's Hampton."

"Is he dead?" another asked.

"Barely alive," a third voice said.

"It's just his shoulder. He'll make it," the second man to speak opined.

The next two shots, evenly spaced, made Sawyer flinch. Another cop, one that he hadn't heard before, informed the rest, "He's good and dead now."

Men were closing in on Sawyer, rapidly surrounding him. One of them kicked him in the ribs, asking him, "What about you, nigger? You alive?"

"I doubt it," said another, and the loudest noise Sawyer had ever heard eclipsed all conscious thought, spinning him off into the void.

———

Saigon: December 20, 1969

HARDY GANTT FOUND IT IRONIC, though perhaps predictable, that he should draw assignment to the very theater of operations where his father had been stationed with the OSS, then later sent back by the CIA. In fact, despite the heat, humidity, insects, and the persistent threat of being picked off by the Việt Cộng, he didn't even mind.

He'd made it through The Farm with high marks and had done his "finishing" courses at the Harvey Point Defense Testing Activity facility, outside Hertford, North Carolina. Hardy had kept his fingers crossed for posting to an active duty station, and he had that now, in spades.

Next door, Laos was seething with sporadic back-and-forth campaigns, pitting the Royal Lao Army against Pathet Lao and the People's Army of Vietnam's 174th Vietnamese Volunteer Regiment. Only bad weather seemed to interrupt fighting around the Plain of Jars, despite American B-52s doing their best to slaughter every Red below.

Closer to Saigon, National Security Advisor Henry Kissinger pressed for air strikes on more "lucrative targets" in North Vietnam—pipelines and such—but Agency analysis found hostile traffic teeming along the Hồ Chí Minh Trail, particularly on Cambodia's side of the border. In Saigon itself, President Nguyễn Văn Thiệu flailed about pathetically, launching a new National Social Democratic Front to counteract Red progress, but it hadn't helped. A rival group, the National Salvation Front, refused to join the NSDF, and both factions deplored the Phoenix Project's campaign of assassination, muddled as it was by double agents boring from within.

By April, U.S. troop levels had peaked around 543,000, while the toll of U.S. dead—33,641—topped that of the Korean War. In May, the *New York Times* published reports of American warplanes bombing Cambodia. June saw President Nixon announce "Vietnamization" of the conflict, promising gradual withdrawal of American troops. A month later, he aired the "Nixon Doctrine," promising to honor all existing treaties, keep supplying arms and economic aid to allies backed by a "nuclear shield," but dismissing any future provision for boots on the ground. By then, peace talks in Paris had been dragging on for six months with no end in sight, but V.C. raids continued in South Vietnam.

September was a hectic month. A heart attack killed Hồ and his replacement, General Secretary Lê Duẩn, read Hồ's will publicly, urging all North Vietnamese to fight "until the last Yankee has gone." Three days later, the U.S. Army charged Lieutenant William Calley with mass murder for last year's My Lai massacre. On September 16, Nixon withdrew 35,000 troops, followed by another 50,000 three months later. Another Air America C-47A went down, en route from Phu Bai to Da Nang, killing a dozen passengers and crewmen.

Hardy was starting to believe he had arrived just in the nick of time, before a golden opportunity was lost. When Nixon pulled the plug, polishing up his "legacy" while turning a blind eye to falling dominoes, where would a young agent like Gantt, just starting out, find any other combat zone in which to hone his skills?

———

Flint, Michigan: December 28, 1969

IT WAS a new day for the FBI, beyond a shadow of a doubt, and newly-minted Agent Wyman Gantt figured he owed it all to Edgar Hoover's combination of senility, his daily "vitamin" injections, and the paranoia that had dogged the Chief throughout his adult life at Justice.

Finally, after forty-one years of spit-and-polish grooming and dress codes, the Old Man was permitting long hair, whiskers, and slovenly clothes for handpicked agents nicknamed "Beards," chosen to infiltrate subversive groups as part of COINTELPRO-NEW LEFT operations. Hardy, fresh from the Academy at Quantico, with no time on the streets —and thus no scumbags who could finger him for their associates—had made the cut, assigned to penetrate the SDS and its new radical spin-off, the Weatherman Underground.

For years now, SDS had been the leading faction among

anti-war protesters, campus free speech activists and bridge-builders between white radicals and ghetto militants, but that had changed of late. The Weatherman Underground—or WU, in Bureau files—leaned heavily toward Maoism and "propaganda of the deed." Its name derived from Bob Dylan's song "Subterranean Homesick Blues," ranting against G-men in trench coats and warning revolutionary youth that they didn't need a weatherman to know which way the wind blows. While other groups eclipsed the SDS in protests over Vietnam, WU adherents turned to guns and homemade bombs as instruments of change.

That all played out against the backdrop of an epic federal trial for the "Chicago Eight"—alleged ringleaders of wild rioting throughout last year's Democratic National Convention. The cast of characters included Black Panther Bobby Seale, Yippies leader Abbie Hoffman, Vietnam Day Committee founder Jerry Rubin, David Dellinger from the Young People's Socialist League, SDS spokesman Tom Hayden, Rennie Davis from the National Mobilization Committee to End the War in Vietnam, Yale-educated chemist John Froines, and social worker Lee Weiner. After Judge Julius Hoffman separated Seale's case from the others, over his repeated courtroom outbursts, trial proceeded for the truncated "Chicago Seven," sure to drag on till sometime next year.

Meanwhile, the WU was raising holy hell. Founded officially in June, seizing control of the national SDS office, it sent six members to Cuba a month later for meetings with Castro and North Vietnamese officials. August found a representative in Hanoi, while others rehearsed for October's "Days of Rage" in Chicago. A group of female members, the "Pittsburgh 26," awaited trial for staging a student "jail-break" at South Hills High School. During the Chicago mêlée, WU bombers struck the Haymarket Police Statue commemorating another blast in 1886. Cambridge, Maryland police charged two WU members with sniping at police headquarters, then dropped the case when their witness recanted his statement. On December 6, bombers demolished Chicago patrol cars to protest Fred Hampton's death two days earlier.

Now, Gantt was one of some 300 Weathermen gathered for a "War Council" at a seedy ballroom in Flint's mostly-black inner city, dried blood still visible in a corner of the room where a shooting had occurred two days earlier. Hasty decorations included posters of Malcolm X, Fred Hampton, Che Guevara, Mao Zedong, Fidel Castro, Lenin, and Hô Chí Minh. Hanging banners called for "Sirhan Sirhan Power" and "Piece Now," over the picture of a gun. To drive the point home, a giant papier-mâché gun was displayed, with bullets affixed to photos of President Nixon, Vice-President Agnew, California Governor Ronald Reagan, Chicago Mayor Richard Daley, and Manson "family" victim Sharon Tate.

Speechmaking would go on for three more days, interspersed with sing-alongs, calisthenics and karate practice, but Gantt already had the gist of it, duly reported back to Bureau Headquarters. The WU was "going underground," committing calculated acts of sabotage against the government. As keynote speaker John Jacobs proclaimed, "We're against everything that's 'good and decent' in honky America. We will burn and loot and destroy. We are the incubation of your mother's nightmare."

And Gantt was in the middle of it, even as his cousin Hardy worked to aid "The Man" in Southeast Asia. Smiling as he listened to the next speaker in line, he wondered if, between them, they could finally give Reds around the world their just deserts.

CHAPTER 6

Lanman Center, New Haven, Connecticut: May 18, 1970

TO ANY CASUAL OBSERVER, MARK AND ISABELLA BARNES seemed proud as punch to watch adoptive son Stephen receive his Juris Doctor from Yale Law School, though in fact, Stephen surmised, they'd be relieved to see him out and on his own after so many years under their roof. They still had work to do for Moscow, after all, while Stephen followed his own path.

Before the law school ceremony, 1970's commencement for the university at large consumed the best part of an hour on the Old Campus, while those receiving law degrees were gathering at Lanman Center's Payne Whitney Gymnasium on Tower Parkway, one block west of Grove Street Cemetery. It was fairly cut and dried by then, tomorrow's lawyers anxious to get on with future plans.

For all of them, that meant sitting for bar exams. New Jersey and New York both offered this year's final round during the third week of July, and Barnes still hadn't made his mind up as to which one he would take. His home address in Trenton made him lean toward Jersey, but New York seemed more prestigious from the view of an alleged American with money on his mind.

Whichever test he tried, if Stephen failed—about as likely as a UFO landing in Central Park—he wouldn't have another chance in either state for seven months. He had no plan to practice law per se, but any failure on his record, at that level, would look bad when he applied to join the FBI.

As usual, he had been following events from Bureau headquarters and in the field. The Ten Most Wanted list had started out with nine names added during 1968-69, but only one of those had been arrested so far, during 1970. Meanwhile, for the first time since its creation twenty years ago, the Top Ten had expanded with addition of six "New Left" radicals: Lawrence Plamondon, founder of the kiss-ass White Panther Party; David Fine and Karleton Armstrong, bombers of Sterling Hall, involved in Pentagon research at the University of Wisconsin–Madison; and three Weathermen—make that Weather*women*, Bernardine Dohrn, Katherine Power, and Susan Saxe.

Barnes wished them well in terrorizing upper-class America but guessed the only real damage they'd do was to themselves.

At home, in Moscow, peace was all the rage this year. America, Britain, the USSR, and forty other signatory states had ratified a Treaty on the Non-Proliferation of Nuclear Weapons two years earlier, taking effect in March of 1970. Its goals: preventing the spread of nuclear weapons, promoting cooperation toward peaceful uses of nuclear energy, and—in a wild-eyed flight of fantasy—achieving world disarmament at some unfathomable future date.

Now, still trying to deceive the capitalist nations, Vice Chancellor Willy Brandt and Soviet Chairman Alexei

Kosygin had signed the Treaty of Moscow, striving for "normalized relations" between the USSR and West Germany. Of course, behind the scenes, Barnes knew the KGB was still at work, and he still bore the burden—no, the *gift*—his father had bequeathed to him at birth, ultimate ruination of the FBI.

He didn't plan to let the old man down.

————

FBI Field Office, Jackson, Mississippi: June 23, 1970

EVERY TIME NOLAN O'HARA hoped that the Magnolia State might try to close the rift between its races, something else cropped up, and all the superficial progress went to hell again.

In April, it was Rainey Pool, a fifty-four-year-old black sharecropper from tiny Midnight, population somewhere under 200. There, a gang of white men had attacked Pool, fracturing his larynx and some vertebrae, then dumped him in the Sunflower River, where he had surfaced two days later. Officers broke with tradition and detained four suspects, but the county prosecutor nolle prossed murder charges and dismissed the case.

A short month later, there was worse in store, the headlines coming this time from Jackson State College on the same day Ohio National Guardsmen killed four unarmed student protesters at Kent State University, wounding nine others. The Jackson State bloodletting was "minor" by comparison—two dead, twelve rounded—but the twin events made global news and gave the Eastern Bloc another reason to ignore American demands for granting broader human rights.

The Jackson trouble had occurred on Lynch Street, named for a black Reconstruction-era congressman, when student demonstrators rallied following false rumors that Charles Evers (Medgar's brother) had been slain by whites. Jackson police and state highway patrolmen rolled out, firing some 200 shots into a women's dormitory, later claiming that a sniper they could never find shot first. Their fusillade killed two black students—one a high school track star—and some dumb cop made it worse by getting on his radio, hailing an ambulance with the announcement that "we got a couple of dead niggers here."

Dick Nixon formed a President's Commission on Campus Unrest, but no lawmen were fired or prosecuted, despite the panel's conclusion that "the 28-second fusillade from police officers was an unreasonable, unjustified overre-action. A broad barrage of gunfire in response to reported and unconfirmed sniper fire is never warranted."

The Mississippi Klan kept making news, most recently when killer James Seale's Cessna collided with a twin-engine Bonanza at Louisiana's Concordia Parish Airport. Five others died in the crash, ironically including Dr. Charles Colvin, who'd treated Ku Klux arson victim Frank Morris six years before. Now Seale was facing lawsuits from the victims' families and two insurance companies, while gloating to the media, "It just wasn't my time to go."

Too bad, Nolan had thought, when he heard that gem on TV.

Despite the Bureau's low conviction rate for Delta terror-ists, author Don Whitehead tried to polish Edgar Hoover's halo with another book in June, titled *Attack on Terror: The FBI Against the Ku Klux Klan in Mississippi.* As with *The FBI Story,* Whitehead's new tome was long on praise for Hoover and his G-men (most anonymous in print), off-loading blame for scuttled prosecutions onto state authorities, but half a dozen pages talked about Frank Morris and the Silver Dollar Group, without identifying any terrorists.

Nolan wondered how much of the publisher's advance had found its way to Hoover's pocket, but decided that he didn't care. The Chief would never change, but now, in failing health at seventy-five, he must be running out of time.

Who isn't? Nolan asked himself, and wondered now, with thirty-four years spent in service to the Bureau, how much longer he would manage to hang on.

————

Little Italy, Manhattan, October 16, 1970

"THEY KEEP PASSIN' these goddamned laws, we may as well pack up and move," Ange Giordano said.

"Move where?" his brother Dominic replied. "Go back to Italy?"

"Mebbe."

"*Morto,* we never even been to Italy. You can't go *back* someplace ya never been. Wha's wrong wi' you?"

Ange had a point, though. Yesterday, Congress had passed something it called the Organized Crime Control Act of 1970. Its key provision was the RICO statute—short for *R*acketeer *I*nfluenced and *C*orrupt *O*rganizations—that imposed long prison terms for "predicate offenses" linked in any way to racketeering as the term was normally applied. The list included all the hinky things that mobsters normally got up to in their daily lives outside the law: gambling, murder, kidnapping, extortion, arson, robbery, bribery, peddling obscene matter, drug dealing, bribery, counterfeiting, theft, embezzlement, fraud, human trafficking, obstructing justice, slavery, or money laundering.

In short, a wise guy couldn't do a frigging thing without being indicted for conspiracy somehow and sent away. Already Angelo "The Gyp" DeCarlo from New Jersey was en route to prison for conspiracy to murder, looking at a twelve-year minimum. Still, Dom didn't suppose that he'd trade places with Bonanno family *caporegime* Gaspar DiGregorio, killed by cancer in June.

And now, Louisiana moralists were probing what reporters called "high-level corruption" in their state—no secret to lords of *Cosa Nostra* who'd been banking loot from New Orleans and environs since Prohibition. A state committee had subpoenaed *Don* Carlos Marcello but he gave them squat, hiding behind the Fifth Amendment when they asked about his empire and its ties to Santo Trafficante's family in Florida.

That wouldn't get far, Dominic predicted, since between them, Carlos and Santos could spill an ugly can of worms about the CIA. The Giordanos, in New York, had played no part in the Agency's Cuban fiasco, thus had no federal buffer against any future. RICO charges.

Now, the question: what could Dom do to prevent them all from landing in the shit?

———

Harlem: October 28, 1970

NYPD Sergeant Payton Sawyer was remembering lost members of his family again. Just yesterday, passage of the federal Comprehensive Drug Abuse Prevention and Control Act had categorized controlled substances based on their medicinal use and potential for addiction, prompting a White House declaration that drug abuse was now "Public Enemy Number One."

If Papa Ike had been alive, Payton supposed he would've asked if that meant Tricky Dick had stopped accepting contributions from drug-dealing mobsters and the unions they controlled.

His answer would've been a belly laugh.

Payton was also tracking the Chicago raid from last December that had killed three Black Panthers, one of them his brother Frederick. He'd seen news footage of the cops toting corpses in black body bags, smiling, and knew they'd beaten up seven survivors of the raid—two of them seriously wounded by police gunfire—then charged them all with aggravated assault and attempted murder, holding them on $100,000 bond apiece. The word was out that their primary target, chapter boss Fred Hampton, had not only been asleep when he was shot, but also drugged by something slipped into his food before he went to bed.

As far as the attempted murder charges went, he knew police had fired ninety-nine shots, compared to one triggered by a young dying Panther, drilled before he had a chance to aim his weapon. At a morning-after press conference, a police department spokesman called the Panthers "vicious" and "extremely violent." He'd praised his boys in blue for their "bravery" and "professional discipline," claiming they'd shown "remarkable restraint" by letting any Panthers live.

Problems began to surface right away. Police posed for the media, pointing to bullet holes they claimed were made by Panther guns during the "shootout," but police weapons made most of those, and some were nail heads in the walls. An "internal investigation" cleared all officers, but now there was a federal lawsuit in the works against them, threatening exposure of the truth plus a $47 million bill for taxpayers, resulting from Chicago's brand of reckless law enforcement. Backing that up was a DOJ "Commission of Inquiry into the Black Panthers and the Police," finding December's raid unjustified, including "summary punishment" of the survivors that breached their constitutional rights.

Payton had been invited to participate in the lawsuit but let it go. Aside from what he saw as the futility of bucking City Hall, how would it look at BOSS to have it known his brother was a militant picked off by Chicago's "brothers in blue"?

Speaking of trials, the "Panther 21" were finally in court, the D.A. trying to support his feeble case by reading passages from Mao's *Little Red Book* and having jurors watch a four-year-old Italian film, *The Battle of Algiers,* which had no more to do with plots in Gotham than it did with green cheese on the moon.

The year's "good" news, as viewed by cops and FBI agents, was the impending dissolution of the Panther Party nationwide. In May, an appellate court had overturned founder Huey Newton's manslaughter conviction, ordering a retrial, but two successive hung juries put that to bed at last. Instead of celebrating, though, Newton had quarreled with Eldridge Cleaver and they'd split up, Cleaver heading for Algeria with wife Kathleen, while his adherents in the feud spun off to form a new, more militant Black Liberation Army.

And whatever praise liberals lavished on the Panthers, members of the BLA appeared to be a gang of hard-core revolutionaries. They declared themselves "anti-capitalist, anti-imperialist, anti-racist, and anti-sexist," then added that "in order to abolish our systems of oppression, we must utilize the science of class struggle, develop this science as it relates to our unique national condition." So far, BLA members were suspected of bombing St. Brendan's Church in San Francisco during the funeral of Officer Harold Hamilton, killed by bank robbers.

Payton reckoned worse still lay in store, and from the literature circulating around Harlem, he suspected that New York would be the BLA's primary battleground.

———

Birmingham, Alabama: November 5, 1970

DAVE JORDAN and Fiona O'Hara lay in bed at his apartment on Sutherland Place, in the Homewood district, talking over Tuesday's election between rounds of sex. George Wallace, four years out of office, was winning a second term as governor thanks to the worst racist campaign the state had seen since 1962.

Wallace's literature asked white voters, "Do you want the black bloc electing your governor?" A typical campaign flier featured a photo of a young white girl surrounded by seven shirtless black boys, its caption trumpeting: "WAKE UP ALABAMA! (June 3 Could Be Too Late) Is This the IMAGE You Want? BLACKS VOW TO TAKE OVER ALABAMA."

June third had been primary day, sending Wallace to November's runoff against moderate incumbent Albert Brewer, now entitled by a constitutional amendment to succeed himself. Wallace branded Brewer "Sissy Britches" and maligned his family, while Brewer claimed Wallace was planning on another White House run in two years' time, telling voters, "Alabama deserves a full-time governor."

White voters, still in a majority despite the Voting Rights

Act, clearly disagreed. They'd swallowed George's lie that he had no more federal ambitions—then had watched him fly off to Wisconsin one day after votes were tallied in his favor, launching his presidential run for 1972.

The only bright spot in the primary election, if you chose to see it that way, was the beating Asa Carter had received as one of five contenders for the governorship. Trying to submerge his rancid past, Carter swapped "busing" for the hated label "integration," but he couldn't make it stick. On June 3 he'd run last amidst the field of five, with barely 1.5 percent of ballots cast.

In Wallace's quaint turn of phrase, his onetime speech-writer had been resoundingly "out-niggered" by his former boss.

"More wine," said Fiona. "Seriously, more."

"I'll get it," Dave said, rolling out of bed and padding naked toward the kitchen, still vaguely amazed that he could show himself to her that way, with all his scars.

"On second thought," she said, "get back here. Now."

————

CIA Headquarters: November 18, 1970

JUST AS EUROPE'S Cold War tension seemed to be subsiding, Colby Gantt found the Western Hemisphere was heating up again. He wondered at those cyclic outbreaks sometimes, but he didn't let it trouble him for long.

Trouble was what kept Colby employed.

In Haiti, on a noisy April afternoon, all five ships of the country's Coast Guard had begun to shell the National Palace, but none of the incoming rounds eliminated Papa Doc, and the hoped-for army uprising failed to materialize on schedule. The Coast Guard's commander sought asylum in Cuba, more hundreds were slain, and Duvalier remained ensconced as president for life.

The heat in Uruguay was worse. By 1970, the U.S. Office of Public Safety had trained at least 1,000 Uruguayan cops in riot control and torture techniques, prompting retaliation from the Tupamaros via kidnapping of hostages held at their secret Cárcel del Pueblo ("People's Prison") where they got a taste of their own medicine before large ransoms sent them home. One target was Aloysio Dias, Brazil's consul in Montevideo. Others, including soldiers and police with no money behind them, simply got mowed down in bombings and drive-by assassinations.

That was all embarrassing, but nothing hit home at Langley quite like the abduction and subsequent murder of Dan Mitrione, the Italian-born ex-FBI agent and Agency torture teacher who educated his students in application of "the precise pain, in the precise place, in the precise amount, for the desired effect." A Tupamaros snatch squad grabbed him on the last day of July and put him through the ringer, offering to swap him for 150 political prisoners. Backed by Washington, Uruguayan officials refused the demand, whereupon Mitrione was left in a car, shot twice in the head.

So the ritual stateside mourning began. Nixon PR flack Ron Ziegler praised Mitrione for "devoted service to the cause of peaceful progress in an orderly world." Secretary of State William Rogers attended Mitrione's funeral with presidential son-in-law David Eisenhower and other notables. Mitrione's widow called him as "a perfect man," their daughter lauding him as "a great humanitarian." Frank Sinatra and Jerry Lewis staged a benefit concert for the Mitrione family in Indiana.

Colby, who had once been introduced to Mitrione

without being too impressed, had other matters on his mind by then.

Stateside, he'd donned a wig and fake beard, clipped a bogus PRESS pass on his jacket, and sat through most of the Manson murder trial without Charley or any of his naughty nymphets recognizing him from their fleeting encounter in Haight-Ashbury, before the mayhem started. One of Manson's girls had turned state's evidence against the "family," and with forensic evidence thrown in, that sealed the deal, but it was still in progress, Charley and his women putting on a daily show for the reporters present. Lately, they'd carved Xs in their foreheads, symbolizing their removal from society, with daily outbursts rivaling the strange Chicago Seven trial.

Bobby Beausoleil was already awaiting execution at San Quentin, for the Gary Hinman murder, and unless Gantt missed his guess, at least six other members of the Manson tribe would soon be joining him. Good news for Langley: they were too whacked-out on drugs to make much sense in interviews, and too enthralled by TV cameras to give a damn.

Worse news: public acceptance of a plot behind the death of JFK was at an all-time high, but the death clock kept running for troublesome witnesses. In January, Darrell Garner—once accused of wounding Tippit murder witness Warren Reynolds, alibied by Ruby stripper Betty McDonald before she's "hanged herself" in jail—died from an overdose of drugs. In September, unknown gunmen in Big Spring, Texas, murdered George McGann, a hoodlum friend of Ruby's whose wife had filmed the Dealey Plaza shooting. One week later, *mafioso* Salvatore Granello, closely tied to Santo Trafficante, Jimmy Hoffa, and the Agency's attempts to murder Castro, turned up in a car on

Gotham's Lower East Side, shot four times at point-blank range.

The Dallas case was a self-cleaning oven, turning leftovers to ash.

With any luck, none of the dust would settle anywhere in Gantt's vicinity.

———

Tenleytown, Northwest Washington, D.C.: November 26, 1970

IT WASN'T OFTEN Devon Gantt got back to his old family home, but this Thanksgiving felt like time to join his wife Camille and Devon's widowed mother Gwendolyn, now well into her so-called "golden years" and living mostly on her own.

Son Wyman wasn't with them, off somewhere with Edgar Hoover's "Beards" in hot pursuit of Weathermen, and that drew Devon's thoughts back to the Bureau, even with a feast laid out before him and the women in his life discussing recipes.

At headquarters, Bill Sullivan had been promoted to the FBI's third-highest post, presumably the heir apparent when time finally caught up with Hoover and his failing alter ego, Clyde Tolson. Clyde hadn't bounced back fully from his stroke in '64, now seventy years old to Hoover's to seventy-five, both prone to long naps in their offices—at least, when Edgar wasn't soaring from his daily booster shot of speed.

Devon remained in charge of COINTELPRO—BLACK HATE operations for the moment, tracking targets of the Chief's personal spite and some actual felons who had stumbled in almost coincidentally. In Maryland, SNCC organizers Ralph Featherstone and William "Che" Payne had died in a March car bombing outside the courthouse where Rap Brown's riot trial was supposed to convene the next day. It looked like murder, but police preferred to think the victims had been transporting a bomb when it went off by accident. Brown skipped bail and went underground, missing the debut of his memoir, presciently titled *Die Nigger Die!* While he was on the run and posted to the Ten Most Wanted list, a judge in New Orleans slapped him with a five-year sentence and $2.000 fine *in absentia*.

In Detroit, prosecutors had charged three Republic of New Afrika members with killing Officer Michael Czapski last year, but jurors freed them all on grounds of insufficient evidence. Devon consoled himself with one defendant's later ghetto stabbing death. Meanwhile, the RNA upped stakes and moved its headquarters to Jackson, Mississippi, despite failure to acquire an eighteen-acre lot they craved.

In Cleveland, court proceedings from the Glenville shootout finally wrapped up. Two juvenile defendants saw their charges nullified by the Supreme Court of Ohio, whereupon the D.A. dropped it, claiming they "were not ring leaders and besides, many key witnesses are no longer available."

More FBI attention was devoted to the Panthers and their hostile rivals from the BLA. The Alex Rackley murder trial in New Haven had flopped, big-time. Jurors acquitted all accused Panthers, except for two who had confessed participating at the instigation of an FBI *agent provocateur,* sent off to spend four years apiece in prison.

The Black Liberation Army, meanwhile, seemed intent on racking up a score of murdered cops. In April, they's slain Baltimore Patrolman Donald Sager and wounded his partner. May saw Officer James Sackett gunned down in Saint

Paul. August's victim was Sergeant Francis Van Colln in Philadelphia. September's murder claimed Patrolman William Miscannon of Toledo. Three weeks later, Officer Harold Hamilton died when he interrupted BLA bank robbers in San Francisco. Officer Glenn Smith fell that same month, from sniper fire in Detroit. Suspects were being hunted down in all those crimes, but other militants were standing by to fill their places on the firing line.

The Black Guerrilla Family generated more headlines. George Jackson and "comrade" William Nolen had been transferred from San Quentin to Soledad Prison in January 1969, then one year later, tower guard Opie Miller shot Nolen and two other black inmates, killing all three on the exercise yard. Four days later, while parents of the victims sued Miller in federal court, Jackson, Fleeta Drumgo and John Clutchette faced charges of murdering another guard as retaliation.

That prosecution was still pending in August, when Jackson's younger brother Jonathan invaded the Marin County courthouse with a duffel bag full of weapons, briefly liberating "Soledad Brothers" William Christmas, Ruchell Magee, and James McClain. They took Judge Harold Haley, Deputy D.A. Gary Thomas, and three jurors hostage, but prison guards with rifles were coincidentally staked out, ready to fire as they emerged. When the smoke cleared, Christmas, Haley, Jackson and McClain were dead; Magee, Thomas, and one of the jurors lay wounded. Two months later, bombers hit the courthouse in reprisal for the ambush.

In the meantime, G-men traced Jonathan Jackson's weapons to their owner, Communist Party member Angela Davis, whom he'd served as a volunteer bodyguard. Under pressure from Governor Reagan, Davis had been fired in

1969 from her position as an acting assistant professor at UCLA, soon striking up a correspondence with George Jackson in prison. Now her name had been appended to the Ten Most Wanted list on charges of conspiracy. Arrested in Manhattan, five days after the Marin courthouse bombing, she returned to California for a trial that might drag on into the next White House campaign.

At one point, Gantt had wondered whether Davis's childhood in Birmingham, where she'd been friends with four girls murdered by the Klan in church, had somehow set her on her present course—but if the truth be told, he didn't give a damn.

Then, there was AIM, still on the warpath and involved in occupying Alcatraz. The siege claimed its first life in January, when a thirteen-year-old girl fell down the former prison's concrete steps. Aside from that, The Rock was running short on water and the government had shut off its electric power, though that failed to silence "Radio Free Alcatraz." In June, a suspicious fire razed several of the island's buildings, and the occupiers started fading fast.

Not so, the militants of AIM. On Thanksgiving Day, they'd "celebrated" the Pilgrims' landing on Plymouth Rock by seizing a *Mayflower* replica anchored in Boston Harbor. Certain that he hadn't heard the last of them, Devon put on a happy face and asked his wife, "Can I get seconds on those mashed potatoes, please?"

———

Manhattan: December 17, 1970

THE "BEARDS" wouldn't be home for Christmas, but that didn't bother Wyman Gantt. He'd done the family thing for years and much preferred his risky but invigorating duty for the Bureau, tracking radicals.

In Illinois, five of the Chicago Seven had reached the end of their road, jurors convicting all but John Froines and Lee Weiner of violating the 1968 Anti-Riot Act. Judge Hoffman sentenced those convicted in late February, and they'd entered prison one month later, their first round of appeals exhausted.

Shortly after that, Dick Nixon copped to an American "incursion" in Cambodia, and holy hell broke loose on campuses across the country. It was worst at Kent State, where National Guardsmen fired sixty-seven rounds at unarmed protesters within a span of thirteen seconds. Governor Jim Rhodes called the victims "un-American," while down in Mississippi, white cops simply called the black students they'd gunned down "niggers." The nearest student slain at Kent had been 265 feet from his killers; those in Jackson died in a bullet-riddled dorm. The trigger-men, North and South, would face no charges for the shootings.

And of course, Wyman could understand why members of the Weathermen were so pissed off, no matter that the bulk of them were white and came from affluent backgrounds. The boys had no desire to die in Vietnam, much less Cambodia; the girls were simply in the mood to kick a little ass.

It still boiled down to terrorism though, in Gantt's view, illustrated by the self-destruction of a Greenwich Village bomb-making operation in March. Three WU members died in that blast, while two others—both women, and wounded—escaped. The bombs, informers said, were earmarked for Fort Dix, seeking to "bring the war home" with a vengeance.

Nor was that incident a one-off. Bureau headquarters might claim the WU had less than forty members, but insiders placed the number closer to 600. Either way, they had been keeping busy: a January bomb placed at Seattle's ROTC building; February's bomb in Golden Gate Park, killing police sergeant Brian McDonnell, plus Molotov cocktails hurled at the home of Judge John Murtagh from the "Panther 21" trial; discovery of a second WU "bomb factory" in March, on Chicago's north side; May's blast in Washington, at the National Guard Association's headquarters, followed by a formal "Declaration of a State of War"; June's explosion at NYPD headquarters, together with a dud planted at San Francisco's Hall of Justice; July bombings at the U.S. Army's Presidio in Frisco and Wall Street's Bank of America headquarters; September's California jailbreak liberating Dr. Timothy Leary, for which the WU banked $25,000 from the "Brotherhood of Eternal Love."

Also, in September, Katherine Power and Susan Saxe had teamed with ex-cons William Gilday and Robert Valeri to help arm and finance the Black Panthers. First, they'd robbed a National Guard armory in Newburyport, Massachusetts, stealing guns and ammo before they torched the place, causing $125,000 in damage. Next, they'd hit a bank in Brighton, killing the first cop on the scene, Patrolman Walter Schroeder. Gildray did the shooting, while Power drove one of their getaway cars, fleeing with $26,000 in cash.

October was a crazy month, including a second blast at Chicago's Haymarket Police monument, others at the Marin County courthouse, a traffic court in Queens, and a courthouse on Long Island. Eight bombings marked Columbus Day: five in Rochester, New York; two in Manhattan; and one in Orlando, Florida. Two days later, the WU's "Proud

Eagle Tribe" bombed Harvard's Center for International Affairs.

The campaign wasn't all one-sided, though. In April one of Hoover's "Beards"—not Wyman but a colleague—tipped NYPD to the whereabouts of WU fugitives Dianne Donghi and Linda Evans. In July, a federal grand jury in Detroit indicted thirteen members on firearms and explosives charges. Fugitives Bernardine Dohrn, Katherine Power, and Susan Saxe hit the Ten Most Wanted list in October but were still at large. December's bag included member Caroline Tanker, busted in Pittsburgh after a side trip to Havana; seven nabbed in two separate firebomb attacks on Manhattan banks; and fugitive Judith Clark, jailed in New York on an indictment from Chicago's Days of Rage.

We're winning, Wyman told himself, but it was still an uphill battle, with a long, long way to go before America was finally made safe and sane again.

———

Vientiane, Laos: December 23, 1970

HARDY GANTT WAS on the road again. If Southeast Asia only had one lesson for Americans, it was that moving targets were more difficult to hit. And Gantt intended to come through his Far East tour of duty without being killed or maimed.

As for being *embarrassed,* well, that might be something else. He'd been ordered to Vientiane following claims by the *Christian Science Monitor* that the Agency was "cognizant of, if not party to, the extensive movement of opium out of Laos." Specifically, the article quoted one charter pilot who said that "opium shipments get special CIA clearance and monitoring on their flights southward out of the country." The guy was right, of course, but wasn't that beside the point? You couldn't just go blowing whistles on the dope trade when an estimated 30,000 U.S. servicemen in Vietnam were hooked on heroin, taking their habits home with them if they survived that long.

Gantt knew that Air America was both inserting and extracting U.S. personnel from Laos, further providing backup for the Royal Lao Army, to Hmong guerillas under Major General Vang Pao, and to volunteers from Thailand, shuttling refugees around, and flying photo recon missions in their "down time," using two-dozen twin-engine transport planes bearing civilian markings. All of that took money, and with Langley's budget under strain, where better to go looking for a covert fortune than the poppy fields?

In Vietnam, meanwhile, there were at least 700 Project Phoenix "advisers" directing assassinations, an ongoing effort that prompted the Việt Cộng to retaliate with hit lists of southern officials. Agency operatives also conducted raids across the DMZ, sabotaging pipelines, torching storage buildings, but they'd fallen out of favor now, with half of twenty-two incursions rated total failures, the rest yielding only "meager results." On the flip-side, Langley enjoyed more success with "Operation Wandering Soul," a propaganda campaign urging VC desertions based on native superstitions that persons dying while away from family doom their souls to wander aimlessly throughout eternity.

Another ploy involved broadcasts of tigers roaring in the Bangkok Zoo, played over loudspeakers around Nui Ba Den Mountain amid Agency rumors that man-eaters were gobbling up Reds. Reports to headquarters claimed that 150 Việt Cộng had fled their posts as a result, but who could really say?

Then came America's Cambodian invasion, and shit hit the fan on both sides of the world. B-52 strikes on the Hồ Chí Minh had done little to slow down Red traffic, and General Lon Nol had deposed Cambodia's Prince Sihanouk in March, imposing military rule with CIA support. Of course, Khmer Rouge communists immediately escalated their attacks upon the government, prompting the Nixon White House to invade, even as another 150,000 troops came home from Vietnam. It might not prove to be the single dumbest thing that Nixon ever did—how could you even list them all?—but it was up in the Top Ten.

White House ambivalence continued in October, with a TV speech in which Nixon proposed a "standstill" cease-fire, but Hanoi didn't respond, so South Vietnamese troops launched a new offensive—in Cambodia. Two months later, Nixon warned he might order new bomber raids above the DMZ if Reds continued fighting in the south. Twelve days after that, fed up with the whole mess, Congress tacked on an amendment to their new defense appropriations bill, forbidding use of U.S. ground troops in Cambodia or Laos.

Wyman was leaning toward belief that simply pulling out was best. though he would never say that to his Agency superiors. They should be able to read all the signs themselves. With 30,000 junkies now in uniform, an equal number who admitted to "experimenting" with assorted drugs, while racial brawls became an epidemic and "fragging" of unpopular officers had military brass watching their backs.

Reap what you sow, Gantt thought, *so long as I still have a job.*

CHAPTER 7

Birmingham, Alabama: January 18, 1971

GEORGE WALLACE WAS IN FINE FORM, BEING SWORN IN FOR the second time as governor of Alabama, while a constitutional amendment passed during 1968 allowed him to succeed himself in four years' time, provided nothing better came along.

By then, of course, George hoped he would be President of the United States.

Dave Jordan figured he was dreaming, if he clung to that belief, but Wallace was already lined up for another White House run next year on the American Party ticket. Flanked by his new wife, nineteen years his junior, Wallace preened as if he thought he was a hero to all voters.

Meaning *white* voters, of course.

After his rank racist campaign, Wallace had switched from flaying integrationists to castigating the U.S. Supreme Court's ruling in *Swann v. Charlotte-Mecklenburg Board of Education*, addressing residential segregation in the South by granting lower courts the power to bus students into better schools from their impoverished ones. Striking a pose of modern populism, Wallace prompted journalist Jack Newfield to report that George had "recently has been sounding like William Jennings Bryan as he attacked concentrated wealth in his speeches."

Which, naturally, didn't mean that he would turn Big Money down, by any means.

The only sour note at Wallace's inauguration came from former friend Ace Carter and a few of his old Klansmen, bearing placards reading "Wallace is a Bigot" and "Free Our White Children." It was Carter's swansong in the Cotton State, however, as he hit the road to Texas, seeking rebirth as a novelist under the pseudonym of "Forrest Carter," borrowing his pen name from original Klan wizard Nathan Bedford Forrest.

David wished Fiona had been with him, watching the inauguration on TV, but she was visiting her brother Nolan, with the FBI in Jackson, Mississippi. They still hadn't talked about Dave's family, its history of criminal activity, and he'd begun to think they never would.

Which might, he told himself, cracking another beer, *be just as well.*

———

Saigon: July 3, 1971

THE WAR in Southeast Asia might or might not be approaching its conclusion. From the daily news and CIA reports crossing his desk, it was impossible for Hardy Gantt to say.

In early January, Nixon told America, "The end is in sight." Then, two weeks later, he'd ordered heavy air strikes against North Vietnamese Army bases in Cambodia and Laos. Over the next four months, an "all-South Vietnamese ground offensive" into Laos met with defeat, killing 215 U.S. servicemen, leaving 700 helicopters downed or damaged, while southern troops were chased back home, trailing 7,600 casualties. In March, Nixon's approval rating dropped to 50 percent, while support for the war hit 34 percent, half of those who opposed it calling the effort "morally wrong."

The end in sight? When China pledged complete support for North Vietnam's war against America? When U.S. deaths in Vietnam topped 45,000? When "Vietnam Veterans Against the War" staged a week of national protests, one march drawing 200,000 demonstrators? When the White House confessed that 30,000 CIA-sponsored guerillas were active in Laos? When full-scale bombing raids around Hanoi resumed?

Behind the scenes in Laos, secret Agency inquiries continued into drug trafficking. Langley's conclusion: the opium trade was "legal" in Laos, permitted as the only source of income for impoverished hill tribesmen. Of course, that hardly covered Prince Sopsaisana, wealthy head of the Asian Peoples Anti-Communist League and chief political advisor to Vang Pao, Vice President of the Laotian National Assembly and military commander of the CIA-controlled Laotian Hmong army. In April, as his country's new ambassador to France, Sopsaisana was busted while smuggling 123 pounds of pure heroin valued at $13.5 million through Orly Airport. The largest French drug seizure to date, that smack was earmarked for shipment to New York, but Customs officers seized it. The Agency's chief of station in Paris persuaded the *Police Nationale* to bury their report, and Prince Sopsaisana was back in Laos two weeks later, free and clear.

Meanwhile, stateside, the war was hitting home, thanks primarily to a Report of the Office of the Secretary of Defense Vietnam Task Force, commonly known as the Pentagon Papers. Compiled between 1945 and 1967, reams of secret documents and correspondence told Americans they'd been sold a bill of shoddy goods on Indochina from the days of Harry Truman to the fall of LBJ. Secretary of Defense Robert McNamara ordered the collection, with an eye toward future publication of an "encyclopedic history" detailing America's long drift toward war, but now his bid had blown up in Washington's collective face.

One memo sent to LBJ quantified U.S. motives for involvement in Southeast Asia: 70 percent to avoid humiliating defeat as a feeble ally; 20 percent to keep Indochina out of Mao Zedong's hands; and only 10 percent to grant Vietnam's people "a better, freer way of life." Other motives, assigned no percentage, were "to emerge from the crisis without unacceptable taint from methods used," and to remain despite the will of Indochina's people, although "it would be hard to stay in if asked out."

The leak was traced to RAND Corporation staffer Daniel Ellsberg, who fled into hiding with wife Patricia after the *New York Times* revealed him as its source. The *Times* ran its first exposé on June 13, followed two days later by the White House securing a temporary injunction against further publication. Alas, that only applied to the *Times*, and excerpts soon appeared in the *Washington Post*, followed by seventeen other newspapers. Alaska Senator Mike Gravel staged a midnight coup, reading the Pentagon Papers aloud for three hours, entering them into the untouchable *Congressional Record*. Ellsberg finally surrendered to face charges under the Espionage Act, while the Supreme Court tossed out

Nixon's unconstitutional bid for prior restraint of publication.

Never one to quit when he was proven wrong, Nixon created a special investigations unit—dubbed "The Plumbers," as in plugging leaks—to smear Ellsberg, following Henry Kissinger's sage advice that "the most dangerous man in America had to be stopped." To that end, a federal grand jury indicted Ellsberg and RAND colleague Anthony Russo on fifteen felony counts, Ellsberg facing 115 years in prison, while Russo stood to serve thirty-five.

Gantt didn't know how long that case would drag on through the courts, but he was crystal-clear on one thing: the damage had been done.

———

FBI Field Office, Manhattan: August 9, 1971

SOME MIGHT HAVE SAID that Fate had smiled on Stephen Barnes, but he didn't believe in Fate, only planning and dogged perseverance. Those two things, he was convinced, had brought him to his present posting as a rookie special agent of the FBI.

The Bureau's background checks on Barnes and his adoptive parents in New Jersey had revealed nothing to bar him from acceptance as an agent, buttressed by his academic records from Princeton and Yale Law. Nor had his training at the FBI Academy at Quantico proved daunting, either for his agile mind or strong body. A new facility had been approved in 1965—also at Quantico—but its construction hadn't started until 1969, and it would not receive its first class of prospective agents for another nine months yet.

At the Academy, Barnes had been quick to purchase all

the "recommended" books by Edgar Hoover and his PR man, Don Whitehead, even though he'd read them thoroughly in their original editions. Nothing must disturb his well-rehearsed façade as one of Hoover's fledgling agents, anxious to begin his service to America—and, more importantly, to the Great Man himself.

No new additions had been made to the inflated Ten Most Wanted list so far this year, nor had G-men traced any of the fugitives already listed. New Left radicals had proved adept at going "underground" while striking at the U.S. government, and anything that cast the Bureau in a bad light was of benefit to Stephen's goal.

His posting to Manhattan's field office *was* providential in its way, considering his father's handling by the Gotham FBI that sparked Leonid Babin's lifelong passion for revenge.

Barnes had reviewed the office's long history and was aware that its first Special Agent in Charge had been appointed weeks *before* the Bureau's predecessor agency was certified in July 1908. His name was I. C. Sauer, and if history had now forgotten him, the same couldn't be said for the field office he commanded, presently the largest in America, with current leader John Malone rating designation as Assistant Director.

Long before Malone's appointment in 1962, however, New York City's Bureau office had been famous—or, depending on your viewpoint, *in*famous. Its agents led the "slacker raids" of World War One, arresting hundreds of alleged draft dodgers who were minors or among the elderly, disabled—and in one case, even blind. A year later, the "Red raids" had determined Stephen's future course in life, with deportation of his father, Leonid Babin, back to Mother Russia in what Edgar Hoover would've called disgrace. The Wall Street bombing of September 1920 was unsolved, despite a vow by Edgar Hoover to pursue the terrorist as long as he drew breath. Stephen's blood father had returned years later, as a spy, and he had been deported once again—thankfully overlooked that time, as journalists focused their cameras and tiny minds on agent Valentin Gubitchev and his family, also among those outward bound.

Today, under Assistant Director Malone, the New York City office faced a revolution in its own backyard: Black Panthers, the Black Liberation Army and the Weather Underground, hijackers seizing airliners, violent bank robbers, plus untold numbers of suspected spies serving Russia, the Eastern Bloc, and China.

It was where he'd longed to serve, and his arrival coincided with a most auspicious scandal rocking Bureau headquarters.

The big news out of Washington—Barnes thought of it as a political earthquake—had struck in early March. A self-styled Citizens' Commission to Investigate the FBI had burglarized a two-man Bureau office in Media, Pennsylvania, west of Pittsburgh, making off with countless COINTELPRO files. Before long, they were popping up in leftist publications nationwide and shocking those Americans who still believed the FBI was a straightforward law enforcement agency, neutral and incorruptible.

Analysis of the reports published so far revealed that 1 percent of COINTELPRO actions had targeted organized crime, mostly gambling; 30 percent comprised "manuals, routine forms, and similar procedural matter"; 40 percent involved political surveillance on two right-wing groups, ten immigrant associations, and 200-plus left-wing or "liberal" groups; 14 percent covered draft resistance and military desertion; while 15 percent concerned "normal" crimes such as bank robbery, interstate theft, murder and rape.

Thus, Edgar Hoover's paranoid obsession with the left, driving him to rubber-stamp hundreds of crimes committed by his agents, was revealed. A bulletin from headquarters immediately canceled COINTELPRO's scheming, although Barnes was certain the same underhanded tactics would continue, suitably renamed. The backlash was immediate, with lawsuits filed by various targeted groups and their members seduced into crime by FBI *agents provocateurs*. Congressional hearings were likely, but would they drive Hoover from power?

Barnes hoped not. He was hoping that the Old Man hung on long enough to feel the wrath of Stephen's true father, reaching out beyond the grave to crush Hoover and soil his legacy.

Jackson, Mississippi: August 18, 1971

THE FBI in Mississippi still hadn't procures justice for Vernon Dahmer, Wharlest Jackson, or a list of other victims dating back to 1963—much less dismantle the bomb-crazy Silver Dollar Group—but now it found time to join forces with local police to mount a military-style assault on the Republic of New Afrika.

Agent Nolan O'Hara looked around him at the mob of uniforms on Lewis Street, a half-mile north of Jackson State, where cops had felt obliged to kill two "niggers" fifteen months ago. Aside from every weapon in their arsenal, Jackson PD had rolled out their "Thompson Tank," an armored vehicle named for ex-Mayor Allen Thompson, who'd splurged for it at the tag end of his twenty-year tenure.

Few whites in Jackson thought the RNA had any rights when leader Richard Henry—aka "Imari Abubakari Obadele"—moved headquarters south from Philadelphia in '68. Since then, the group had been embroiled in feuding with Hinds Justice Court Judge William Skinner Jr., and "coincidentally," the judge's father, a police lieutenant, was leading the assault planned for today. Nolan was sorry when the Bureau fell in line with that plan, but it came as no surprise.

Now, Special Agent James Sammon was on his bullhorn, warning anyone inside 1148 Lewis that they had one minute to leave the house with empty hands held high. In fact, by Nolan's watch, a minute and a quarter passed before Agent Bill Crumley shouldered his Federal Riot Gun and fired a 37-mm teargas projectile through one of the home's front windows.

It went to hell from there in nothing flat, with gunfire crackling from the house, police and G-men firing back with everything they had. Searching for targets, Nolan witnessed Lt. William Skinner dropping, his peaked cap flying from the impact of a buckshot charge. O'Hara fired a few shots back at the defenders with his .38, unlikely to hit anyone or anything except the home's half-brick façade. A vehicle in the attached carport was being riddled front to back, although immobile and unoccupied.

The battle sputtered out after ten minutes, give or take, and someone called out from the inside of the house to say they were surrendering. In single file, seven young blacks emerged—one of the women obviously pregnant—as police rushed forward, swinging clubs and gun butts, slapping on handcuffs once they were down.

Nolan felt vaguely sick but knew the raid would be reported as another job well done by editors of the *Clarion-Ledger*, still fighting a rear-guard action in defense of Jim Crow. Local blacks called it "The Klan-Ledger," and Nolan still recalled a headline from the Medgar Evers slaying, when G-men captured Byron De La Beckwith. Beckwith had been born in California, but his widowed mother brought him to her former home in Mississippi at age five, and he had lived there ever since, except for his Marine Corps service during World War Two. Regardless, on the day of his arrest, the *Ledger* had proclaimed: "Californian Arrested in Evers Murder."

Was it any different today? In May, drive-by gunmen had slain Jo Etha Collier in Drew, Sunflower County, less than an hour after her high school graduation. The sheriff had three whites in custody but claimed he "couldn't figure out" their motive for the murder.

August brought the year's first gubernatorial primary, "moderates" Charles Sullivan and Bill Waller defeating a hard-core racist candidate, Waller trailing Sullivan by 129,000 votes. In the runoff three weeks later, Waller reversed that trend, defeating Sullivan by 60,000 ballots, rolling on to November and a 77-percent victory over black rival Charles Evers. What made the difference in August? FBI informers said that Sullivan had vowed to free the state's imprisoned Klansmen within one year of inauguration. Waller, who'd defended one of Vernon Dahmer's killers back in '69, allegedly said he'd release them all inside six months.

Some things never appeared to change, and now, Nolan felt soiled by contact with the local strain of bigotry.

Manhattan: September 19, 1971

PAYTON SAWYER HAD JOINED NYPD two decades earlier, in part to spare himself from combat in Korea, but another war had found him now and it was spreading on all sides.

It wasn't Richard Nixon's "War on Drugs," although the White House had declared drug abuse America's "Public Enemy Number One" in June, committing his administration to "prevention of new addicts and the rehabilitation of those who are addicted" nationwide, while stepping up police pressure on smugglers. How he hoped to do that, given Nixon's close ties to the Syndicate since 1946, was anybody's guess, but Payton knew it would've made his father laugh.

The war that troubled him today was based on race and politics, a conflict being fought out in the courts and on the streets. Exposure from the FBI break-in in Pennsylvania, revealing cozy ties to BOSS, had spawned lawsuits by some of NYPD's targets, including Black Panthers, Yippies, and anti-war activists. Those cases might drag on for years, but the Panther 21 had scored a major victory in May, with all defendants cleared on each of their 156 charges.

And in the meantime, bodies dropped in Gotham.

The east-west Panther split drew first blood in January, with Party member Fred Bennett slain by purported Oakland loyalists. Two months later, Panthers killed BLA member Robert Web in retaliation, then the BLA hit back for that with the torture-slaying of Panther Samuel Napier. Two days later, BLA member Harold Russell died in a Harlem shooting that left two detectives wounded.

A surprise entry to April's list was JoAnne Chesimard, aka "Assata Shakur," a Queens native and college graduate who'd briefly joined the Panthers, then switched to the BLA.

On April 6 she'd barged into a private party at Midtown Manhattan's Statler Hilton Hotel, demanding money. Instead, she'd wound up shot in the stomach, then released on bail pending trial for attempted robbery, felonious assault, reckless endangerment, and possession of a deadly weapon.

Left with egg on his face from May's Panther 21 acquittals, Edgar Hoover ordered "intensification" of harassment against those found innocent, prompting furious response from the Black Liberation Army. Seven days after the trial's conclusion, black gunmen wounded Officers Nicholas Binetti and Thomas Curry, guarding Manhattan D.A. Frank Hogan's home on Riverside Drive. Two nights later, shooters killed Officers Waverly Jones and Joseph Piagentini in Harlem. Jones's pistol, stolen from the scene, was later used to fire on a police station in San Francisco.

After BLA communiqués claimed credit for both shootings, Hoover opened a "NEWKILL" file—for *New* York *kill*ings—targeting the former Panther 21 defendants without any evidence. On May 26, Hoover met with Dick Nixon, receiving the president's order not to "pull any punches in going all out in gathering information on the situation in New York."

Ten days later, NYPD nabbed BLA member Richard Moore, aka " Dhoruba ('The Storm') Wahad," at an after-hours club in the Bronx, catching him with a submachine gun. The tip came from a diagnosed paranoid schizophrenic who first claimed Moore shot no one, then changed her tune after BOSS jailed her as a material witness. Still, ballistics evidence linked Moore's weapon to the Binetti-Curry shootings, and his fingerprints were on a BLA communiqué claiming credit, resulting in a July indictment for attempted murder.

In the Jones-Piagentini case, police named BLA suspects Herbert Bell, Anthony Bottom, Francisco Torres, Gabriel Torres, and Albert Washington. San Francisco police caught Bell in August, after he and two other BLA members killed a police sergeant there.

Five days before the California arrest, BLA members had robbed a bank in Queens. Security cameras filmed fugitive bail-jumper Joanne Chesimard, gun in hand.

Then, yesterday, the action had shifted to Plainfield, New Jersey, where Patrolman Frank Buczek was slain while working security at St. Mary's Church. As with Waverly Jones, his pistol was stolen. Police there were hunting three BLA members, presently hiding in the Dominican Republic.

As if those deaths weren't bad enough, nine days before Buczek's murder, 2,200 prisoners had seized control of Attica Prison, 350 miles northwest of Gotham, ostensibly in reaction to George Jackson's death at San Quentin. Governor Nelson Rockefeller, harboring presidential ambitions, dispatched state troopers on September 13, with orders to retake the prison at all costs. Their indiscriminate gunfire killed ten hostage guards and twenty inmates before survivors were lined up and systematically beaten. In the wreckage, cops also found four snitches executed by their vengeful fellow prisoners. Newspapers called it America's bloodiest day since the Civil War, and Rockefeller saw his White House dreams go up in smoke, whining, "On a much smaller scale, I think I have some feeling now of how Truman must have felt when he decided to drop the A-bomb."

Not to be left out, five days after the massacre, Weatherman Underground members bombed the office of New York Correctional Services Commissioner Russell Oswald. Survivors of the slaughter and the families of those who'd died were lining up to sue, one more long-winded case that stood to cost the state tens of millions before it was settled.

Payton wondered what his father would've said, if Ike had been around to see the present age of chaos, then decided that it didn't matter. Death cured all mortal headaches, while the folks still standing had to soldier on, wading through shit.

———

FBI Headquarters: November 6, 1971

DEVON GANTT sipped coffee at his desk, trying to decide how he could personally profit from the Bureau's recent string of setbacks. Was there some way for him to emerge from it triumphant, where his late father had so abjectly failed?

Spring's burglary in Pennsylvania remained unsolved, but journlalists exaggerated its impact. So what, if COIN-TELPRO had been formally disbanded under that once-secret designation? In the next breath, Edgar Hoover had established a new, improved "Special Target Development Program" against the Weatherman Underground, using the same illegal "black bag jobs" as in the past, and once again buried the scheme in secret files.

But the Old Man was also fighting battles in his own backyard, clinging to power at the FBI with little help from doddering Clyde Tolson. Hoover kept resisting White House calls to "centralize" intelligence and help Dick Nixon plug the countless leaks in his regime, but then he'd been blind-sided by a Judas literally next-door to his office. Having reached the Bureau's number three spot, touted in the press as next in line to rule the roost, Bill Sullivan had thrown it all away. His claims that Hoover's antiquated emphasis on Reds ignored real problems here and now were true, but when had that ever mattered? One month ago, Sullivan had come to work and found his office lock changed, his nameplate on the door removed. He was "retired" now, desperately peddling his insider tales to anyone who'd listen, working on memoir that had yet to find a publisher.

As far as FBI pursuit of ghetto blacks and other militants, nothing had changed except the operation's label. In January, reporters disclosed that Maryland state's attorneys admitted fabricating an arson charge against Rap Brown, but Brown remained in hiding till October, when NYPD shot and captured him on new charges of robbing a neighborhood bar that, Brown claimed, "exploited the community." Convicted and dispatched to Attica, he'd watched as one of the lying Maryland prosecutors pled guilty to contempt of court and walked free on probation. In jail, Brown had converted to Islam, changing his name to Abdullah Al-Amin ("the trustworthy").

In Cleveland, eight cops and a tow truck driver were suing the city for $8.8 million, claiming black Mayor Stokes had funded militants, thus leading to their wounds during the 1968 Glenville shootout. After a three-week trial, their judge dismissed the case for lack of evidence, but cops remained embittered against Stokes, bad-mouthing him at any given opportunity.

Out west, where skirmishes between Black Panthers and Ron Karenga's US commandos continued, Karenga and two male adherents drew ten-year prison terms for false imprisonment and felonious assault. Two of his female acolytes, whom he'd christened "African queens," accused Karenga and his codefendants of caging them naked and whipping them with electrical cords. Ex-wife Brenda Karenga confessed sitting on one victim's stomach while Ron forced water down her throat. Strangely, other female followers kept recruiting for US after Ron went away.

In Connecticut, the Rackley murder case against New Haven Panthers had collapsed. The Bureau's *agent provocateur* and two of his stooges confessed in return for lighter sentences, while jurors deadlocked on defendants Bobby Seale and Erica Huggins. Prosecutors planned a second trial until Judge Harold Mulvey said, "I find it impossible to believe that an unbiased jury could be selected without superhuman efforts—efforts which this court, the state and these defendants should not be called upon either to make or to endure." With that, the case was closed, another flop.

Meanwhile, the BLA was going strong, riding a wave of violence and taking losses in the process. In January G-men in Tampa killed member Frank Fields, sought in New York for slaying Panther rival Sam Napier, and in Miami for a bank heist.

In August the BLA distracted San Francisco cops by bombing the Stonetown Mall, then raided the Ingleside police station, killing Sergeant John Young and wounding a civilian staffer. Police soon nabbed members Anthony Bottom and Albert "Nuh" Washington in that case, reporting that "Nuh" was Swahili for "Noah." Both were also suspected in Gotham's Jones-Piagentini murders.

On November 3, in Atlanta, two BLA members executed Officer James Greene, stealing his badge, pistol, and wallet. Eight days later, also in Atlanta, Lieutenant Ted Elmore made a traffic stop unusual for someone of his rank and took three bullets from the suspect auto's occupants, leaving him paralyzed. Cops found the shooters' car abandoned, containing shotguns, rifles, 14,000 rounds of ammunition, and a bazooka.

Meanwhile, the Black Guerrilla Family had suffered a critical loss with George Jackson's death at San Quentin under most peculiar circumstances. Officially, Jackson had met with lawyer Stephen Bingham on a civil lawsuit against the California Department of Corrections. Before the meeting, he was searched from head to toe, Afro hairdo included, but when he returned to his cellblock, a guard "noticed a metallic object in Jackson's hair" and ordered him to remove it. At that point, authorities said, he'd whipped off a wig concealing a pistol, announcing, "The dragon has come!"

When the shooting ended, Jackson, two white convicts, and three guards lay dead; three other guards were wounded. Jackson's death came just three days before his scheduled trial for slaying another guard in 1970. Prosecutors charged Bingham with smuggling the gun and alleged wig to Jackson, despite San Quentin's rigid security screening, but by then he'd disappeared. Relatives buried George beside his brother Jonathan in Illinois, his grave unmarked.

In related news, Angela Davis, captured in New York, represented by Communist Party attorney John Abt, pled not guilty to charges stemming from the 1970 Marin courthouse shootings. By February, supporters in 200 cities nationwide and 67 foreign countries were laboring on her defense. Ex-Beatle John Lennon and wife Yoko Ono wrote a song titled "Angela" in her honor.

While most of the media focused on militant blacks, AIM was still on the warpath and trying to garner attention. Federal officers removed the last live-in protesters from Alcatraz in June—the only time cops ever threw anybody off The Rock—but AIM just shifted gears, attacking perceived failures by the Bureau of Indian Affairs. One member briefly faced "unlawful entry" charges, soon dismissed, and AIM leaders received a brief audience with BIA Commissioner Louis Bruce. Thus ended the first Indian raid on Washington, but Devon reckoned they'd be back.

And when they came, a new improved COINTELPRO squad would be waiting to receive them.

———

Seattle, Washington: December 3, 1971

DESPITE COINTELPRO's embarrassing demise in April, Edgar Hoover's "Beards" were going strong and Agent Wyman Gantt was in the thick of it.

Remnants of the weakened SDS were catching on to Bureau tricks, producing a pamphlet titled "Who Are the Bombers?" that accurately blamed FBI *agents provocateurs* for acts of violence designed to excuse homicidal police reactions, but most of America yawned and moved on.

In March, President Nixon denounced a bombing at the U.S. Capitol—retaliation for his Laotian invasion—as "a shocking act of violence that will outrage all Americans." A month later, G-men claimed discovery of a "Pine Street Bomb Factory" in San Francisco, but the Weathermen who'd manned it escaped. August saw California Department of Corrections offices bombed in Frisco and Sacramento, responding to George Jackson's death at San Quentin. Attica, in turn, provoked September's blast at the New York Department of Corrections in Albany. A month later, bombers struck the government-funded Center for International Studies at MIT, in Cambridge, Massachusetts.

The Bureau's only win so far this year had happened in Seattle yesterday, with the arrest of Capitol bombing suspect

Matthew Steen, a WU member charged with bank robbery and conspiracy. Gantt had played a covert role in Steen's capture, but that was strictly under wraps unless the Bureau needed him to testify at trial.

He hoped that wouldn't happen. It would be a shame to blow his cover, just when he was having so much fun with hippie chicks, love grass, and living like a renegade while still drawing his Bureau salary.

Hell, who could ask for more?

———

Little Italy, Manhattan: December 24, 1971

"SOME SHITTY CHRISTMAS, EH?" Angelo Giordano asked his brother Dominic.

"I can take it or leave it," Dom replied.

Their mother hadn't lived to see the holidays this year, and who was left out of their family? Their cousin Dave—who used the last name Jordan, given to him by their skittish Uncle Greg, a missing person since the early days of the "Banana War"—steered clear of Gotham, practicing civil rights law somewhere in the South. Dave's sister Gemma was in mourning for her daughter Lucia, Dom and Ange's cousin, who'd been blown up by some psycho redneck, also in the wilds of Dixie.

Fuckin' civil rights, Dom thought. *Who needs 'em, anyhow?*

Or maybe he and Ange would, if the feds ever resumed their crackdown on the *Cosa Nostra* and decided to come after them. They were comparatively small fish in the gangland ocean, but Dom tried to learn from the example of his elders when he could.

Take Jimmy Hoffa. Teamster leaders had been lobbying

and bribing Richard Nixon to cut Jimmy loose, but with a nasty twist. In February, Hoffa had ceded the union presidency to protégé Frank Fitzsimmons, but Frank wanted to run the show for real. His payoffs to the White House, rumored to be $1.7 million, had sprung Hoffa yesterday, just five years into his thirteen-year sentence, but as a condition of parole, Hoffa was barred from holding any union office for the next nine years. Jimmy was pissed, and rumor had it that he was already seeking ways to make an earlier comeback.

The year's shocker had come in late June, when a black gunman shot *Don* Joseph Colombo during his second "Italian-American Unity Day" rally, leaving him a comatose vegetable. Bosses of the other Gotham families had criticized Colombo for creating the Italian-American Civil Rights League two years earlier, making headlines, picketing *Godfather* film sets, even aligning his group with terrorist Meir Kahane's Jewish Defense League. Of course, Colombo wouldn't listen, and now he couldn't hear a thing, only alive because machines were keeping him that way.

Why would a black street hustler—killed immediately by Colombo's bodyguards—come gunning for a top-ranked *mafioso*? Wise guys knew Colombo rival Joey Gallo had been chummy with black drug dealers before making parole last year, and soon after he'd hit the streets Gallo declined peace feelers from Colombo, demanding a $100,000 payday instead of the paltry $1,000 he'd been offered. After that, it wasn't hard to read between the lines.

Meanwhile, a heart attack had finished squealer Joe Valachi off in Texas, at the La Tuna federal lockup. He'd outlived his ex-boss Vito Genovese by two years, and *Don* Vito's $100,000 contract on Valachi went unclaimed.

In a weird, twisted way that made Dom jealous: not

about the heart attack but wondering if anyone would ever care enough about him to put that kind of price on his head. The way things looked to him these days, he had begun to think nobody ever would.

———

CIA Headquarters: December 24, 1971

COLBY GANTT HAD FALLEN into his late father's bad habit of shopping late for Christmas presents, but so much had happened with the Agency of late that it was hard to tear himself away.

For one thing, he'd been supervising background checks on more than 26,000 potential CIA agents. James Bond films and Nixon's foreign policy had overcome Agency setbacks from the years of JFK and "Camelot." Now everybody longed to be a spy, licensed to kill if possible, and it was time-consuming, weeding out the jerk-offs who had no idea what they'd be signing up for.

Haiti was a prime example. President-for-life François Duvalier had finally dropped dead from heart disease and diabetes, but his son Jeanne-Claude—inevitably nicknamed "Baby Doc" although, unlike his old man, he had never been to med school—had succeeded him. Jeanne-Claude turned out to be Earth's youngest living president, barely twenty, but he had his father's flair for graft and crushing peasants underfoot.

In Uruguay, the Tupamaros had peaked as a terrorist army, battling a new National Directorate of Information and Intelligence created in large part by CIA officer William Cantrell. Fielding death squads from Montevideo, the NDII had defeated the Broad Front's leftist election campaign, while Tupamaros fought back with assassination and kidnapping—notably of British Ambassador Geoffrey Jackson. In September, more than 100 guerillas had escaped from the capital's Punta Carretas Prison, tunneling from their cellblock to a nearby private home, leaving the NDII to play catch-up with raids in the countryside.

Stateside, remnants of MKULTRA and MKOFTEN lived on, still testing drugs on animals and humans, with a weird sideline called "Subproject 139" at Pennsylvania State University, described for public consumption as "bird disease studies."

MKULTRA's most infamous crop of alumni to date, Charles Manson\s "family," had finally reached the end of their Tate-LaBianca murder trial in late January. Jurors convicted Charlie and three of his women on all counts, then moved on to the penalty phase, for which the defendants shaved their heads, Manson telling reporters, "I am the Devil, and the Devil always has a bald head." Jurors recommended death in March, affirmed by Judge William Holder three weeks later.

A second, men-only trial followed, resulting in Tex Watson's conviction on seven Tate-LaBianca counts, plus Clem Grogan's conviction for helping Watson kill Spahn Ranch employee Donald "Shorty" Shea in August 1969. Judge James Kolts accepted the panel's death sentence for Tex, but gave Clem life instead, declaring, "Grogan was too stupid and too hopped on drugs to decide anything on his own."

Langley insisted that the sudden end of Operation MKSEARCH, decreed immediately after Manson's trial, was mere "coincidence." No one was facing charges yet for the January murder of defense attorney Ronald Hughes, who'd missed the sentencing when someone stuffed his corpse between two boulders in Ventura County.

Some heat landed on Lynette "Squeaky" Fromme in April, slapped with a ninety-day sentence for trying to feed Tate murder witness Barbara Hoyt a burger laced with LSD. It didn't work, and Squeaky got off light, considering.

The same couldn't be said for stray survivors of the JFK assassination case. In March, Clayton Fowler—lead defense attorney for Jack Ruby and a lawyer for Lee Oswald bene-factor George de Mohrenschildt—died in Dallas from a heart attack. A month later, General Charles Cabell, CIA deputy director during the covert war on Castro, collapsed and died shortly after his service physical at Florida's Fort Myers. In mid-September persons unknown strangled *mafioso* James Plumeri and dumped his corpse on a sidewalk in Queens, thus ensuring silence on his involvement with Agency plots to murder Fidel.

Dealey Plaza was the gift that kept on giving, making Colby hope its long arm never reached for him.

CHAPTER 8

FBI Field Office, Manhattan: June 19, 1972

THE PRESIDENT HAD STEPPED IN SHIT BUT DIDN'T SEEM TO recognize it yet, which tickled Agent Stephen Barnes no end. For now, he simply had to watch and wait for the disaster to play out while attending to his duties with the local Bureau's Criminal Investigative Division.

Granted, the year had started strong for Nixon with his February visit to the People's Republic of China. No president before him had set foot on Chinese soil, and even critics hailed him as a "great statesman" after he'd met with Mao Zedong and Prime Minister Zhou Enlai. Three months later, he had signed the First Strategic Arms Limitation Treaty and Anti-Ballistic Missile Treaty with Moscow, both considered major steps toward global peace.

But then came Watergate.

The name belonged to a ten-acre, six-building complex in the Foggy Bottom neighborhood of Washington, D.C., along New Hampshire and Virginia Avenues. Its high-rises included a hotel, two office buildings, and three blocks of cooperative apartments.

Yesterday, five men had been caught in the act of burglarizing Democratic National Committee headquarters in the office building at 2600 Virginia Avenue. Public details were sparse at the moment but Barnes had gleaned intriguing details on the burglars from hourly-updated FBI memos.

The team's leader was James McCord Jr., a one-time Bureau agent who'd shifted to the CIA, rising to a GS-15 position in the Agency's Office of Security. In 1961, after he led a counter-intelligence program against Lee Oswald's Fair Play for Cuba Committee, CIA Director Allen Dulles had called McCord "the best man we have." After retiring from the Agency, still a lieutenant colonel in the U.S. Army Reserve, McCord became security coordinator for the Republican National Committee and the Committee for the Reelection of the President—Nixon's "plumbers," aka CREEP. The morning after his arrest, the GOP had fired McCord from both positions, trying to save face.

Second-in-charge of the burglars was Bernard Barker, a Miami realtor with a checkered past. He'd flown bombers over Europe in World War Two, was shot down and imprisoned in 1944, liberated thirteen months later by the Red Army. From there, he'd joined Fulgencio Batista's secret police in Cuba while doubling as an FBI agent, then enlisted with the CIA in time to participate in the disastrous 1961 Bay of Pigs invasion.

Frank Sturgis, né Fiorini, served with the Marine Corps in World War Two, wore a cop's badge in Norfolk, Virginia, then joined the army in time to witness the 1949 Berlin Blockade as part of an intelligence unit spying on Russia. He'd changed his surname at age twenty-eight, joined

Castro's rebels as a captain in 1959, briefly serving as Fidel's gambling czar while doubling as director of security and intelligence for the Cuban air force. Seven months after the revolution, he'd defected to the CIA in Miami and supported anti-Castro exile operations ever since.

And speaking of exiles, the last two burglars were both Cuban refugees from communism. Eugenio Martinez was one of Barker's real estate agents, with CIA connections on the side. Virgilio Gonzalez, recruited to handle the break-in's grunt work, was Miami locksmith.

Barnes had no idea how far the Watergate scandal would spread, but he hoped it went all the way to the Oval Office, taking down as many members of the GOP regime as possible.

Chaos could only make his own work at the Bureau that much easier.

———

Birmingham, Alabama: August 5, 1972

KARMA, Dave Jordan thought, could be a bitch. Over the past decade, George Wallace had sown seeds of violence to boost his burgeoning political career, but now it had caught up with him, his fate delivered—oh, sweet irony—at a Caucasian adversary's hands.

Despite his hollow promise to forego another White House race, Wallace had picked up chasing that dream one day after his inauguration for a second term as governor. This time around, he'd abandoned his American Party supporters, leaving them to nominate a pair of John Birch Society members, California congressman John Schmitz and Thomas Jefferson Anderson, supervising editor and author of the *Straight Talk* column carried in 375 newspapers nationwide. Wallace declared himself as a Democratic candidate, claiming 42 percent of all primary ballots in Florida, 68 percent in Tennessee, and 50 percent in North Carolina.

And then came Maryland.

On May 15, at a rally in Laurel, white assailant Arthur Herman Bremer stepped out of the crowd and emptied a .38-caliber revolver, critically wounding Wallace and three bystanders. After his arrest, police discovered that a second pistol—a Browning 9-mm automatic holding thirteen rounds—remained in Bremer's car nearby, thus averting more slaughter.

All those whom Bremer shot survived, with Wallace paralyzed from the waist down. Despite his injuries, he still won Maryland's primary with 39 percent on May 16, and Michigan's with 51 percent the same day. He placed second in two others, Oregon and New Mexico, ran third in California, but failed to place at all in New Jersey, New York, and South Dakota.

Whatever impact the shooting had on Wallace's presidential obsession, he remained as Alabama's chief of state. Lieutenant Governor Jere Beasley held his place until July, when George returned from Silver Spring's Holy Cross Hospital, then handed the reins back to Wallace.

But what of Arthur Bremer?

Media reports identified him as a Milwaukee native, product of a tumultuous home that included three other sons, two illegitimate and sired by different fathers. Friendless through high school, he quit a technical college after one semester to work as a busboy, demoted to kitchen work when customers complained about him talking to himself. He left that job to be a school janitor, then lost his only adult friend to a game of Russian roulette one year before the Wallace shooting. Arrested for carrying a concealed weapon in November 1971, he paid a $38 fine and underwent court-ordered psychiatric counseling.

Unemployed by March 1, 1972, Bremer told his diary, "It is my personal plan to assassinate by pistol either Richard Nixon or George Wallace. I intend to shoot one or the other while he attends a campaign rally for the Wisconsin Primary." He'd missed that target date, despite attending a Wallace campaign function in Milwaukee on March 2, but popped up in Maryland ten weeks later, nearly achieving his goal.

From Fiona O'Hara's brother Nolan, an FBI agent in Mississippi, David knew that burglars from Dick Nixon's CREEP had invaded Bremer's Milwaukee apartment—abandoned six days before he shot Wallace—in search of any evidence that might connect him to the GOP. Now, with the revelations spinning out of Watergate, some critics of the president suspected that someone from CREEP, perhaps Bernard Barker, had altered Bremer's diary or helped fund his travels while stalking Wallace.

None of that mattered at Bremer's August trial, where defense attorneys claimed Bremer was schizophrenic with "no emotional capacity to understand anything." Jurors preferred the prosecution's line, casting Bremer as one more in a long line of lone glory-seekers. Convicted on four counts of attempted murder and related firearms charges, Bremer received a sixty-three-year sentence, soon reduced by ten years on appeal.

But would the whole truth ever be exposed? Considering that question, Jordan was surprised to find that he no longer cared.

———

FBI Academy, Quantico: August 14, 1972

SOMETIMES, Erin O'Hara thought, it took a stroke of Fate to realize a dream.

From childhood she'd admired her father's service with the Bureau, even though it often kept him late at work or gone from home entirely for long intervals. She had gone on to law school after college, with the goal of someday managing to join the FBI herself, but that had been impossible while sexist Edgar Hoover ruled the Seat of Government. Upon promotion to Director back in 1924, he'd fired two of the Bureau's female agents, while the third resigned in 1928, later detained in an asylum, ranting threats to murder him. Since then, no women had been hired—the FBI's final remaining prejudice, since it was forced by Robert Kennedy to hire black agents during 1962.

But Hoover was no longer a concern. On May 2, one of his black servants found him sprawled lifeless beside his bed, killed by a heart attack at age seventy-seven. Doddering Clyde Tolson spent one day as Acting Director, then resigned, citing his obvious poor health. President Nixon replaced him with Louis Patrick Gray III, a DOJ official with no FBI experience who spent most of his time at home in Connecticut or touring Bureau field offices nationwide. His absenteeism became an office joke in Washington, where working agents dubbed him "Three-Day Gray" after his short workweeks.

And even when Gray tried to serve his White House masters, he almost invariably failed. His first task, on orders from Nixon, was to find and seize his predecessor's secret files. At headquarters, retiring secretary Helen Gandy claimed that no such files existed, showing Gray a row of empty filing cabinets. Gray had no way of knowing that

Gandy had passed 167 of the "nonexistent" files—some 1,800 pages in all—to Associate Director Mark Felt before Gray reported to work.

Finally, the late Director's passing mingled pomp and slapstick comedy. Two young U.S. Marines collapsed with hernias while carrying his flag-draped, lead-lined casket into the Rotunda of the U.S. Capitol, where he laid in state before a funeral service at National Presbyterian Church. President Nixon kept a straight face while he read the eulogy, calling Hoover "one of the giants, whose long life brimmed over with magnificent achievement and dedicated service to this country which he loved so well." Afterward, Hoover was buried at Washington's Congressional Cemetery, beside his parents and a sister who had died in infancy.

The grave was barely filled in before a press release from Gray announced that "women applicants will now be considered for the FBI special agent position." Erin had missed the two first spots—Agents Joanne Pierce and Susan Roley, sworn in on July 17—but she was one of nine in the next class at Quantico, determined to succeed despite any chauvinist roadblocks she might encounter.

And her new career was starting at a brand-new FBI Academy, opened to students only five days after Hoover's death. The new, improved facility included more than two dozen classrooms, eight conference rooms, twin seven-story dormitories, a 1,000-seat auditorium, a dining hall, a full-sized gym and swimming pool, a well-equipped library, a new firing range, four identification labs, and thirteen darkrooms. Overall, its classroom space expanded tenfold, accommodating 200 prospective agents, plus other students from U.S. regional police departments and foreign agencies.

Aside from classroom work, the Academy's core curriculum included Tactical and Emergency Vehicle Operations training, the usual firearms instructions with up-to-date weapons, plus simulated raids and arrests carried out in a mock-city setting complete with storefronts, houses, apartments, and a bank subjected to twice-weekly holdups. Erin had been acing all her courses so far, looking forward to her graduation and rookie assignment to a field office where she could prove herself.

It was a shame her grandfather hadn't lived to see this day, but Erin still hoped that in some way she could make him proud.

———

Harlem: September 30, 1972

THE WAR between Black Liberation Army members and NYPD was had gathered steam this year, with bloodshed on both sides. The BLA wasn't hunting for Payton Sawyer yet, thanks to his covert work for BOSS, but how much longer could that respite last?

In January, multiple gunmen had ambushed Officers Gregory Foster and Rocco Laurie, killing them both while they walked their 9th Precinct beat, stealing both their sidearms. Eleven days later, Police Commissioner Patrick Murphy named nine suspects at large: Ronald Anderson, Herman Bell, Ronald Carter, Joanne Chesimard, Twyman "Olugbala" Myers, Cooper Stewart, and Robert Vickers.

Carter didn't last long, killed by St. Louis police in mid-April, with BLA members Robert Brown and Thomas "Blood" McCreary captured at the same time. Early August saw Vickers arrested in Newark.

Two days before the St. Louis shootout, there'd been more bloodletting in Gotham. It began with an short anonymous call declaring an "officer in distress" at 102 West 116th Street in Harlem—Nation of Islam Mosque No. 7, currently led by Minister Louis Farrakhan. Patrolmen Phillip Cardillo and Vito Navarra, first on the scene, were surprised to find the temple's front door—normally bolted and covered by Muslims—unlocked and unguarded that day.

Barging inside, they'd been repelled by ten guards from the Fruit of Islam before nine more cops arrived and the usual mêlée broke out, gunshots killing Officer Cardillo five minutes after the fake alarm call was received. Another cop was wounded, while sixteen Muslims were "detained," refusing to identify themselves. Chief of Detectives Albert Seedman finally showed up and reached a compromise with black congressman Charles Rangel, fifteen months into his federal job. To avert a riot, Rangel and Seedman had agreed police would pull back from the mosque, pending surrender of the sixteen suspects later in the day.

Accordingly, the cops bailed out, leaving their suspects and a crime scene rife with bloodstains and ballistic evidence. NYPD was suitably embarrassed when the day passed, then more days, with no suspects presented for arrest. The hunt was on now for one NOI member, Louis 17X Dupree, but another haunting question remained: who'd made the 911 call that started the whole shebang?

Theories abounded, from a simple "prank" to a BLA setup, but Payton had another idea. Having observed the FBI in action and having his one-time G-man brother Fred explain their tactics in detail, Payton now thought the tip-off might have been what Bureau agents called a "pretext call," made as a part of their malicious COINTELPRO—BLACK HATE operation. It was right up Edgar Hoover's alley to provoke killing between black militants and any handy adversaries, whether street gangs or police, in hopes of dropping bodies on the street and justifying further para-military action by lawmen.

Meanwhile, with that investigation going nowhere, BLA "den mother" Joanne Chesimard had come into her own. In January she'd apparently wounded a Brooklyn cop during a traffic stop. Five weeks later, she or her double was caught by security cameras during an $89,000 Brooklyn bank robbery. May found her named as a suspect in four cop-killings, Jones-Piagentini and Foster-Laurie. Chattanooga officers allegedly spotted her with other BLA members during a brief road trip to Tennessee. In May, she and two companions killed a New Jersey state trooper during another "routine" traffic stop.

Now, even the Catholic Church was involved. Just yester-day, Brooklyn Monsignor John Powis claimed that Chesi-mard had robbed Brownsville's Our Lady of the Presentation Church at gunpoint.

How much of all that did Sawyer believe? He wasn't sure yet, but he'd seen first-hand how NYPD and the FBI piled on felony charges in such cases, only to stand back and watch them fall apart in court. Hell, cops abetted by an FBI informer had slaughtered his own brother in Chicago, and that civil lawsuit was still dragging on, without Payton listed among the plaintiffs.

Wait and see, he thought. And if he thought that Chesi-mard was innocent on any of the charges filed against her...then, what would he do?

———

CIA Headquarters: October 17, 1972

COLBY GANTT WAS THINKING of retirement, though he hadn't

worked his nerve up to proceed with it so far. He'd served a quarter-century in harness with the Agency, plus more time with the OSS during the last World War, and he was getting...tired.

But was he tired enough to quit outright at fifty-one?

Granted, he had a son serving the CIA today, who'd carry on the family tradition in his own way, but the thought of cutting loose disturbed him nonetheless, with so much still remaining to be done.

In Uruguay, for instance, great strides had been made against the Tupamaros, hampered by their record of assassination and kidnapping, damaged when the state recruited several leaders as informers, killing or arresting many more, and when firebrand Héctor Amodio Pérez fled to Spain with his wife. Still, some left-wing propagandists hailed the rebel movement, like Greek-French film director Costa-Gavras with his recent movie *State of Siege*, in which French actor Yves Montand portrayed the Agency's own torture master, Daniel Mitrione, thinly disguised as character "Philip Michael Santore."

Stateside, Agency Director Richard Helms had all hands busy, shredding files from Operations MKSEARCH and MKULTRA while the Watergate scandal expanded in Washington. As far as CIA drug "research" went, however, the worst news had come from the Supreme Court on June 29.

Split five-to-four, the court had ruled in *Furman v. Georgia* that capital punishment as presently conducted in America violated the Constitution's Eighth Amendment bank on "cruel and unusual" punishment. Two more cases roped into the mix, *Branch v. Texas* and *Jackson v. Georgia*, banned the time-honored Dixie tradition of executing rapists—at least if they were black, their victims white.

Clearly, there was nothing "unusual" about capital

punishment in America. Between 1608 and 1967, at least 14,290 prisoners had been executed by various U.S. colonies and states on wide-ranging charges. Ten of the fifty states had abolished capital punishment between 1853 and 1957, which left forty raring to go. Still, there had been no executions in America for five years prior to *Furman*, a lull that abolitionists called a "moratorium," while eager advocates termed it "foot-dragging."

Personally, Colby didn't give much of a damn who lived or died outside of his own family, but *Furman* automatically commuted all standing American death sentences to life imprisonment—and that posed certain problems for the Agency.

Sirhan Bishara Sirhan was one of the lucky bastards, spared execution for the highly suspicious murder of Robert Kennedy in 1968, now scheduled to remain alive and talking without hope of parole until Mother Nature eventually knocked him off.

Equally dangerous to MKULTRA went, despite ongoing destruction of its files, was the Manson "family" case. All five of the defendants facing death for murders during 1968-69 saw their penalties commuted to life—and in liberal California, that meant life *with* possible parole. Gantt could imagine Charley and his four disciples talking up a storm with future interviewers. Worse yet was the prospect of their ultimate release to roam at large.

At least Colby took consolation in the fact that one more nagging problem from the JFK assassination had been solved by sudden death. Congressman Hale Boggs of Louisiana, a Warren Commission member who'd voiced "strong doubts" about the panel's silly single-bullet theory, had risen to become House Majority Leader last year, granting him increased access to meddling journalists. That ended in October, when Boggs traveled to Alaska in support of fellow Democrat Nick Begich in a dicey reelection bid. Their twin-engine Cessna had vanished en route from Anchorage to Juneau, taking the congressmen, their pilot, and Begich's aide along for the ride into limbo. Massive airborne searches continued for thirty-nine days but found nothing at all.

Easy peasy, Colby thought, relieved that one problem, at least, had been effectively disposed of.

And how many others did that leave to be resolved?

———

FBI Headquarters: December 7, 1972

PEARL HARBOR DAY reminded Devon Gantt of how far he had come since the surprise attack thirty-one years ago. He'd followed his father's advice, joining the Bureau while twin brother Colby went off to the OSS, later the CIA, and while they had discussed Colby's consideration of retirement, Devon didn't feel like going anywhere.

Not yet.

The nonstop circus in D.C. and nationwide still fascinated and amused him. Take Dick Nixon for example: even with the albatross of Watergate around his neck and growing heavier each week, he'd cruised to reelection in November by a landslide, claiming 520 of the Electoral College's 537 votes. He'd also carried forty-nine states, while only one, plus Washington, D.C., had gone for George McGovern, a pallid ghost of 1968's Bob Kennedy and Gene McCarthy.

At Bureau headquarters, beginning with Chief Hoover's death in May, the road forward had been a rocky one. In

California, jurors had cleared Angela Davis of any involvement with the Marin County courthouse slayings, while codefendant Ruchell Magee pled guilty to aggravated kidnapping and drew a sentence of life with possible parole. A separate trial led to acquittal of the two surviving "Soledad Brothers," John Cluchette and Fleeta Drumgo, on charges of murdering a white prison guard.

The Bureau had better luck in April, when four imprisoned Panthers faced additional charges of killing Corrections Sergeant Brent Miller with a sharpened lawnmower blade at Louisiana's Angola Prison.

Success against the Black Liberation Army was more dramatic. In January police captured Russell "Maroon" Shoatz for an August 1970 cop-killing in Pennsylvania. A month later, Georgia jurors had convicted two BLA members of killing Lieutenant Ted Elmore last November, one drawing a life term, the other a piddling five years. June brought New York arrests of Victor Cumberbatch for killing Transit Patrolman Sidney Thompson and capture of suspect Andrew Jackson in the Foster-Laurie murders. September saw Herman Bell nabbed in New Orleans, for Gotham's Jones-Piagentini slayings, plus the arrest of Robert Hayes for helping Cumberbatch murder Patrolman Thompson. That same raid netted Henry Brown and Melvin Kearney, wanted in the Foster-Laurie case and for multiple bank heists. October saw BLA brothers Francisco and Gabriel Torres booked for the Jones-Piagentini ambush.

The Bureau's big loss for this year so far had occurred in July, when five BLA members with three of their children hijacked Delta Air Lines Flight 841 en route from Detroit to Miami. One of the hijackers, George Wright, came aboard in priest's garb with a pistol stashed in his hollowed-out Bible. Landing in Miami as scheduled, the terrorists released eighty-six other passengers, then refueled and flew to Boston with seven hostage crew members, collecting a $1 million ransom, food, and a flight engineer qualified for trips overseas. They'd touched down in Algiers, where local lawmen freed the remaining hostages but soon released the hijackers, who made their way to Spain, then Portugal, where extradition was refused.

A big win for the Bureau, from Gantt's view as an alumnus of the COINTELPRO—BLACK HATE program now officially defunct, had broken in Chicago three months after the Delta hijacking. According to police and rabid crime reporters in the Windy City, six black members of an outfit called "De Mau Mau" had shot and killed nine whites during suburban home invasions. If that wasn't frightening enough, the *Daily News* announced that the group had 300 to 400 members at large in Chicago, as many as 4,000 nationwide. All the accused were military veterans, supposedly involved in "fragging" their white officers in Vietnam.

Okay, what if the *Sun-Times* came along days later, noting that the *Daily News* reports were "probably false"? And so what if Chicago PD had reversed early claims of a "national anti-white terrorist organization"? The *Daily News* hung in there, linking De Mau Mau to the Oklahoma murders of a state trooper, plus a convenience store manager and his family. Their "evidence": a toll-road ticket found in one alleged shooters car—which Chicago cops had seized two weeks *before* the Oklahoma slayings. It was smoke and mirrors, Bureau-style, but what the hell? White panic reelected Cook County State's Attorney Ed Hanrahan in a race he'd been expected to lose, based on chicanery in the 1969 Fred Hampton raid. Instead, he'd hold onto his office for another term, while six black vets went off to prison for mass murder and conspiracy.

Another target of the Bureau, in Philadelphia—where Panther-hating Police Commissioner Frank Rizzo now served as mayor—was MOVE, a "black liberation" group founded this year as the Christian Movement for Life by functional illiterate Vincent Leaphart, aka "John Africa." Pushing a platform that echoed the Panther Party's, MOVE members changed their surnames to "Africa," sported dreadlocks in the style of Caribbean Rastafarians, and broadened their call to liberation for all species of life on Earth. They scavenged food from supermarket dumpsters, while protesting zoos and puppy mills, blaring bullhorn-amplified "sermons" rife with profanity from their commune in West Philadelphia's Powelton Village district. So far, police complaints were mostly limited to noise, but Devon knew that cycle could be ramped up with strategic applications of brute force and Bureau know-how.

Meanwhile, AIM had worn out its welcome at the Nixon White House, rallying marchers nationwide for an October trek along the "Trail of Broken Treaties." Five days before Nixon's reelection, activists had occupied Bureau of Indian Affairs headquarters in Washington, whereupon Nixon threw up his hands in disgust and declared that he was "through doing things to help Indians." Calling that tantrum white business as usual, AIM pursued a program that included restoration of treaty-making (ended by Congress in 1871), Senate review of treaties never ratified, reparations for past treaty violations (including restoration of 110 million acres stolen from Native Nations), abolition of the BIA, and removal of Indian issues from state law enforcement.

AIM informers on the Bureau payroll now reported plans to occupy the 1890 Wounded Knee massacre site, located on South Dakota's Pine Ridge Indian Reservation, and Devon was watching closely to see what came of that.

In fact, he couldn't wait.

———

Little Italy, Manhattan: November 14, 1972

DOMINIC GIORDANO SAT in the darkened movie theater, watching *The Godfather* for the tenth time since it had premiered in March. Some might call it a waste of time and money, but to hell with them.

Dom hadn't read the novel it was based on—books had never been his friends—but now he damned near had the movie's dialogue down pat. The last six times he'd seen it, he had come alone, finding that chicks only distracted him from what was happening on-screen, preventing his total immersion in *La Cosa Nostra*'s legacy.

He loved Brando as Vito Corleone, but naturally, Dom felt a closer kinship for the Godfather's sons. Not Fredo, he was just a fucking clutz, but Sonny or Michael. Depending on his mood when he sat down with popcorn in the theater, Dom couldn't say which of the brothers he admired the most.

Other Mob-related movies he'd enjoyed this year: *Prime Cut,* with Gene Hackman and Lee Marvin, plus two with Charley Bronson in the leads. One, *The Mechanic,* cast him as a hitman with a reputation to protect; the other, *The Valachi Papers,* featured Bronson as the *Cosa Nostra*'s worst real-life turncoat to date. Call that one an instruction booklet on what not to do.

Out in the world, mobsters and their associates kept making news. Jimmy Hoffa had announced a run against ex-protégé Frank Fitzsimmons for the Teamsters presidency in 1976, troubling "Big Fitz" and White House pal Dick Nixon, not to mention sundry *mafiosi* who'd grown tired of Hoffa's tossing shit into the nearest handy fan.

In April, Joey Gallo had been gunned down at Umberto's Clam House on Mulberry Street, clearly retaliation for Joe Colombo's shooting last year, followed swiftly by the murders of Gennaro Ciprio at his Bath Beach restaurant and "laundryman" Frank Ferriano getting capped on the Lower West Side. Four months later, drive-by machine-un fire took down Thomas Eboli, "front boss" of the Genovese family, outside his girlfriend's home in Crown Heights, Brooklyn. In August, a shooter killed two men and wounded two more at the Neapolitan Noodle on East 79th Street, apparently missing several intended targets from the Colombo family. Cops were blaming that on Joey Gallo's younger brother Albert, called "Kid Blast," but they weren't filing any charges yet.

The courts weren't idle, though. Just yesterday, indictments had been handed down on four Colombo soldiers, charged with obstructing a comrade's prosecution for murder.

Screw them guys, Dom thought, and returned his full attention to the scree in front of him. Sonny Corleone was approaching a trap set for him by his scumbag brother-in-law Carlo and the rival Barzini family on the Long Island Causeway, headed to get blown away by toll booth Tommy-gunners.

Definitely Sonny, Dom decided. Michael Corleone might always overcome his enemies, but Sonny died with style.

———

Washington, D.C.: November 21, 1972

LATELY, Agent Wyman Gantt suspected time was winding down for FBI pursuit of fugitive Weatherman Underground members. Granted, they were still active—claiming credit for twenty-two of the year's 1,500 New Left bombings, including a Pentagon blast to celebrate Hô Chí Minh's birthday in May—but court decisions lately were restricting prosecution of white radicals.

Eight days before the Pentagon bombing, the Seventh Circuit Court of Appeals reversed Judge Hoffman's contempt citations of the Chicago Seven defendants and their two dense lawyers. Then, just yesterday, the same court had reversed the riot convictions of defendants Rennie Davis, Dave Dellinger, Tom Hayden, Abbie Hoffman and Jerry Rubin.

As for surviving remnants of the SDS, now calling themselves the SDS-Worker-Student Alliance, a June Supreme Court ruling in *Healy v. James* found that members had been robbed of their First Amendment rights by Central Connecticut State College's refusal to welcome a chapter on campus. In July and August, respectively, SDS-WSA pickets had protested both the Democratic and Republican National Conventions condemning Nixon for the obvious and candidate McGovern for retreating from his early hard-line stance on Vietnam.

Aside from bombs and bombast, Weatherman news boiled down to member Mathew Steen's indictment for bank robbery and conspiracy. In June, he'd tried to curry favor with the Bureau by becoming an informer on his "comrades," but it didn't fly. Headquarters much preferred him jailed for ten years on the charges filed against him.

As for Wyman and the other "Beards," they faced intensi-fied suspicion lately from the radicals they'd been assigned to infiltrate and undermine. That was no wonder, with ongoing COINTELPRO revelations from the Pennsylvania burglary, but Wyman wasn't worried yet—at least, not much.

In fact, he'd learned that danger was the spice of Bureau life.

———

Jackson, Mississippi: December 25, 1972

CHRISTMAS ON MONDAY made for a long weekend, but it brought no respite from Agent Nolan O'Hara's troubled thoughts.

Echoes from last year's raid on the Republic of New Afrika still haunted Nolan, like a nagging case of acid reflux. Prosecutors charged eleven RNA members with murdering Lieutenant William Skinner, then dismissed three of those cases, including that of Richard Henry who, the state discovered, wasn't even present when the raid went down. Eight others were convicted on reduced charges, handed minimal prison terms, but now the DOJ was pursuing Henry for weapons violations and conspiracy to assault a federal officer.

Klansmen were back in headlines too, thanks to new Governor William Waller freeing the killer of Vernon Dahmer he'd once defended at trial. Waller granted ex-client Charles Wilson a work-release program in Laurel, Wilson's home town, where he spent nights with his family after taking day shifts at Southern Mississippi State Hospital, a charity institution chiefly serving indigent blacks.

When the storm broke over that deal, Waller cited Wilson's previous work designing artificial limbs, adding that inmate records from Parchman Prison called Wilson "well-balanced, without psychosis, even-tempered, mild, timid and nonviolent." That failed to placate Dahmer's family, nor did it please some members of the Klan. A "former" White Knights officer in Laurel, pleading anonymity, complained that Waller had reneged on his promise to free all imprisoned Kluxers within a year of his inauguration, favoring only his erstwhile client, whom he'd failed to spare completely from incarceration.

One bright note to Nolan's Christmas, other than some time alone with wife Keely, had been a morning call from his sister Fiona, still in Alabama working night and day for Legal Aid. Some nights, of course, she managed to reserve for other things, primarily her paramour Dave Jordan.

Nolan felt like Judas, but he'd run a background check on Jordan, just for safety's sake, gobsmacked to learn he was the son of missing and presumed dead New York mobster Gregory Jordan, né Gregorio Giordano. More astounding still, said Jordan-Giordano was a former college classmate of Nolan's own father and Fiona's grandfather, departed G-man Declan O'Hara. The Bureau's file revealed no links between Dave Jordan and his father's shady business, and yet....

What could he do about that liaison? What *should* he do about it, when the guy had no record except for heroism during World War Two, and both parties were free consenting adults?

Nolan knew he'd have to think about that further, but he wasn't dropping any nasty bombs on Fee during the holidays. Even a special agent had to draw the line somewhere.

———

Saigon: December 30, 1972

Hardy Gantt had been tracking the Pentagon Papers through CIA files and occasional newspaper headlines from 14,000 miles away, sometimes uncertain whether he should laugh hysterically or fly into a rage. Most times, he settled for a pissed-off feeling somewhere in between.

It figured that the scandal only broke with Richard Nixon in the White House, and considering his record, the administration's fumbling response was all you could expect. Back in 1962, Nixon had published a memoir he called *Six Crises,* covering the years between the Alger Hiss fiasco and his first defeat running for president. The book was barely printed when his race for governor in California crashed and burned, now there was Watergate, unending revelations about Tricky Dick's collusion with the Mob and crooked labor unions.

Whose fault was it when each major step along life's road became a personal and national crisis? Who should step up and take the blame, except the fool at center stage?

The latest minnow in the government's Pentagon Papers net was a Harvard assistant professor, jailed for a week when he'd refused to answer a grand jury's questions. That was a drop in the bucket and estimates of *New York Times* coverage showed that the paper had only published 5 percent of the papers so far. What remained was bound to be another Nixon crisis—maybe even two or three.

Meanwhile, in present-day Southeast Asia, statistics from the Phoenix Project listed 81,740 Việt Cộng agents "neutralized," 26,369 of whom had been killed without trial. Air America had moved its headquarters again, to 1725 K Street Northwest, while its stateside maintenance base operated from Arizona's Pinal Airpark. Its only crash this year had involved sabotage of a C-7A Caribou loaded with Nationalist Lao troops, thankfully killing no one.

In January Nixon had announced an eight-point peace plan for Vietnam negotiated between Henry Kissinger and North Vietnamese President Tôn Đức Thắng, but two months later U.S. diplomats quit the Paris peace talks, Nixon claiming that Hanoi refused to "negotiate seriously." That sparked a six-month Eastertide Offensive by 200,000 North Vietnamese soldiers under General Võ Nguyên Giáp. That, in turn, prompted more U.S. bombing raids, Nixon telling his aides, "The bastards have never been bombed like they're going to get bombed this time."

That, plus no end to other vulgar tirades, thoughtfully recorded by a hidden tape deck in the Oval Office by the Quaker president who, legend had it, never used profanity.

The peace talks resumed in late April, followed three days later by U.S. troop levels dropping below 69,000, then in a classic turnaround, the talks were suspended again after only four days, while Nixon shipped 125 more warplanes to Saigon, announcing that he planned to mine North Vietnam's harbors under "Operation Linebacker." It was a weird path toward peace, especially when TV cameras caught South Vietnamese children "accidentally" burned by napalm.

In another bout of seeming schizophrenia, soldiers dismantled Saigon's U.S. Army headquarters in mid-May, a week before Nixon visited Moscow for cozy chats with Presidium Chairman Leonid Brezhnev. Once again, Nixon put on his "statesman" had and reaped world accolades—until Watergate broke and knocked him back on his heels. Seesaw battles continued in Nam, minus U.S. soldiers once the last of them pulled out on August 23. Bombing raids continued through September, until Kissinger finally struck a bargain with Lê Đức Thọ, telling his aides, "I want to end this war before the election."

Five days before Halloween, Kissinger told reporters, "We believe that peace is at hand. We believe that an agreement is in sight." Twelve days later, the largest landslide in U.S. history bought Nixon four more years, yet bombing of the north continued through Christmas, with 125 B-52s shot down while inflicting 1,300 civilian casualties around Hanoi.

Joy to the world, Gantt mused. *And peace on Earth, unless we say otherwise.*

Meanwhile, journalist Alfred McCoy had published a book titled *The Politics of Heroin: CIA Complicity in the Global Drug Trade.* It flew off bookstore shelves and resonated in the media, while admitting that "the CIA did not handle heroin, but it did provide its drug lord allies with transport, arms, and political protection. In sum, the CIA's role in the Southeast Asian heroin trade involved indirect complicity rather than direct culpability."

No one who'd spent a week in Vietnam since 1954 could honestly deny the truth of that, even if libel laws prevented McCoy's publisher from saying more. Gantt would be glad when he got out of there for good, but he had no idea when that might be.

CHAPTER 9

FBI Field Office, Jackson, Mississippi: May 23, 1973

NOLAN O'HARA WAS CONSIDERING A TRANSFER OUT OF Jackson to some other field office, but he hadn't submitted any paperwork so far, a part of him still hoping he could see his present cases through to something like a satisfactory conclusion.

The Klan, of course, kept raising hell whenever possible. Bureau informers passed on word that Byron De La Beckwith planned to murder Adolf Botnick, New Orleans regional director of the Anti-Defamation League, who'd helped bankroll an ambush of Klan bombers five years earlier. Police caught Beckwith on the Lake Pontchartrain Causeway Bridge, relieving him of a dynamite timebomb, several loaded guns, and a map of Bornick's neighborhood, but legal maneuvers would likely stall his trial until next year, if not longer.

Meanwhile, Ku Klux killer James Seale had contrived to cheat death once again, crashing his crop-duster in a Louisiana cottonfield. Perhaps fearing his luck had soured for good, Seale swapped his pilot's license for a badge, now working as a cop in Vidalia, Louisiana. Despite his failure as a sheriff's candidate in Mississippi, he had finally achieved his dream of infiltrating law enforcement.

Elsewhere in Louisiana, college-educated David Duke, just twenty-three, was busily recruiting members for a new Klan, calling himself grand dragon and billing realtor Jim Lindsay, aka "Ed White" or "Jack Lawrence," as the imperial wizard. The group had done nothing to speak of so far, but Nolan had Duke marked as one to watch.

And once again, as in his father's time, the Klan had reared its ugly hooded head above the Mason-Dixon Line. In Michigan, back in September 1971, bombs had destroyed ten school buses slated for court-ordered integration of Pontiac's schools. Police had charged six Klansmen, led by Robert Miles, and now, just yesterday, five of the six had been convicted on federal charges, facing ten years each in prison and $10,000 fines.

Would that stop them, or even slow the Kluxers down? After the maddening frustration he'd been through in Florida, then Alabama, finally in Mississippi, Nolan seriously doubted it.

Hate never died, as far as he could tell. It just changed costumes and moved on.

———

FBI Field Office, Manhattan: July 9, 1973

Agent Stephen Barnes was keeping his nose clean, doing his job, and watching while the Bureau suffered through continuing convulsions after Edgar Hoover's death.

In February, President Nixon had nominated Acting

Director Louis Gray as Hoover's permanent replacement, but that hadn't lasted long. Ten weeks later, prior to Senate confirmation, Gray resigned when proof surfaced that he'd removed files on Watergate plotter Gordon Liddy from the White House safe and shredded them. Disgraced, Gray suggested Associate Director Mark Felt as his replacement, seconded by Attorney General Richard Kleindienst, but Nixon had other ideas.

Acting on advice from White House Chief of Staff Alexander Haig that Felt was "a bad guy," prompting Felt's resignation, Nixon named Assistant Attorney General William Ruckleshaus as Acting Director while he went in search of someone better.

That someone, in Nixon's view, was sixty-two-year-old Clarence Kelle, a G-man from 1940 to '61, Assistant Special Agent in Charge for Houston, Seattle, and San Francisco, then SAC of Birmingham until his retirement. From there, he'd served as K.C.'s police chief, later joining the National Advisory Commission on Criminal Justice Standards and Goals and the FBI National Academy Review Committee. The Senate confirmed him in June, and he'd assumed office this very day as FBI Director.

In the field, Barnes had been present but he hadn't fired a shot when NYPD killed Bureau "Top Ten" fugitive Mace Brown in April, caught robbing a Harlem bank and holding forty-two hostages. His two accomplices awaited trial on charges of robbery, attempted murder, and possession of dangerous weapons.

Before that, in North Carolina, a robbery suspect had slain Agent Gregory Spinelli. Barnes felt zero sympathy for either of the dead men, but he'd gone through the motions, bad-mouthing Brown to his fellow agents, mourning Spinelli like a long-lost brother.

All for show, as he pursued his lifelong goal of ruining the FBI.

————

Little Italy, Manhattan: August 29, 1973

SURVEYING the stolen guns on a table before him, Dominic Giordano wondered if he'd need the weapons soon, of if he was surrendering to paranoia.

Screw that, he decided. Being paranoid was what it took to stay alive these days, within *La Cosa Nostra.*

The Senate's McClellan Committee had finally taken a breather, shifting its attention from the Mob to political corruption, as if there was any difference. Around the same time, Lansky partner Morris Landsburgh had pled guilty in Miami to conspiring with Meyer to cheat the IRS.

Mother Nature also did her share, hitting Frank Costello with a fatal heart attack in February, following that up in July by knocking off Genovese Family *capo* Big Mike Miranda—who'd planned the bungled hit on Frank in 1957 —at his semi-retirement home in Florida. A third casualty of natural causes, one month later, was Bonanno Family boss Natale Evola, replaced in turn by underboss Philip Rastelli.

On the violent side, nothing was settled for the feuding Colombos and Gallos so far. Joey's widow had spoken up at his funeral, promising that Gotham's streets would "run red with blood," and while it hadn't come to that, sniping continued, driving Colombo boss Joe Yacovelli out of town, tossing the reins to Carmine "The Snake" Persico in his federal prison cell.

And who'd be next?

Starting to check the guns again, Dom figured it was better to be safe than sorry any day.

Santiago, Chile: October 24, 1973

MOST OF THE killing was done now, but Colby Gantt still couldn't step outside his air-conditioned hotel room without smelling odors of explosives and burnt gunpowder hanging over the capital.

Long story short, Chile's deluded citizens believed they had the right to vote for any president they liked—in this case Salvador Allende, formerly the Minister of Health and Social Welfare, viewed by most of those *Yanquis* who pulled important strings from the United States as a committed Marxist no one in his right mind would elect as dog-catcher, much less as president. The CIA had spent $3 million to defeat him, while Henry Kissinger's highly suspect "40 Committee" in Washington bent over backwards to swing the election against Allende, all in vain.

His win over incumbent Jorge Allessandri had been touch-and-go in 1970. Since then, Allende had pissed off CEOs of sundry U.S. copper mining firms, as well as International Telephone and Telegraph, a major copper consumer, by nationalizing Chile's mines. When manipulation at the polls proved fruitless, the Agency and its corporate backers had gone with Plan B, fomenting armed rebellion led by General Augusto Pinochet and like-minded neo-fascists.

The result had been predicable. Officially, the *coup d'état* had cost fifty military lives, along with one slain media photographer and an uncertain number of Chilean civilians. President Allende was among them, various stories claiming that he'd "died fighting," committed suicide, or else been executed by a Pinochet hit team. An estimated 50,000 so-called Reds were presently in jail, their number likely to expand as Pinochet and his junta locked down control of the country. As for U.S. interests in Chile, there'd be no more silly talk about seizing copper mines or otherwise using natural resources to benefit the country's citizens. In Washington, Kissinger had assured Nixon "we didn't do it," and the president was either sly or dumb enough to act like he believed it.

Colby was on hand to guarantee that things ran smoothly after the rebellion, and he hoped he could get out of there before some bastard shot him by mistake.

At Langley, ex-Atomic Energy Commissioner James Schlesinger had replaced Richard Helms as CIA Director in February, launching a personnel shakeup that included renaming Clandestine Services as the Directorate of Operations. At the same time, Deputy Director William Colby began compiling a list of Agency misdeeds reported in the press, codenamed the "Family Jewels." When he succeeded Schlesinger as DCI in September, that file got buried in the deepest, darkest hole that he could find.

Chile aside, matters kept running hot throughout the length and breadth of Latin America. Nixon's new Drug Enforcement Administration already had agents all over the region, supplanting the former Office of Public Security while it wasted away from neglect.

In El Salvador, a mounting oil crisis sent food prices through the roof while decreasing agricultural output, driving President Arturo Molina to enact a series of land reform measures that hit the nation's landed elite where it hurt most, in their wallets. Those reforms fell flat, thanks in equal part to native oligarchs and Agency interference, but Colby had the country marked as a likely site for future revolution.

Uruguay kept lurching down the path toward ultimate suppression of the Tupamaros, with its military stealing power from parliament and the civilian executive branch. Nine leading Tupamaros had dodged punishment with a mistrial in 1971, but a second round in court had recently convicted them, imposing sentences of twenty-five years to life.

Stateside, Operation MKULTRA was officially defunct, but ugly echoes of its countless drug experiments on various unwitting subject kept reverberating in the media, albeit without any public knowledge—*yet,* at least—that agents of the CIA had been involved. The latest guinea pig turned homicidal psychopath was a black ex-convict named Donald David DeFreeze.

Cleveland born in 1943, DeFreeze had grown up in a "home" that sounded like a concentration camp. Three times in childhood, Donald's worthless father had chastised him for some minor misbehavior by breaking both of his arms. At age fourteen, DeFreeze quit school and fled to Buffalo, New York, joining a street gang while he lived with a funda-mentalist preacher's family. Said preacher called DeFreeze a "get up and go kid," while branding his companions "99 and 44/100 percent bad." From age twenty onward, DeFreeze logged arrests and served time for auto theft, deserting his wife, attempted burglary, kiting bad checks, and various weapons charges. One prison shrink diagnosed him as "a schizoid personality with strong schizophrenic potential," fascinated by guns and explosives. Sometimes he doubled as a stoolie for police and sold guns to Black Panthers whom the cops were eager to arrest. In 1969 he'd wound up at

Vacaville Prison, which included the California Medical Facility. Coincidentally or otherwise, one of his fellow inmates there was Manson robo-killer Bobby Beausoleil.

At Vacaville, DeFreeze had joined the Black Cultural Association, sponsored by a Berkeley professor and run by his students, preaching a mixture of pop psychology and far-left politics. He also met imprisoned Black Panther Thero Wheeler, recruiting him for a revolutionary group DeFreeze called the Symbionese Liberation Army, led by himself as "Field Marshal Cinque Mtume." He'd mispronounced "Cinque" to sound like "sink you." Transferred to Soledad in 1972, he'd escaped the following year, but the damage was already done. MKULTRA fiddling with his brain had produced a delusional monster, by no means under anyone's control.

On the lam, DeFreeze had gone to Oakland where, like Charley Manson, he'd begun collecting members for his SLA. Like Manson, he preferred young women over male recruits, but he'd take anyone willing to fight and mouth the party line as he dictated it. Joiners included Patricia "Mizmoon" Soltysik; Soltysik's lesbian lover, Berkley artist Camilla "Gabi" Hall; Vietnam vet and ex-convict Joseph "Bo" Remiro; ex-con Willie "Cujo" Wheeler; topless blackjack dealer Nancy "Fahiza" Perry; New Jersey native Angela "General Gelina" Atwood; Berkeley student Angela Siem; former "Revolutionary Army" member Wendy Yoshimura; Kathleen Soliah, aka "Sarah Olson," and her brother Steven; James Kilgore, Soliah's boyfriend of the moment; plus married Hoosiers William "General Teko" Harris and wife Emily, nicknamed "Yolanda."

One funny quirk about the SLA was that its women all wished they were black. In time, they took to wearing Afro wigs and dark makeup, both as disguises at crime scenes and a whacked-out political statement. Members studied DeFreeze's "Symbionese Liberation Army Declaration of Revolutionary War & the Symbionese Program." In it, DeFreeze explained: "The name 'symbionese' is taken from the word symbiosis and we define its meaning as a body of dissimilar bodies and organisms living in deep and loving harmony and partnership in the best interest of all within the body."

Apparently, that "deep and loving harmony" included stockpiling guns and explosives. In early November, it expanded to incorporate assassination, when SLA shooters ambushed Oakland school superintendent Marcus Foster and aide Robert Blackburn after a school board meeting. Ironically, Foster was black, and while the SLA accused him of welcoming cops on school campuses, also supporting a student I.D. card system, they were wrong on both counts. He'd publicly opposed both measures.

The hollow-point slugs used on Foster were packed with cyanide as backup insurance. Blackburn was luckier and managed to survive.

Now "Cinque" and his gang were on the loose, presumably plotting their next adventure in the murky realm of crackpot New Left politics.

If that was troublesome, the JFK case was beginning to wind down, Gantt thought, with mixed results. One of the early MKULTRA victims, Dimitre Dimitrov, had started telling people that he knew who'd murdered Kennedy and Dr. King, five years apart. The good news: his long-term detention, drugging and torture in Panama, back in the early 1950s, had convinced most listeners that he was nuts.

Less easy to discount was Thomas Davis, a mobster and bank-robbing pal of Jack Ruby who'd served the Agency over a span of twenty years in Algeria, the Caribbean,

Indochina and Indonesia. He'd been jailed in Morocco when JFK died, helped to escape by his CIA handler, but he still knew too much about Dallas. In September, providentially, he'd been electrocuted "accidentally," supposedly while trying to cut down and steal a high-voltage power line.

Jim Garrison was still alive, but not exactly loving it these days. Tried for accepting bribes from mobbed-up pinball distributors, he'd been cleared despite testimony from his former chief investigator, Percy Gervais, who swore Garrison had banked $3,000 monthly from the Mob to let it operate freely. Although acquitted, he had lost his bid for reelection as D.A. to Harry Connick Sr., a devoted Catholic who vowed that child-molesting priests would never be charged "as long as I'm District Attorney."

It was business as usual in the Big Easy then, where Carlos Marcello still had things well in hand, and one less thing to fret about when Colby had so many other problems on his plate.

———

Birmingham, Alabama: October 3, 1973

"So, Wallace is all set to run again next year?" Dave Jordan asked.

"That's what I hear," Fiona O'Hara replied.

The news had come as no surprise to anyone in Alabama or in politics at large. If he could occupy no higher office in the land, George Wallace was determined to exert control over the Cotton State for as long as he could do it from his wheelchair, with his wife of two years by his side.

Ace Carter, on the other hand, seemed to be out of politics entirely—or was he? As novelist "Forrest Carter," he'd lately published a Western adventure of Reconstruction titled *The Rebel Outlaw Josey Wales*, spinning the tale of a bold Confederate survivor whose family was massacred by evil Yankee "Red Legs" in Missouri, lighting out for Texas after Appomattox with manhunters on his trail.

And yet...

From Fee, through her G-man older brother in Mississippi, Jordan knew that Carter had been caught addressing meetings of a hard-core racist group whose members called themselves The Southerners. One FBI informer in the clique claimed it was "Carter's group" and said he preached the "Christian Identity" fable that southern white folks were "the true Israelites." Mixing business with pleasure, Carter also touted his novel, predicting that ex-General George Patton would endorse it—quite a trick, since a car wreck in Germany had claimed Patton's life four days before Christmas 1945.

Setting her purse down on a table in the entryway of Dave's apartment, Fee now turned to him with a solemn expression on her face. "We need to talk," she said.

"Uh-oh. What did I do?"

"It's what you *didn't* do," she said.

"Which is...?"

"Tell me about your family."

Jordan tried to keep his shoulders squared away but couldn't manage it. Slumping against the breakfast bar in his kitchen, he said, "Let me guess. Your brother's been playing detective?"

"He doesn't have to *play,* David. I mean, he *is* a special agent of the goddamned FBI!"

"And I'm a suspect now? Of what?"

"Try lying by omission for a start."

"It's not something I've ever bragged about to anyone," he said.

"Screw bragging. No one's asked for that."

"What, then? Why drag it all out now?"

"Because we've been together like, forever, and I'm wondering if I know you at all."

"What do you want from me?"

"The truth."

"All right, you asked for it. Let's have a seat, shall we?"

They sat almost together on the couch, a safe two feet of empty air between them, and he told her everything.

———

FBI Field Office, Chicago: October 10, 1973

ERIN O'HARA'S first assignment to the field turned out to be a bittersweet homecoming of sorts. Her grandfather had been posted to Chicago back in 1933 and spent the next few years pursuing "public enemies" under the leadership of SAC Melvin Purvis. First celebrated, then disgraced and driven from the Bureau by his ex-friend Edgar Hoover, Purvis and he men had been involved, for good or ill, in several of the FBI's most famous manhunts and had seen three fellow agents slain by trigger-happy fugitives.

Her grandfather had also witnessed major travesties of justice, laying out their details to his family in secret as a kind of cautionary tale, yet Erin had admired him so much —to the point the some might call idolatry—that she was following his footsteps both professionally and geographically.

Meanwhile, upheavals triggered by the Nixon gang had rocked Bureau headquarters and America at large.

In Washington there'd been the fall of Louis Gray and his successor, William Ruckleshaus—the latter quitting Justice with Attorney General Elliott Richardson in what reporters called the "Saturday Night Massacre," after refusing Nixon's order to fire Watergate special prosecutor Archibald Cox. Great Quaker Nixon dubbed Cox "Cocksucker" in Oval Office conversations with his cronies, either forgetting or not caring that his hidden tape recorders captured every word.

Clarence Kelley seemed like an able director at first glance, trailing decades of experience behind him, but Erin also knew from her father Nolan, another G-man once assigned to Birmingham, that Kelley's clumsiness and affable collaboration with Bull Connor had prevented capture of the Klansmen who destroyed the Bethel Baptist Church with dynamite in 1958.

As far as Watergate, it seemed to be the scandal that would never die, at least as long and Nixon and his criminal accomplices remained in power. Break-in plotters Howard Hunt and Gordon Liddy had been convicted in January. Three months later to the day, top Nixon aides John Ehrlichman and Harry Haldeman had both resigned, in preparation for their own criminal trials. And that same day, Judge William Byrne scuttled the Pentagon Papers trial of Daniel Ellsberg and Anthony Russo, when he confessed to huddling with Ehrlichman before the case convened. After that, he had procured admissions of illegal wiretapping and burglary by Nixon's "plumbers" and dismissed all charges, ruling that "The bizarre events have incurably infected the prosecution of this case."

May had seen the beginning of congressional Watergate hearings, but the *Washington Post* was well ahead of government investigators, reporters Carl Bernstein and Bob Woodward printing reams of information served up by an anonymous source they'd nicknamed "Deep Throat." That might be giggle-worthy, remembering last year's porn film of the same title, but few outside the Bureau knew that "Deep Throat" was Mark Felt, ex-Associate Director who'd resigned when Nixon denied him promotion in favor of Clarence Kelley. A COINTELPRO overseer prior to Watergate, Felt was a prime "Deep Throat" suspect, but no one had collected enough evidence to nail him for it yet.

And if all those shenanigans weren't bad enough, tough-talking Vice President Spiro Agnew had gone down in flames, snared in a corruption scandal dating back to his days as Baltimore County's highest elected official, then as Maryland's governor. Prosecutors in that case initially told Agnew he "wasn't under investigation," but mounting evidence soon changed their minds. He'd resigned his present office on October 10, and on the same day pled guilty on one count of tax evasion, paying a $10,000 fine and receiving three years' "unsupervised probation"—in short, a virtual free pass. As his successor, Nixon chose congressman Gerald Ford, best known as "the FBI's man" on the Warren Commission in 1964.

The government, it seemed, was on the verge of collapsing, but Erin didn't mind. She wasn't a Republican, had never liked Nixon or his appointees, and whatever happened to the White House had no impact on her Bureau life.

In fact, she thought America today needed its G-men and G-women more than ever.

———

Chicago: December 11, 1973

BEING a Bureau undercover agent kept Wyman Gantt on the move, but lately he'd sensed that his days as a "Beard" infiltrating the New Left were numbered. It had started with the Supreme Court's ruling in the case of *United States v. U.S. District Court*, finding that despite whatever Attorney General John Mitchell claimed, the Fourth Amendment's demand for search warrants applied to domestic surveillance wiretaps based on the "inherent vagueness of the domestic security concept" and its potential abuse.

The defendants in that case, White Panther Party leaders John Forest, Lawrence Plamondon, and John Sinclair faced charges of conspiring to bomb a Michigan CIA office. Judge Damon Keith ruled the wiretaps that bagged them unconstitutional, the DOJ appealed, and it had lost resoundingly, by a unanimous vote of 8-0.

Four months later, realizing nearly all the Bureau's COINTELPRO—NEW LEFT cases hinged upon illegal taps or bugs, Justice dismissed charges filed against most Weatherman Underground fugitives. Ever Bernardine Dohrn got a pass of sorts with her removal from the Bureau's Ten Most Wanted list on Pearl Harbor Day, fourteen months after she first made the roster.

Dohrn was staying underground, along with most of her WU compatriots, who still had a war to fight on the home front. In May they'd bombed New York's 103rd Police Precinct after one of its cops killed an unarmed ten-year-old black boy. In September bombers struck ITT offices in Manhattan and Rome, retaliating for the CIA's coup in Chile. On the side, Weathermen published a *Prairie Fire* newsletter, drawing its title from Mao Zedong's comment that "a single spark can set a prairie fire."

As for the parent SDS—now formally the SDS-WSA— its recent actions were positively tame by comparison to the late Sixties. In Newark, where Anthony Imperiale's para-military white-supremacist North Ward Citizens' Committee opposed construction of Kawaida Towers, a housing project sponsored by black nationalist poet Leroy Jones, the SDS-WSA rallied to picket Imperiale's picketers, reminding everyone that in his spare time Tony taught karate to New Jersey's Ku Klux Klan.

On other fronts, the SDS-WSA protested the published works of Richard Herrnstein, Arthur Jensen and William Shockley, all hyping the long-discredited canard that blacks scored poorly on IQ tests due to genetics. In New York the SDS-WSA also joined the Progressive Labor Party to create an International Committee Against Racism, quickly expanding to claim chapters scattered in Canada and Latin America.

Gantt wasn't sure what he'd do next, when the New Left ran out of steam, but he knew the Bureau would endure. First thing to do, he guessed, was get a haircut and a shave.

―――――

San Francisco: December 25, 1973

IT WAS an odd way to spend Christmas, hunting zebras in Frisco, within sight of Alcatraz, but Devon Gantt thought he was equal to the task. In fact, with all the Bureau roadwork he'd performed of late, hotels felt more like home than Washington, where he'd have been idling around the house with wife Camille, missing their absent son Wyman.

Of course, he wasn't *really* stalking zebras in the City by the Bay. That was a tag that local cops and journalists were using for a string of racial murders, wherein blacks targeted random white victims. No doubt, somebody thought the name was clever, but it was already drawing protests from the black community at large.

The first known crime occurred in mid-October, when a vanload of blacks snatched Richard and Quita Hague from Telegraph Hill, hacking both with a machete, killing Quita, leaving Richard gravely wounded but alive. Ten days later, a black man blocked victim Frances Rose's car near the UC Berkeley Extension, demanded a ride, then shot her multiple times.

In early November, gas company clerk Robert Stoeckmann disarmed his black assailant and returned fire with the would-be slayer's gun, leading police to jail one Leroy Doctor for assault with a deadly weapon. Three days after Thanksgiving, black gunmen bound and executed Jordanian immigrant Saleem Erakat in his store's restroom.

On December 11, artist Paul Dancik took three slugs in a public phone booth but lived to describe his attacker. Two days later, politician Arthur Agnos survived two gunshots in Portrero Hill. On December 20, black gunmen wounded a young college coed in her apartment, then killed octogenarian janitor Ilario Bertuccio in the Bay View district. Two victims—Neal Moynihan and Mildred Hosler—died within six minutes of each other, shot four times apiece near the Civic Center. The victim slain on Christmas Eve was listed as "John Doe."

Panic gripped white Frisco residents, while blacks endured more than usual police harassment. Devon wondered how much worse it might've been had locals known what he knew: that the crimes were traceable to a Nation of Islam offshoot calling its members "Death Angels," earning "wings" drawn on their Polaroid photos for confirmed kills of "Whitey." It wasn't Charley Manson's

Helter Skelter race war, but it had tempers on both sides flaring, gun stores selling out in record time.

And black rebellion seemed to be ongoing everywhere Gantt looked. In the sunny U.S. Virgin Islands, 3,700 miles from Frisco, a "Mau Mau-type rebellion" had seen eight tourists gunned down on a St. Croix golf course owned by Rockefellers. G-men and U.S. Army troops had swarmed the islands, near martial law resulting in arrest of five black men inevitably dubbed the "Virgin Island Five." They'd allegedly confessed, then recanted, claiming they'd been hanged and beaten, shocked with cattle prods, waterboarded, and nearly suffocated by plastic bags over their heads. Judge Warren Young admitted those confessions, seating a jury that included a police detective's wife, and ignored complaints from nine jurors claiming intimidation by police and FBI agents. With the panel "hopelessly deadlocked," Young insisted that they try again, resulting in convictions. He'd slapped each defendant with eight consecutive life sentences, while the archipelago's black populace seethed with fury.

More work needed there, Devon thought, but his hands were full at home.

In March, New York jurors had convicted ex-COINTELPRO target Rap Brown on six counts of robbery, three counts of first-degree assault, and two weapons charges, deadlocking on three counts of attempted murder. His maximum cumulative sentence totaled 149 years. In November, a Maryland judge added one year and a $1,000 fine on federal riot charges.

Death Angels aside, the Nation of Islam suffered more bad PR in January, when its members slaughtered seven breakaway Hanafi Muslims in Washington, D.C., including four children shot or drowned, with two more victims gravely wounded. From New York, NOI spokesman Louis Farrakhan denied any involvement by his sect, blaming instead a criminal gang the styled itself the Black Mafia.

Meanwhile, the Black Liberation Army remained top priority among law enforcement officers nationwide and would until the last of its adherents had been tracked down, killed or caged. February witnessed seizure of a BLA arms cache, along with bank-robbing suspect Oscar Washington. In August the BLA killed Park Ranger Kenneth Patrick during a traffic stop at California's Point Reyes National Seashore, fleeing with his service pistol.

One day before Halloween, G-men and NYPD had bagged Thomas "Blood" McCreary, a fugitive from Miami bank robbery charges. Two weeks later, still in Gotham, cops and G-men killed Twyman Meyers, sought since November 1971 for murdering Atlanta Patrolman James Greene. For good measure, a quartet from the BLA's Atlanta chapter was also jailed pending trial on sundry counts.

The other big news, spanning eight days in December and January, involved Mark Essex, a black Kansas native and U.S. Navy dental technician who'd joined the Black Panthers following a general discharge for "character and behavior disorders" in February 1971. No one seemed to know if he was still a Panther when he ran amok in New Orleans nearly two years later.

What they *did* know was the outcome of his rampage. On New Year's Eve, Essex killed police cadet Alfred Harrell, wounding NOPD Lieutenant Horace Perez and Sergeant Edwin Hosli in separate shootings with a .44 Magnum carbine. Oddly, though Essex had preceded those attacks with statements that he planned to kill "just honkies," Cadet Harrell was black.

After New Year's, Essex had taken a hiatus until January

7, when he shot grocer Joe Perniciaro, then carjacked motorist Marvin Albert for a ride to the Downtown Howard Johnson's Hotel on Loyola Avenue. There, he fatally wounded vacationing Dr. Robert Steagall and his wife Betty, draping their bodies with a Pan-African flag and setting their room afire. He next mortally wounded hotel manager Walter Collins and assistant manager Frank Schneider. Essex was setting more fires when police and firefighters arrived. Officers Phillip Coleman and Paul Persigo tried to enter the hotel via a firetruck's ladder, but Essex shot them both, subsequently killing NOPD Deputy Superintendent Louis Sirgo and wounding Officer Ken Solis.

By then, the whole shebang was playing live on local television, prompting the Marine Corps to loan police a Huey helicopter for the firefight. Firing from the hotel's roof, Essex damaged the chopper, then collapsed under a hail of lead, 200 separate wounds enumerated at his autopsy. The final tally for his short-lived war: nine victims slain, including five policemen, with another thirteen wounded.

America's new Indian war was also heating up, particularly on South Dakota's Pine Ridge Reservation, site of the 1896 Wounded Knee massacre. In November 1972, with violence escalating between reservation internees and county law enforcement agencies, the Oglala Sioux Tribal Council authorized tribal president Dick Wilson "to take whatever action that he felt would be necessary to protect the lives and property and to insure the peace and dignity of the Pine Ridge Indian Reservation." His answer was GOON (Guardians of the Oglala Nation), a vigilante group that did more to suppress dissent than stamp out crime. As reservation rapes and murders multiplied, AIM activists moved in and occupied the town of Wounded Knee in February, holding out for Wilson's impeachment.

Inevitably, politicians, journalists and feds flocked to the scene, and mayhem increased. Someone shot and paralyzed a U.S. marshal in March; federal fire killed at least two Indians in April; and AIM protester Ray Robinson vanished without a trace, seemingly kidnapped and murdered by GOON. Despite a law enforcement cordon, weapons kept arriving on the reservation. Wilson sold grazing rights to white farmers at cut-rate prices, pocketing the dough, and leased much of the reservation's mineral-rich land to outside mining companies. Arsonists torched various buildings in Wounded Knee, including the Chamber of Commerce and the unfortunately named Custer Courthouse before a blizzard struck. Feds turned Angela Davis away as "an undesirable person."

The siege lasted for seventy-one days, and with its end, Dick Wilson's GOON squad remained in charge, ongoing violence against Wilson's opponents now a matter of routine. Devon expected more trouble ahead and hoped that he might lend a hand when it resumed.

———

CIA Headquarters: December 29, 1973

HOMECOMING FROM A WAR zone was supposed to be a festive change of pace, but Hardy Gantt had found he missed the constant drums of war beating in Vietnam and Laos. What were the odds of that?

At home, the Nixon White House had little to celebrate, despite January's signing of the Paris Peace Accords, cessation of the military draft, and Nixon's proclamation that he'd achieved "peace with honor." Maybe so, but U.S. bombing continued till mid-August, when Congress cut off further funds for war in Indochina. American combat troops were gone by March 29, leaving a record of 47,244 personnel killed in action, 10,446 non-combat deaths, 153,329 seriously wounded, and some 2,400 missing servicemen still unaccounted for. Henry Kissinger came out smelling like a rose, promoted to Secretary of State, and everyone pretended not to notice that combat continued apace between North and South Vietnam.

Against that "triumph," on the home front, Watergate dragged on, Gerald Ford succeeded Spiro Agnew as vice president, the Pentagon Papers trial ended in chaos, and pundits talked at length about the Nixon regime's "credibility gap." Worse yet, for the CIA, feds in Chicago busted Thai national Puttapron Khramkhruan with fifty-nine pounds of opium, an informant for Nixon's newly-formed Drug Enforcement Administration claiming that the Agency knew all about it and approved the smuggling. Langley wasn't talking publicly about it, but staffers at Justice acknowledged that the Agency had quashed that case from fear that it "might prove embarrassing because of Mr. Khramkhruans's involvement with CIA activities in Thailand, Burma, and elsewhere."

Fools never learn, Gantt thought, but they kept making money in the name of national security, and while he went on earning his fair share of it, who was he to complain?

———

Manhattan: December 31, 1973

SOMETIMES, against his will, NYPD Sergeant Payton Sawyer wondered what his dad would think about the world today if he were still alive.

Nothing about the Nixon "War on Drugs" would have surprised him. Creation of the DEA, merging the old Bureau of Narcotics and Dangerous Drugs with the Office of Drug Abuse Law Enforcement, amounted to little more than paper shuffling. Nixon had appointed psychiatrist Robert DuPont as his "Drug Czar"—one of those royal titles specifically banned by the Constitution—thrilled to hear the doctor spurn the bulk of medical opinion by calling marijuana "the most dangerous drug." That helped the administration criminalize and disrupt both minority communities and leftist "hippie"-types.

What else was "new"?

Payton shrugged it off and concentrated on his work for BOSS, beginning with mayhem at Newark's Muslim Temple No. 25. Police accused Warren Marcello and ten other members of the offshoot "New World Muslim" sect of murdering Minister James Shabazz at his home in September, in a presumed takeover bid. Before that case saw trial, while free on bond, Marcello and comrade Michael Hufff were found beheaded at Weequahic Park, a block from Minister Shabazz's home. It smelled like war coming, but so far, that was the extent of it.

Meanwhile, the BLA was still fighting, still dying, its members still going to prison. In January NYPD detectives caught Woodie Green and Anthony White robbing a Brooklyn bar and killed them both in a gunfight that left the officers wounded. February sent Alfredo Estremeara and Pedro Monges to jail, pending trials for bank robbery and explosives possession, respectively. March saw Richard Moore sentenced for shooting two Gotham cops back in '71. Another firefight, in April, killed fugitive Harold Russell in Brooklyn, while Robert Vickers escaped.

May brought more mayhem from the Garden State, with

a shootout on the New Jersey Turnpike near East Brunswick. Once again, a "routine" traffic stop had gone to hell, leaving State Trooper Werner Foerster and ex-New York Black Panther James Coston dead. A second trooper suffered wounds, as did BLA fugitive Joanne Chesimard, hospitalized with gunshots to one shoulder and both arms. Another BLA member, Clark Squire, was also in jail, pending trial on various felony charges.

It looked like the end for the BLA's "den mother," charged with multiple murders and kidnapping a Harlem heroin dealer, but Payton knew better than to count her out just yet.

A month later, in the Bronx, two BLA members shot and killed Transit Police Officer Sidney Thompson when he tried to arrest them for ducking fares at an Interborough Rapid Transit station. Gunman Robert Hayes was now in custody, awaiting trial. Come September, FBI "Top Tenner" Herman Bell was captured in New Orleans, far from the Manhattan killing grounds. G-men and Bronx officers teamed up to kill fugitive Twyman Meyers in mid-November, prompting Police Commissioner Donald Cawley to claim that his death "broke the back" of the BLA.

Maybe. But Payton would believe it when the guns stopped going off around New York. And in his personal experience, they never had.

EPILOGUE

Birmingham, Alabama: January 30, 1974

"I can't believe we're really watching this," said Fee O'Hara.

David Jordan smiled and sipped his beer, sitting beside her on the couch in his apartment. He'd have liked to say *I can't believe you're here at all* but thought it through before speaking. Instead, he answered, "We should always try to stay informed."

"By lies?"

"We ought to wait and see."

"Why? He's been lying to us since the run six years ago."

"Maybe he's changed?"

"As if. I need more wine for this," she said, and grabbed the bottle to refresh her glass.

Somehow, he'd managed to explain about his family, that he wasn't a part of them except for rare obligatory meetings such as funerals, and she had seemed to understand, insisting only that he keep nothing from her in future. That had been an easy promise, both to make and keep, since he had nothing else to hide.

"And here he comes," Dave said.

On television, Richard Nixon took the podium before a joint session of Congress, shuffling the notes for this year's State of the Union Address.

"Why does he need those, with the teleprompter?" Fee asked the TV. "They've been using it since 1950, for God's sake."

"Temper," said Dave, and took the hand that didn't have a glass in it.

Nixon began. "Mr. Speaker, Mr. President, my colleagues in the Congress, our distinguished guests, my fellow Americans. We meet at a time when we face great problems at home and abroad that will test the strength of our fiber as a nation. But we also meet at a time when that fiber has been tested, and it has proved strong."

"Tell that to all the guys you've fired!" Fee jeered at him.

"It was five years ago on the steps of this Capitol," Nixon droned on, "that I took the oath of office as your president. In those five years, because of the initiatives undertaken by this Administration, the world has changed. America has changed. Five years ago, our cities were burning and besieged. Five years ago, our college campuses were a battle-ground. Five years ago, crime was increasing at a rate that struck fear across the Nation..."

Fee interrupted him, saying, "And five years ago, some fools still didn't know you were a criminal!"

He blathered on awhile, at one point saying, "We will make an historic beginning on the task of defining and protecting the right of personal privacy for every American."

Fee interrupted him again, hooting, "By spying on each one of us!"

As if he'd heard her, Nixon answered back, "One measure of a truly free society is the vigor with which it protects the liberties of its individual citizens."

Dave had to laugh at that, while Fee replied to the TV, "You're such a goddamned hypocrite!"

This time, the president seemed to ignore her. "Throughout the five years that I have served as your President—"

"You've screwed us every way you could!" she shouted back at him.

And then he got down to the crux of it, the basic reason all of them were present, saying, "I would like to add a personal word with regard to an issue that has been of great concern to all Americans over the past year. I refer, of course, to the investigations of the so-called Watergate affair. As you know, I have provided to the special prosecutor voluntarily a great deal of material. I believe that I have provided all the material that he needs to conclude his investigations and to proceed to prosecute the guilty and to clear the innocent. I believe the time has come to bring that investigation and the other investigations of this matter to an end. One year of Watergate is enough."

Fee scooped up Dave's remote control and switched off the TV. "I can't take any more of this, not one more frigging lie," she said. Setting her empty class down on the coffee table, she stood up and said, "It's time I was in bed."

Keeping his disappointment to himself, Dave nodded, rose, and said, "I'll get your sweater, then. Be careful driving home."

"Driving?" she said and glanced off toward his bedroom. "Do I need a car for that?"

"Um..."

She took his hand and asked him, "Well, are you coming or not?"

A LOOK AT PRICE OF HONOR:
THE BUREAU SERIES BOOK 8

Book No. 8 of *The Bureau, Price of Honor,* follows the surviving protagonists through the turbulent years between 1974 and 1983. For the FBI and NYPD's BOSS, pursuit of black militants and white radicals continues, sometimes with fatal results. President Nixon resigns in disgrace, while revelations made in recent years prompt formation of multiple congressional committees probing illegal acts by both the FBI and CIA. Despite cancelation of COIN-TELPRO before Hoover's death, the Bureau still pursues lawless tactics against perceived subversives, including a new Indian War of sorts against Native American activists. The Vietnam war ends in communist triumph, while two single-term presidents seek to salvage America's image on a global scale. A new grassroots demand for "law and order" at home, with greater security abroad, propels Ronald Reagan into the White House and toward a new would-be assassin's gunsights. Nolan O'Hara leaves the Bureau to cooperate with Senate investigators, while the CIA cleans house of all possible living embarrassments. New frontiers of conflict open in Latin America and the Caribbean.

COMING SOON FROM MICHAEL NEWTON AND
WOLFPACK PUBLISHING

ABOUT THE AUTHOR

A California native, Michael Newton has published 215 books under his own name and various pseudonyms since 1977. He began writing professionally as a "ghost" for author Don Pendleton on the best-selling Executioner series and continues his work on that series today. With 104 episodes published to date, Newton has nearly tripled the number of Mack Bolan novels completed by creator Pendleton himself.

Newton's first book under his own name was *Monsters, Mysteries and Man* (1979), a survey of unexplained phenomena for younger readers. While 156 of Newton's published books have been novels—including westerns, political thrillers and psychological suspense—he is best known for nonfiction, primarily true crime and reference books.